Unspeakable Truths

By

ALICE TRIBUE

Photos by Lindee Robinson Photography

Cover Designed by Najla Qamber Designs

Models: Ahmad Kawsan & Destiny Mankowski

Editing by Editing4Indies
https://www.facebook.com/editing4indies
Formatting by CP Smith

Other Titles
by
Alice Tribue

Translation of Love (Of Love #1)
Desperation of Love (Of Love #2)
Shelter You

Dedication

To Arbin for listening to all my new book ideas and giving me your amazing suggestions.

For Eva Rose, because to me you're everything...my very own 'happily ever after'. For anyone whose ever experienced the beauty of a second love.

Prologue

"Tyler, do you take Everly to be your lawfully wedded wife, to have and to hold from this day forward, for better or for worse, for richer, for poorer, in sickness and in health, until death do you part?"

"I do," declares Tyler, his deep voice cracking slightly.

My own eyes are now moist with the threat of unshed tears. His beautiful smile shines down on me, making the butterflies in my stomach take flight. I turn my head to the priest as he begins to speak again.

"Everly, do you take Tyler to be your lawfully wedded husband, to have and to hold from this day forward, for better or for worse, for richer, for poorer, in sickness and in health, until death do you part?"

"I do," I agree joyfully tilting my head up and looking into Tyler's chocolate brown eyes, the tears pooled in them reflecting my own. This is the kind of moment that every girl dreams of, the happily ever after that we read about when we're little.

"You have declared your consent before the Church. May the Lord in his goodness strengthen your consent and fill you both with blessings. What God has joined let no man divide. Do you have the rings?"

Tyler nods, turning around and taking the rings from his best man. As he turns I take in the sight of him, really look at this man standing before me, loving the way he looks in his black suit and tie. Tyler is slender with lean well-defined muscles. His light brown hair is short and perfectly groomed for the occasion. Tyler likes to look good; he's always so well put together. He takes pride in his appearance—even in sweats and a t-shirt he looks styled to perfection. He's tall, so tall that he hovers over me even in the highest heels I could find I still have to look up at him. His thin lips and perfectly chiseled nose make him look almost like the typical boy next door.

I focus on Tyler as he shakily picks up my left hand and grins as he slides a platinum diamond band on my finger.

"With this ring, I thee wed," he says softly, so low that no one past the first few rows likely heard him.

I wipe away a stray tear, turn to my maid of honor who hands me his ring, and turn back to Tyler. I take his hand in mine repeating the same words he's just spoken.

"With this ring, I thee wed."

"You place these rings upon each other's fingers as a visible sign of your vows this day. And now by the power vested in me by the state of New Jersey, I hereby pronounce you husband and wife. Tyler," the priest calls with a smile on his face, "you may kiss your bride."

His lips crush down hard against mine and my arms wrap around his neck as cheers erupt throughout the church. Two hundred of our closest friends and family are in attendance, but I don't see any of them. I barely register the fact that they're here at all. The only thing I know is that we did it, that as of this moment I'm Tyler's wife and he's my husband. Mine. And this is the day I've been waiting for since I met him on campus four years ago.

We slowly break apart, and I swear it feels more like a fantasy than reality. Tyler looks down at me with his perfect smile and whispers, "I love you Mrs. West."

"I love you Mr. West." I giggle as he takes my hand leading me down the rose-covered aisle and out of the church. Life with Tyler hasn't always been perfect, it hasn't always been easy, but my life is so much better with him in it. I've never doubted his love — not ever once. He's steady, grounded, focused; that's what I love about him and Tyler would do anything to make sure I'm happy. He would move mountains if it meant giving me something that I want. How can I not love someone like that?

The rest of the day passes in a series of beautiful scenes filled with happiness and laughter. Endless food and alcohol is consumed, music fills the air as our guests dance and mingle. It's been prepared to be the wedding to end all weddings as two prominent families are united through our love for each other. Everything is as it should be, everything is right with the world, and I'm afraid I might burst because I'm so full of joy right now.

"The moment I saw you in that first class I knew I was going to marry you," he tells me. My arms wrap around Tyler's neck as we sway back and forth to the beautiful ballad.

I laugh and shake my head at him. "Confident huh?"

He always says he had known…well hoped, from the minute I walked into my Econ class, that he and I would be together. I, on the other hand, wasn't so sure. I'd had a crush on someone else, but it didn't take long for me to reciprocate. There was just something about Tyler that got to me. It was more than his looks, although his dark brown eyes and killer smile didn't hurt. He had a level of confidence unlike anyone I'd ever met before. It poured out of him, making him almost infectious to be around; getting to know him, spending time with him became almost necessary to me.

I remember being the envy of every girl in that class when he and I were paired off together to do our semester project. We spent a lot of time together studying and researching during that time and every day we grew closer and closer until I finally realized I had fallen in love with him. That's all it took for us to become inseparable, for us to become Tyler and Everly, and now look at us—married and about to start a life together.

I place a chaste kiss on his lips. "You know, if I could have created my dream man from scratch, he would have been you. I know now that you were meant for me."

"Mmm baby, I'm going to take you out of here in a few minutes and show you exactly why you'll never regret getting mixed up with a guy like me."

I lean into him resting my head on his shoulder and let out a sigh.

"I could never regret you Tyler; you're the love of my life."

"And you're mine," he replies, placing a kiss on the top of my head.

❦

We wanted to make sure to thank every last person who came to celebrate our day with us, so we stayed at the reception till the end. It's after midnight when Tyler and I stumble our way back into our room for the night after the last guests have left the banquet hall located inside the hotel. It's a gorgeous beachfront hotel, the ideal location for a wedding and convenient because a lot of our guests decided to spend the night here too. I stand in the middle of the dimly lit room in my stunning ivory wedding gown, fitted at the top making it almost skin tight and then flaring at the bottom in a mermaid style. The back is see-through with a seam of tiny pearl buttons running up my spine. The details and appliqués are stunning and hand sewn, making it a one of a kind dress. Anticipation courses throughout my body as Tyler pours two glasses of champagne and hands me one.

"To my beautiful bride and the beginning of our life together. I can't wait to spend forever with you."

"To forever," I toast in agreement.

I take a long sip from my flute before placing it on the small table. I step back slowly, watching Tyler take a drink, his eyes never leaving mine. I reach around my back and release the first of many buttons that holds my dress together.

"Let me," he whispers, putting his glass down and making it across the room in two strides. He circles me until he's behind me and begins to slowly take out the pins of my hair, releasing my elaborate up do. Once he's satisfied that he has them all, he uses his fingers to shake out my hair until it falls in soft waves, framing my face.

I sigh as he kisses my bare shoulder, making my body shiver with excitement. His fingers lightly travel up to my ear where he removes my earring then gently tugs on my earlobe with his teeth. This earns a gasp of shock from me, and I've barely recovered before he removes the other earring.

My body grows warmer with Tyler leaving a trail of kisses down my neck, shoulders, and finally the top of my dress. I feel his powerful hands begin to undo the buttons, my dress getting looser as he opens each one.

"Hands up over your head wife," he teases softly. Giving me a command is very unlike Tyler. He's more about asking me what I want, letting me tell him what will make me feel good which is nice...but I really like this.

Hearing him call me his wife is strange, but it's strange in the most incredible way. In the way that makes me believe that dreams do come true, because from the moment I allowed myself to fall in love with him, Tyler West has been my biggest dream. *To Forever*, I think to myself as he continues his sweet seduction.

I lift up my arms for him as he bends down and gathers the hem of my dress in his hands. He effortlessly lifts it up over my head, tossing it on a nearby chair. His hooded gaze scours the entire length of my body, taking in my bare breasts and the flimsy strip of ivory material I was assured were panties. I can see the exact moment when his eyes pool with desire; it's the same moment when my desire pools between my thighs. The look in his eyes is almost too much.

"Jesus Everly, you take my breath away."

I say nothing in return, just stare at him trying my best to memorize his face, memorize how he is looking at me right now. I don't know why I do it—but it feels like it's important, like I should never forget how he looks in this moment. I didn't think it would ever be possible to love him as much as I do or love him more than I did when I woke up this morning, but right now I think I just might. It's the most beautiful and scary feeling in the world to put yourself out there like that, give your heart away so effortlessly to another person.

"Sit down on the bed," he demands in a husky voice laced with desire.

I do as he asks, backing up until the back of my legs hit the edge of the mattress. I lower myself down until I'm sitting and facing him. He reaches for his glass and gulps down the rest of his champagne before striding across the room and bending down before me. He reaches down and grabs hold of my ankle; he releases the strap and slides my bejeweled shoe off of my foot. Once he's divested me of both shoes, I reach down and begin to unbutton his shirt while he undoes his cufflinks.

I waste no time in shoving the shirt off of his shoulders while he helps me slide it off. Tyler gets to his feet, pulls his undershirt over his head, and starts to remove his pants.

"Slide back and lie down for me baby." His voice is even hotter than before, he's taking control in a way that I'm not used to, and it's only getting me more excited. His words make me even wetter, needier for him; he's never been like this before. I do as I'm told while he takes care of the rest of his clothing; I shudder as I take in the sight of him in all his glory. Tyler. My husband. Mine. For as long as we both shall live. He's my life now, my world, and I intend to make him as happy as he makes me.

He climbs onto the bed, crawling up until he's hovering over me and we're face to face. His eyes burn through me, filling me with a heady combination of love and lust.

"Have I mentioned how beautiful you are?"

I let out a sigh and smile shyly. "So are you."

"I love you Everly, I fucking love you so much. I promise you that no matter what, no matter what happens I'll always take care of you."

"Make love to me husband," I whisper, keeping the tears at bay. No wife has ever felt this happy, because there's only one Tyler, and he's all mine.

To forever…

Four Years Later

"God it's cold today Ty," I remark, wrapping my arms around my torso before I burst into a fit of giggles. "Four years of marriage and I've resorted to talking to you about the weather. I guess that doesn't bode well huh?" I let out a sigh, close my eyes, and tilt my head up letting the rays of the sun warm me. It's the start of the summer season here, but the mornings still tend to be a bit on the colder side. "I guess it doesn't really matter anyway."

Growing up, I was addicted to romance novels, reading about the moment when a boy meets a girl and they fall in love, overcoming insurmountable circumstances. But no matter what they faced, no matter how high the obstacles—they would always, always get their happy ending, their happily ever after. I learned the hard way that the romance novels are wrong! Happily ever after doesn't always mean forever. I know this because my happily ever after was stolen, ripped away from me in the most unimaginable kind of way.

I run my hand over the top of the gray headstone and take a look at the dates imprinted on it. It's still surreal when I look at it. Hard for me to wrap my head around the fact that my beautiful husband ended up here—in a cold lonely cemetery, the victim of a random carjacking— hours after we had celebrated our wedding, instead of living a lifetime full of love with me.

In everyone's life there are moments in time, events that define you, instances that effect you in such a way that they alter the way that you think, the way that you choose to live your life. For me, losing Tyler is the thing that defines me because when he died he left a gaping hole in my heart so large that nothing could ever fill it. Not time, not hope for the future, not the idea of a new love...none of those things could ever change the fact that all I'll ever be is broken. In fact the idea of me feeling whole is like trying to get a rose to bloom in the desert...impossible.

I place a small bouquet of flowers on the grave and wipe away my now falling tears. Being here never gets any easier but leaving him here...leaving him here is like a knife in my chest.

"Happy anniversary babe," I whisper, before finally walking away from him. I notice all the beautiful flowers around me, people who just like me have come to pay respects to someone who we once loved. It seems almost wrong having so much beauty in a place that represents so much sadness. I make it back to my car, get in, and let go, sobbing uncontrollably into my steering wheel. This will never get any less painful.

I never thought I'd be the kind of girl who spent her life dwelling on the past, on all of the things that should have gone one way but then went horribly wrong. I always prided myself on being strong, resilient, and capable of making the best out of bad circumstances, but shit, I was so wrong. For four years I've let my grief control everything, I've let it suffocate me and snuff the light right out of my life and the thing of it is...I'm okay with that. I have no desire to forget, to forge ahead and move on without my husband. My husband... Jesus can I even call him that? It's like a cruel joke; the ink was barely dry on the marriage certificate before he died.

To Forever...

Forever—that's what he said. *Well Tyler*, I think to myself, *forever never came*. I sit here in my car gazing at the gloomy sky, the thick clouds that hide away all traces of sunlight for what must be a long time. It usually takes me a while before I'm finally ready to drive away from here, but this time I tell myself I'll stay away, at least for a while. No more monthly visits to this place. It doesn't make me feel any better, and I know that Tyler wouldn't want me to keep coming back. I'm never really going to find what I'm looking for here. This place holds no answers, no solutions, no hope, and it leaves me feeling even more lost and lonely than I did before. It takes me days to start to even begin to feel normal again after leaving here. As normal as I can feel anyway. The truth is that besides going to work, I've managed to detach myself from the outside world and alienate everyone who ever gave a damn about me. *Nice work Everly.*

My parents still try to get through to me because really what kind of parents would they be if they just gave up on me? I guess they still have hope that I'll come back to them as the happy loving girl they once knew, but I know that will never happen, and I feel for them, I really do. Ty's parents make a monthly appearance at my door, and they like to share their grief with me. I almost think it makes them feel better to see just how miserable I am. Like my sadness means something to them—maybe it shows them that their son didn't die in vain. That someone loved him so much that she can't even begin to fathom moving on with her life so she stands frozen, cemented in place, while the whole world goes forth without her. Seasons change, people live their lives—fall in love, get married, have babies, move away, change jobs, buy houses, laugh, cry, feel—and all the while she remains unchanged, unmotivated, unmoving.

That's the cliff notes version of the girl I've become, it sums it up pretty nicely I think. I point my car in the direction of my house and drive. I drive around in the car that Tyler helped me pick out, the car that he haggled with the dealer over for hours and hours trying to get me the best possible deal on. I still have a year's worth of payments on it; one more year of driving a vehicle that reminds me of nothing but him. The anxiety begins as I get closer to home. For most people, coming home is the highlight of their day. I wonder what it would feel like to go home to a place where you can relax, unwind, and feel free to be whoever it is that you want to be. I can't imagine it though, because for me going home feels like serving out a lifelong prison sentence with no possibility of parole, every day it just gets harder and harder.

I park my car in the double garage, a single car in a garage made for two. I think of the irony of that and let out a sigh before making my way inside and flipping on the light switch. This was my dream house, the house that Ty and I had constructed after we got engaged, thinking that we would do it right the first time so that we wouldn't have to move around every few years. A house big enough to accommodate us, our future children, and even our future pets, a Maltese for me and a chocolate lab for him. A house with five bedrooms, a huge backyard, and a massive pool; the house that literally broke the bank to get built but we knew we would make it work. This was the house that all of my dreams were built on, now it's just a constant reminder of what could've been, of what will never be. If I could light a match and burn it to the ground I would. I positively hate it.

Weeks after Tyler died, after the endless stream of visitors left, family, friends, and neighbors paying their respects and bringing me enough food to feed an army, after I finally got my parents to leave me alone here I began to think about my finances. For a while there I thought I wouldn't be able to cover the expense of this house on my own, and I figured I'd be able to sell it. I know it sounds terrible, but I was honestly relieved by that. But Tyler's life insurance policy covered the majority of the mortgage and his parents graciously offered to pay the rest. It was a final gift from my dead husband…worst present ever. Every so often I tell myself that I should sell it. Logically, I know that I should leave everything in it behind, pack up my clothes and just sell it, but the guilt would be too much, or maybe I just like living like this. Perhaps the misery and loneliness I feel here is my way of punishing myself for living.

I climb the marble staircase up to the second level, enter my cavernous bedroom, and toss my purse onto the dresser. I plug my cell in the charger before I strip down to my t-shirt and panties, tie my hair up into a messy bun, and climb onto the massive bed. It's not even twelve o' clock in the afternoon, but I feel emotionally drained after my visit to the cemetery. Sleep is the best thing for me right now—if I'm lucky I can escape my feelings through sleep. In the beginning, I would dream of chocolate eyes, the eyes that I used to love getting lost in which now sadly only haunt me.

I wake to the sound of my cell phone ringing; my eyes try to adjust to the light as I clumsily reach out for my phone.

"Hello," I answer with a groggy voice, not even bothering to check who it is. I don't get many phone calls anyway; realistically it can only be a handful of people.

"Hey Everly, I was just thinking about you and I wanted to check in. Did I catch you at a bad time?"

I let out a sigh doing a poor job of hiding my slight annoyance. "Oh hi Morgan. No, no, it's not a bad time, how are you?"

Morgan is my best friend if you can even call her that anymore. She's one of the many people I've pushed away since Tyler died; she's also one of the only few who haven't given up all hope on me. Every couple of weeks she calls me to "check in". It's nice that she still cares enough to bother, and I guess I don't mind the phone calls, it keeps me somewhat connected to the outside world, but today is just not a good day. It's been four years since the day I married Tyler, and it's just one day shy of the day he died.

"I'm good, I just haven't talked to you in a while, and I thought that maybe you'd want to meet up for dinner or something?"

I lie. "I'm sorry Morgan, I'm coming down with a cold or something and I'd feel terrible if I got you sick."

I hear her sigh on the other end of the line, her frustration with me is so evident that she doesn't even try to hide it anymore. I don't blame her; I'd be frustrated with me too. I've only seen her four or five times in the last two years, and it isn't due to lack of trying on her part, but Morgan always tries to make everything better. The kind of girl who tells you that everything will be alright when you're so deep in shit that you can't see anything else. She's the first one to tell you that everything happens for a reason; that you have to try to find the positive in even the worst situations. Unfortunately I find it difficult to find anything good about having a dead husband.

"Okay, I understand. I'll try you again in a few weeks. Hopefully you'll feel better by then."

"Yeah, well thanks for calling," I respond before ending the call and falling back into my bed. I feel bad for blowing her off, but I'm not so fired up to hear any of the self-help bullshit today. If I wasn't starving, I'd attempt to go back to sleep because I've been known to sleep entire days away. After Tyler died I suffered with bouts of insomnia, and the only thing that helped were the sleeping pills my doctor had prescribed to me after my near nervous breakdown. After a while he refused to keep refilling the prescription, so now when necessary I just chug Nyquil like I would a can of cola.

I get up, putting on the same jeans I discarded earlier, and head downstairs to the kitchen. I decide to peruse the contents of my freezer, quickly coming to find that there *are* no contents in my freezer. I've got to give it to my mom; she's usually right on top of making sure there's enough food in this house to keep me fed. I've never asked her to go grocery shopping for me, but after four years, I've kind of come to expect it.

"Cereal it is then," I murmur to myself as I open the refrigerator door. I look around a moment before finally accepting the fact that there is no milk. I shut the door with a little more force than I intended to use. I can hear the rattling of whatever jars may be situated inside. I walk over to the island in the middle of the kitchen and lean against it, resting my head in the palm of my hands. I'm waging an internal battle—do I order food and pray that my mom actually comes through with groceries in the near future or do I act like an adult and go buy my own.

The mere fact that I have to contemplate this at all sickens me. This isn't how I'm supposed to be, sitting at home with no motivation to do anything. I used to love life. I loved everything about it—the way the sun shines through the window in the morning, and the way it felt on my skin when I'd go for a walk. I loved spending time with my friends, taking trips, having fun. The girl I am now is a far departure from who I used to be, and I'm disgusted with myself. The fact that I've let myself get to a point where the simple act of buying groceries is cause for concern. Have I really become that much of a recluse?

"Fuck this." I push off of the counter and go to grab my purse and car keys. I will not let something as mundane as buying food overpower me. This is where I need to draw the line. I need to start taking better care of myself; I shouldn't have to be reduced to starvation because I'd rather wallow in self-pity. The drive to the grocery store just outside of town takes only 15 minutes; I choose this one with the hope that my chances of running into someone I know will be significantly decreased.

I grab a shopping cart and take my time slowly going up and down every aisle, putting things in my cart as I go. It's silly but I actually feel a sense of power that I haven't felt for years, doing something for myself, making choices for myself, getting what I want. Something as ordinary as going to the grocery store, a task that most people find boring or mundane makes me feel like I've just jumped a tremendous hurdle. I pay for my purchases and push the cart out to the parking lot, popping the trunk and placing everything inside. Just as I move to slam it shut I hear a voice from the past, an all too familiar voice.

"Everly?"

My body stiffens, and I can almost feel my blood begin to boil the instant I hear the deep timbre of his voice. An intense anger fills up every crevice of my body, making me feel nauseated and unsteady. Memories rush back into my head, opening a floodgate of emotions that I didn't need to feel, especially not today. I slowly turn and come face to face with *him*—the sole reason that Tyler is gone today.

15

"Luca," I say on a breath, but looking at him again breaks something apart inside of me. Something that I've been struggling so hard to keep under the surface, and I hate him for it. I hate him just as much today as I did when my life was obliterated four years ago, and suddenly I'm back there again, back to the place where I lost it all.

I'm awoken by the shrill sound of a nearby telephone. I open my eyes and try to get my bearings. It takes me a second to realize that I'm at the hotel. I peek over my shoulder, and Tyler is still sound asleep. Who could possibly sleep through that ringing?

I reach over to the nightstand and grab the receiver bringing it up to my ear.

"Hello?"

"This is your courtesy wake-up call," says the voice on the other line.

"Thank you," I reply before hanging up. I throw my head back on the pillow and stretch my arms up over my head.

"Ty, we have a flight to catch babe," I groan out mid stretch. Excitement starts to build at the thought of Tyler and me on a beach, sipping drinks and soaking each other up.

I roll my head to the side and smile at the sight of my sleeping husband. My husband... I still can't believe that we're married.

"Come on Ty, we have to start getting ready."

He turns his head to squint at me. "It's still early babe. Our flight isn't until later."

"I know honey but by the time we get up, get ready, and have breakfast, it'll be time to go. The airport is over an hour away, did you take travel time into account?"

I hear a low chuckle escape from his lips. "Alright, go hop in the shower. I'll be up by the time you're done."

I smile at him. Tyler has never been a morning person, and getting him out of bed is always a challenge, but he's right we have time. "Okay. But you better be up by the time I come back in here," I say. I place a quick kiss on his lips and make my way to the bathroom. I take a few minutes inspecting my reflection in the mirror, funny... I know it's silly but I thought I'd look different somehow as if getting married changes you somehow.

I take my time in the shower enjoying the feel of the warm water on me. I imagine that Tyler is probably still in bed, the things we can do together if I just went back into the room and crawled in beside him. Tyler knows me like the back of his hand, he knows exactly what to do to set me off and with him it's always sweet. From the beginning it's always been about making love, expressing how we feel about each other intimately. I don't know if it can get any better than that, although him being a little bossy in bed yesterday was a nice change, that might be fun to explore in the future. I turn off the shower and dry myself off before wrapping the oversized towel around my body. I towel dry my hair and run a brush through it before exiting the bathroom. As I walk back into the bedroom I notice that Tyler is up and dressed already.

"You're actually up already?" I question with amazement. "Aren't you going to take a shower?"

He walks over to me wrapping his arms around my waist and pulling me in for an embrace. "I'll grab a shower when I get back babe. Luca dropped by and asked me to give him a ride home. He spent the night at the hotel too and apparently his date ditched him last night."

I make no attempt to hide my annoyance when I use my hands to push at his chest enabling me to disengage from him. "You're joking right?" It comes out like more of a warning than a question.

"No." He sighs. "It'll take me a half hour tops babe. He's my best friend, what do you expect me to do?"

"How about telling him to call a cab?"

"Is that what you'd do if Morgan knocked on the door right now?"

He has me there, I'd never deny my best friend anything, but Luca is different. He's always been a source of contention in my

17

relationship with Tyler. He and I have never gotten along, and I hate the fact that he has the power to cause tension between me and Ty.

"Alright fine, go. You always come to the rescue where he's concerned." Arguments like these are not uncommon for us, but the day after our wedding, when we're about to go on our honeymoon... Even I can't believe this shit.

"Please don't be that way. He's like a brother to me," he says reaching out and grabbing my hand. "But you...you are my wife, and we're about to leave on our honeymoon and have an amazing time. It'll be just you and me." He pulls me closer wrapping his arms around my waist and placing a kiss on my neck. "And when we get to Antigua Ev... I'm not letting you out of the room for at least twenty-four hours... At least!" he declares with a twinkle of mischief in his eyes.

"You promise?"

"Mmm hmm."

I let out a sigh; he knows he's won me over already.

"Get yourself dressed and ready, I'll be back before you know it. I'll take you to breakfast on the way to the airport."

"Alright, but hurry up."

"I will." He releases me and grabs his keys off of the nightstand. "I love you," he calls out right before he walks out the door and just like that he's gone.

My eyes are shut tight and I'm holding on to my car for dear life while I gasp for air and fight for breath as the memory recedes. The panic attack hit too quickly. I haven't had one in over two years, and I'd thought that they were behind me, but seeing *him* again must have triggered it.

My eyes slowly open as my breathing starts to even out. I squint, adjusting to the bright rays of the sun beating down above me.

"Hey, you're okay," he says calmly almost soothingly. "You scared the hell out of me."

I stare into his intense green eyes, the eyes of the man who while I was with Tyler I never really cared for, but who over the last four years I've come to hate. In them I can clearly see his worry for me. He wasn't expecting me to lose it moments ago, but more importantly I see the guilt, the apology that lies just below the surface, looming, hoping that I'll make this easier on him and show him some kindness.

The problem is I don't think that I'm capable of it. No…I know I'm not. I do not have it in me to show him anything but my true feelings. He's the living breathing reason why my husband is dead, why I'm a widow at only twenty-six years old. The best man at our wedding who ended up being the catalyst for tragedy.

"I'm fine," I say, hearing the sound of my own anger laced with my weak attempt at trying to sound unaffected.

"We're drawing a crowd here Ev. Let me at least help you to the car."

I push his hand off of me and quickly turn to close the trunk. The lightheaded feeling returns and I wobble slightly. Luca's arm goes around my waist helping to steady me.

"Look, I know you hate me, but I'm only trying to help. I wouldn't have stopped at all if I'd have known this is how you'd react."

He can't be serious; did he think I would greet him with open arms? "How the fuck did you think I would react?" I reply, my eyes nearly bulging out of my head. "You know what? Get away from me." I try in vain to wriggle out of his grasp. I can almost feel my skin burning at his touch; I don't like to be touched at all anymore but especially not by him.

He says nothing at first, just releases a frustrated sigh and stares at me. He shakes his head after a while and shrugs. "I guess I'd hoped that time might have lessened the anger you feel toward me. I see that that wasn't the case."

He forcefully leads me to the passenger side of my car and helps me in, holding onto me until I'm fully seated.

"What are you doing?" I look up at him through still hazy vision.

"I'm taking you home. I can't just let you drive like this."

"Yes you can. I'll be fine. Turn around, walk away, and leave me the hell alone."

He gives me a curt nod and lets out yet another sigh of frustration. "Okay Ev, I'll do all of those things as soon as I make sure that you're safe at home."

I shake my head and scowl at him. "I'm not giving you my keys Luca, so you can just give up now," I say, feeling especially satisfied with myself. Like hell I'm going anywhere with him, even if I did just freak out.

He grins down at me for a moment looking almost smug before opening the palm of his hands. "You mean these keys? Yeah, I picked them up after you dropped them during your little incident back there."

I open my mouth to respond, but he shuts my door before I can get a word out. He's in the drivers seat and backing out of the parking spot before I can protest at all.

A patch of dark clouds roll in, effectively blocking out the sunlight, and I zone out during the drive home, letting my mind drift off so that I don't have to think about the fact that I'm sitting next to the one person I've focused on hating for so long. I let myself zone out so that I don't have to participate in any meaningless conversation or forced niceties. I try to fight against the memories that linger under the surface when Luca is around. I try but I can't stop myself from thinking back four years ago, to the moments after I realized my life had been irrevocably changed.

Luca came to see me almost immediately after I learned Tyler was gone. My parents had just driven me home from the hospital when the knock came on the front door.

"Everly," he said on a whisper, his bloodshot eyes full of tears.

"Everly I'm so sorry."

He looked distraught, disheveled, and if I didn't know any better, I'd

21

have thought that he was in as much pain as I was. I couldn't think of that though, couldn't let myself sympathize with his grief when my own was so consuming. My body trembled at the sight of him, a mixture of anger and disbelief.

"Get out of here, I don't want to see you," I said, shaking my head. He visibly flinched at my words, but I didn't care. Looking at him made me hurt, made me hurt everywhere, made me hurt even worse. The thought that he was here and not Tyler filled me with rage.

"I just... I don't know what to say Ev. I can't... I don't know how this happened."

"This happened because of you!" I screech. "You did this, you killed him."

His face blanched at my words, but he didn't argue, didn't defend himself, because he knew I was right. I watched him nod his head in agreement as he realized what I was saying. With no other words, he accepted the blame and then turned and walked away. I could have stopped him, could have tried to ease his guilt, but I couldn't make myself care about his feelings. He was the reason I lost Tyler and nothing he could ever say to me would ever make me forgive him.

Luca left town a few days after that. He didn't even go to Ty's funeral, not that he would have been welcome there to begin with. I hadn't seen him since that encounter, not until now that is. The shock of seeing him must have been too much for me, I've carried around all of this anger and resentment toward him for all this time and in the moment that we came face to face it finally just hit me all at once. Normally I'd be embarrassed about blanking out but right now it pisses me the fuck off. I hate that he has any effect on me at all. Any emotion wasted on Luca is too much—he doesn't deserve even my hate but it doesn't change the fact that I still feel it.

It's raining by the time Luca pulls into the driveway.

"Garage door opener?" he says pointing to the remote on the visor. I nod, never looking his way. The less I say the better because acknowledging his presence only makes it worse. He presses the button and secures the car in the garage. I'm out of the car before he can even turn it off. I wait for him as he rounds the hood and hold out my hands for the keys.

"I'm going to call a ride to pick me up. Do you mind if I wait inside until they get here?"

"Yes I mind," I say walking into the house. I hear the distinct rustling of grocery bags being pulled out of the trunk, and moments later footsteps reaching me in the kitchen, but I don't acknowledge him. I don't know how to cope with having him around me. He places the bags down on the granite countertop while I open the refrigerator and grab a bottled water. I'm taking a sip as he begins speaking into his cell phone requesting a taxi to pick him up.

"You might want to get some rest," he finally says almost harshly. If I didn't know any better I could swear I hear a twinge of anger in his voice. That's rich; I'm the only one here with a right to be angry.

I turn around and glare at him. This seems to be my permanent face where this man is concerned. I have no kind words for him, no words of thanks. One word about sums it all up. "Goodbye."

He pauses briefly, looking around the house as if he's taking in pieces of art on a museum wall, carefully inspecting his surroundings. He looks at me, giving nothing away except for a slight nod of his head. His eyes are guarded in a way that I can tell he has something to say but he won't.

"I'll see you around sometime," he says brusquely before turning around and walking out of my front door.

I know it was rude of me to kick him out like that after being decent enough to make sure I got home, but being nice to Luca was never my strong suit. It wasn't his either — he was always a jerk to me. In fact, there was only one day in our history that I can ever recall him being nice, and it was the day we met. Then of course there was today, he'd been nothing but kind to me today and I treated him like a bug that I needed to squash as quickly as possible. The thing is that after getting over the initial shock of seeing him and of being around him, I realized that the hate I felt for him four years ago was just as consuming now as it was then.

I've been extremely isolated since Tyler died, living in my own little world, a bubble of my own creation. I'd gotten used to feeling empty and numb inside. I'd gotten used to a mostly solitary existence, and I've accepted that as my fate, my future — a life spent alone

Luca was closer to Tyler than just about anybody. I admit that I never really understood the bond between them. Never understood what it was about Luca that made him such a necessary part of Tyler's life. I had tried in the beginning to befriend him, to make an effort to see what Ty saw, but Luca never liked me. He never accepted that I was the woman Tyler loved, so I was made to feel like nothing more than an outcast whenever he was around

I feel anger and tension just rolling off of my body in waves. I suppose I never allowed myself to think about the possibility that I would see Luca again. He's been gone so long; I just assumed *or hoped* that it was a permanent move. I'm not stupid or naïve, I understand that Luca didn't actually kill Tyler. He didn't hold the gun to his chest or pull the trigger. I know that technically it wasn't his fault, but his actions were what led to it. If he'd just left Tyler alone that morning he'd still be here with me. I

24

called my mom in an attempt to take my mind off of things, the surprise in her voice making me sad. I never call her, never pick up the phone—I'm always too busy hiding out. If it wasn't for her regular grocery deliveries I might never see her. She was shocked when I'd told her she didn't have to bring any food this week; I think I may have even heard a little bit of relief in her voice. I think it made her happy that I'd finally taken back a piece of my independence, however small it might be. I decided right then and there that I would be getting my own groceries from now on.

~ Luca ~

Seeing Everly really did a number on me. I had thought that with time she would be able to learn how to move on from the tragedy that took Tyler away. I had hoped that time would have lessened her hatred for me and that she could possibly forgive me for what she believes is my role in his death. I thought wrong, I was so wrong, but even though her forgiveness didn't come, seeing her again made me feel something that I hadn't felt toward her in a long time. Anger. Anger toward her and the fucking blinders she's always had where I was concerned. In fact, Everly has spent the majority of her life walking around with her head in the clouds, only seeing what she wants to see. Despite the anger, every feeling, every emotion that I ever felt for her, toward her, about her, came right the fuck back or maybe it never left me at all. She's beautiful, even now with the clear as day mask of pain she wears on her face. Her brown thick brown hair falls down her back in waves and her dark almond-shape eyes show every single expression on her face. She's never been good at masking emotions. She's of average height for a girl, and her body is curvy in all the right places. No one has ever made me feel as intensely as Everly Phillips and she'll never know that. She'll never understand how her presence has always caused a reaction in me. Whether it is good or bad, she gets a rise out of me, and I can't deny that. I tried to cut her out of my life cold turkey when I walked away and left. I was already scheduled to leave for school in Chicago, but Tyler's death just pushed me to go sooner. I wanted to let her move on with her life without a constant reminder of what she lost and who she blamed, but I never truly let go. Ev's best friend Morgan filled me in every couple of months on what was happening while I was away. From what she told me, I knew that she was having a hard time adjusting to life without Ty, but seeing her just made it hit home even more. She's a girl frozen, stuck in her own grief and unable to move forward.

I knew Everly hated me. I could understand it, understand why she'd felt the way she did. I don't blame her, truth be told I was never her favorite person, I made sure of that. It was better for me to let her hate me all those years ago and to let her believe that I was an asshole. This way she never got to see the truth, she got to have her perfect relationship while never knowing how deep my feelings for her really ran. A revelation like that would have ruined my relationship with Tyler, and he was always like a brother to me. Above everything else my loyalty lay with him, it had to.

I sit in my car for a while; I haven't been here before now. I'd left town before the funeral took place, and it's hard to come to grips with this, even now after so much time has passed. I get out of the car and walk across the lawn. It takes me a few minutes of searching before I found the one I was looking for. I notice the fresh flowers as I run my hand over the engraved lettering on the tombstone, *Tyler Maxwell West*. I let out a chuckle and shake my head.

"Dude. *Maxwell?* I knew you practically all your life, and I never knew that was your middle name. I don't blame you for hiding it though." I release a sigh and look around me, unsure exactly of what or who I'm looking for. I crouch down until I'm eye level with the headstone.

"I'm so sorry man." My voice cracks as I say the words that I've been holding in for so long. "I'm sorry for so many things. Mostly I'm sorry for not being there for her, even though she didn't want me around, even though I know it's what you would have expected from me. I couldn't, I couldn't be around her. And she would never have accepted my presence. I've never had such mixed emotions for anyone in all my life."

I close my eyes, pinch the bridge of my nose, and let out a shaky breath. "If I had known how bad things had gotten with Everly, how she shut her whole life down and let her grief take over, I would never have stayed away as long as I did. She may hate me, but I would have at least tried to help her dig out of this hole she's planted herself in. I don't know, I think it might be too late. Her mind is made up about me, and she won't even look at me. And if I'm being perfectly honest, I don't know if I can stand to be around her either. I hate her too."

I finish unpacking the rest of my boxes, putting away the last of my belongings in the closet of the small one bedroom apartment I rented in town. If you'd have asked me a few years ago if I'd ever come back here, I would have told you I would *never* come back to this town again. I knew that Everly and Tyler's family blamed me for what happened, and I guess a part of me blamed myself too. It was just easier for everyone involved for me to go away since I was leaving anyway. No one knew that I had been accepted into law school in Chicago, not even Ty, but I knew even before everything got screwed up that I needed to go. I'd been contemplating coming home for a long time, but the job offer at one of the top law firms in the state is what ultimately drew me back.

"Knock, knock." I smile at the voice coming from the stairway that leads up to my apartment.

"Hey Mom, come on up."

My mother has been on cloud nine ever since I came back to New Jersey. My leaving had been hard on her, I know she would've wanted me to stay, but she supported my move anyway.

"I wanted to stop by and see the new apartment. I hope that's okay," she says as she walks in with bags in both her hands and takes in her surroundings.

My mom and I have always been close, but I don't think I could have gotten through the last few years without her. It was a dark time for me and even though we were living thousands of miles apart, she found a way to let me know that she was always right there.

"You can come by anytime you want, Mom. You know that."

She gives me her megawatt smile, and I know I've made the right decision in coming back. It's been too long. "I brought you lunch."

"Lunch? It looks like you brought enough to feed the whole building."

"Actually this is lunch," she says holding up a large paper bag. "The rest of it is housewarming gifts."

I grin at her, loving the fact that she's so excited to have me here. "I should have known you'd come and try to decorate the place. Knock yourself out Mom."

"I have amazing taste you know."

"I do. I trust you. Plus it's not like I've had the time to go shopping for much, and I'm not sure I'd want to even if I did have the time." Me in a store to purchase home goods is not on the top of my list of shit to do. We're lucky I managed to get furniture in this place.

"I know you've been lying low since you got back in town Luca but I don't want you to live your life that way. You didn't do anything wrong."

"I know Mom. I've just been focused on getting myself settled."

"Alright, I just worry about you."

I hate that she worries so much, I'm sure everything that happened

wasn't easy on her or my dad.

"I actually saw Everly West a few days ago."

"What?" she says, eyes full of shock. "She's probably the last person on the planet I'd have guessed you'd run into, no one ever sees her around anymore."

"Yeah, it was a little awkward at best; she barely said a word to me."

"She still blames you?" There's a definite tone of annoyance in that

question.

"Blames me? Mom, she nearly went postal, she fucking hates me."

"Don't curse," she warns. I respond with a glare. "Luca just stay

away from her, it's obvious that she's a troubled girl. You don't need that kind of drama in your life."

"I know."

"Are you all ready to start your new job tomorrow? I'm so proud of

you." This is her attempt at changing the subject and lightening the now dampened mood.

Finishing law school was one of my proudest and saddest moments. I know what a huge accomplishment it was, but I couldn't help but think that Tyler should have been graduating too. He came from a family of lawyers, his father owns a successful firm in town, and it was destined for him. Me, I had to fight for it, work harder, read more, and study more to get through. That's why the job offer at Harvey, Stone, and Associates is so unbelievable to me. I never imagined I'd get the offer there when I applied; in fact it was the only firm I applied to here in town. It's the best, even better than Tyler's dad, so the fact that I get to start my career there is unreal.

"Yeah, I'm ready. I'm real excited about it."

"You should be. It's an amazing opportunity."

She's right. This is an amazing opportunity. It's my chance to make a name for myself, to do what my best friend couldn't do. I have to let go of the past, let go of the ghost that I still carry with me, the regret that still consumes me, and the woman who still occupies my mind.

~ Everly ~

The days after my run-in with Luca seem to drag on slower than usual. It's been more of the same—I work, come home, cook, watch television, and sleep. The sleeping part is what's starting to get to me. I've been dreaming about Tyler again, and I haven't done that in a while. It's as if Luca's reappearance has triggered something in my brain and opened up the floodgates again. What's even worse is that Luca's been in my dreams too. I dream about the moment when Tyler goes away, he tells me Luca needs him, and I remember feeling angry. I'm waiting, pacing around the room, looking out the window watching for Tyler to come back. When the door opens again, it's Luca standing there. I know it should be Ty, I know that he's gone and Luca's come in his place, but instead of throwing him out, I'm stuck. I'm stopped dead in my tracks by the look of sorrow in his eyes, the deafening sorrow that could only be matched by my own.

Why, why am I dreaming about Luca? It's puzzling and disturbing to me that he holds a place in my subconscious mind. The fact that I feel enough toward him to conjure him in my dreams unsettles me. It's almost like he's trying to tell me something, but I don't really want to know what it is.

I peek at the alarm clock, dreading that I have to get up and get ready for work. Being a paralegal at a law firm was never my ambition. I was supposed to go to law school with Tyler, we were supposed to graduate and open our own law firm, but fate had other plans, and after he died my dreams of practicing law died too. Sometimes I think that I was pursuing law just because he was. I don't know if I have the drive for it now that he's gone. His father tried for months to get me to go to law school and when I refused he tried to convince me to come work for him at his practice. He could never understand why I refused. He didn't understand that I live with Tyler's ghost everywhere I go; I didn't need to live with it at work too. In fact, this job is just about the only place where I'm able to get away from it.

I stretch one more time, throw the covers off of me, and get out of bed. I push away all of the dark memories and focus on the present, on putting one foot in front of the other and willing myself to get through this day. Just one day at a time, that's the only way I've been able to function for the last forty-eight months. Life was never supposed to be like this, it held so much promise before, so much joy, and now it's full of emptiness and monotony.

After sitting at my desk, logging in to my computer, and prepping myself a cup of coffee, I peruse the contents of my email prioritizing my work for the day. The best part about this place is that I've been here long enough that everyone just leaves me alone to do my job. I know what I have to do, and I get it done without anybody hovering over my shoulder. I roll my eyes at the last minute meeting alert that pops up on my calendar—a meeting first thing Monday morning is exactly what I don't need. Word of a new attorney joining the firm has been running rampant in this place, and I'm wondering if that's what this is all about. I grab my coffee, a notebook and pen, and head over to the conference room where others have already started to gather. I pull up a chair next to Lisa. Aside from me, she's been here the longest; she's thin, frail almost, with hair that closely resembles the texture of straw. She's the mousiest and most quiet person here. She's also by far my favorite person, because she doesn't even try to engage in small talk with me, and I'm pretty sure her mentality is similar to mine. She just wants to be left alone; it's a win-win situation.

There's chatter going on around me but I'm zoned out, uninterested in what's happening around me. My gaze travels to the window and my eyes lock on an old oak tree, trying to focus on something other than the mindless conversations of my coworkers.

"Thank you all for being here on such short notice." I hear Mr. Harvey, one of the partners at the firm, say. He personally hired me, and while I'm fond of him, I still can't manage to bring my attention to him. "As you know we've been talking about expanding our firm for some time, looking to bring in fresh new talent to keep up with our growing caseload. I'd like you all to help me welcome the newest attorney to our practice, Luca Jensen."

My breath catches at the sound of his name, and I jerk my head to the front of the room, eyes wide, mouth open, and my body rigid as I take in the sight of him in his dark gray suit, looking like anything but the Luca I know and every bit like a capable attorney. I question whether I'm actually awake right now or stuck in a nightmare, as he looks my way. He pauses in surprise when he sees my face, clearly not expecting to see me here. My anger is rising, and I clench my fists in my lap in order to keep

33

myself from shaking. What is he doing here? When did he even pass the bar and if he did why is he at this firm? This isn't the only fucking law office in New Jersey, why this one? He does his best to disguise his reaction as he addresses the room. I can hear him thanking everyone for the warm welcome, but I'm too pissed to hear much else.

The meeting lasts a few minutes longer and as it comes to a close I gather my things and rush out of the conference room with my head down. I get to my desk and practically throw myself in the chair, place my head in my hands, close my eyes and focus on my breathing. I need to calm myself down before I start throwing things. This was supposed to be my one safe place, the one place where Tyler's memory wasn't always in my face, but now I know that's not possible. No matter what I do, there will always be someone or something that reminds me of him.

I make it through the rest of the day without running into Luca. I have made it my goal to avoid him at all costs, and I succeed for most of the week. I see him in the hall so I turn and walk the other way. He walks into the kitchen while I'm there; I grab my coffee cup and bolt. He's standing next to the water cooler, and I decide I'd rather die of dehydration. I spy him at the printer and figure the documents I need to mail can wait. He pulls into the parking spot next to mine, and I move my car. I don't care about how petty I must look, how absolutely bitchy I must seem. I. Don't. Care. As far as I'm concerned Luca does not exist, he can't touch me, I will not let him phase me, effect me, bother me. He does not exist! That is until two seconds ago when he walked up to my desk. I look up take in his appearance but say nothing. He cleans up nicely, I'll give him that. He looks good in his black tailored suit, almost like he belongs here, but I know better. He's a selfish asshole loser and the fact that he's standing here instead of

Tyler who really deserved a job like this makes me want to scream.

"Hi," he greets, looking down at me uncomfortably.

I continue to stare at him, and it's probably more of a glare at this point but again say nothing. *He does not exist, he does not exist,* I keep chanting to myself. He waits for a reply from me but quickly realizes that it's not coming. Maybe he's not so stupid after all. He lets out a sigh of frustration.

"I was told that you were the go to person for information on the benefits package."

He was informed correctly, I *am* the person to go to for a lot of things in this place, none of which I wish to go over with him. Had he been any other new hire, I would have already gone over everything with him. I open my bottom desk drawer pull out a pre-made manila file and toss...yes toss it to him as if I were tossing a Frisbee to a dog. He catches it (barely), chuckles, and walks away. I'm glad that he thinks my hatred is amusing. "You're welcome," I mumble to myself. "Jerk."

I open my email program and begin to compose a new message.

    From: Everly West
    To: Luca Jensen
    Subject: New Hire Information.

    Dear Mr. Jensen

    Welcome to Harvey, Stone, and Associates. You
    will need to fill out the benefits package, which
    you have received and return to my attention no
    later than close of business day next Friday.

    Please be aware that should you need supplies for
    your office you may email me a list, and I will take
    care of ordering for you.

    I will be ordering your business cards, and you
will receive them within ten days.

    Should you require anything else please do not
hesitate to E-MAIL me.

    Thank you,

    Everly Phillips-West, CP
    Certified Paralegal

I hit send feeling pretty proud of myself. He should get the picture now, the picture being stay the hell away from me.

❦

Avoiding Luca isn't as hard as I thought it would be, probably because I think he's been avoiding me as much as I've been avoiding him. When I came into work on Tuesday, I found the completed benefits package file on my desk. Good to know he was paying attention to my email. I couldn't help but to peek at his paperwork. I noted that his apartment is located right on the beach; he must have gotten a hefty salary to be able to afford a place like that. I was raised to be happy when good things happen for people but with Luca I just can't be. If anything, the more successful he becomes the more pissed off I get and I hate that I feel that way, because this isn't how I want to live my life. I don't want to hold a grudge and carry all of this animosity, but I lost the thing that mattered most to me and Luca was a key player in that loss.

I shut off my computer and tidy up my desk for the night, making sure to lock up all important documents in my desk. I grab my purse and keys and head out to the parking lot thinking of nothing but soaking in a warm bath when I get home. I approach my car and silently curse when I realize that both of my front tires are flat. My nose starts to burn and my eyes start to glass over with unshed tears. *This is stupid, I will not cry,* I tell myself. I look through the glove compartment for the paperwork which includes the number for roadside assistance.

"Everly?"

I sigh and let my head fall back on the headrest. Why? Why do I have to deal with *him* on top of it all?

"Everly..."

"What?" I snap my head in his direction. "What do you want?"

He points to one of my flat tires. "I thought you could use some help."

"Well I don't. I'm calling roadside assistance; they'll come out and take care of it."

"Do you need a ride home?"

"I'm. Calling. Roadside. Assistance."

"I understand that. But you need two new tires, I'm pretty sure your car only has one spare. They're not going to be able to fix it tonight; they're just going to tow it."

Fuck. My. Life.

I get on the phone and call for assistance only to be told that the tow truck will take over two hours to get to me. This couldn't possibly get any worse.

"Come on Ev, let me take you home. You can leave the keys somewhere for the tow truck driver, have him take the car to a repair shop, and you can deal with it tomorrow."

I roll my eyes, dismissing him even though I know at this point I need his help if I want to get home tonight and not be left out here alone in the dark waiting for a tow truck. I'd call my father, but he works in the city and would likely get here after the tow truck.

"Fine," I say in a huff, crossing my arms across my chest and resigning myself to accept my shitty luck. Luca pries the car keys from my fisted hand and hides them inside the car, noting that I should call the tow company and tell them where to find them. He motions for me to follow him to his car and I do so, all the while huffing and stomping my feet. He opens the passenger door for me and I slide into the seat, rolling my eyes as I go. The thought of him pretending to act like a gentleman is actually comical. He situates himself in the driver's seat and maneuvers us out of the parking lot.

The silence is heavy between us, making the drive uncomfortable, almost unbearable. I stare out the window careful not to make any eye contact with him. I don't want to engage him or show him my discomfort. Every second I spend in his presence feels like being thrust in the middle of a war zone waiting for someone to strike first.

"We don't have to be enemies you know?" This is Luca's attempt at an icebreaker.

"You can't be enemies with someone who doesn't exist, and in my world you do not exist."

"He would have wanted me to look out for you. Does it really make you feel any better to act like this?"

"Like what?"

"Like a bitch."

"Excuse me?" I gasp, whipping my head around to give him a dirty look. "Who the hell do you think you are calling me a bitch?"

"I'm trained to see through the bullshit, and you're fucking full of it," he grinds out of his mouth as he pulls into my driveway. It's a direct hit, a blow to my armor, and I'm exposed and vulnerable. But I steady my breathing, steel my spine, and retaliate.

"I'm sure you are! I'm sure you look in the mirror every day and see bullshit staring you right in the fucking face."

"You're right I do. At least I can be honest about it."

"Go. To. Hell!" I yell practically leaping out of the car and slamming the door.

"So I can live like you? No thanks."

He's right behind me now as I rifle through my bag in search of my keys.

"Can you hurry up and open the goddamn door so that I can get the hell out of here."

Realization dawns and I throw back my head and curse the sky. "If I could I would. I left the house key on my keychain which is sitting in my car right now."

"Wow. You couldn't have thought about that, say, fifteen minutes ago?"

"I'm sorry, I was too busy being accosted by a raging asshole," I shout, getting in his face.

"Is that how you talk to people who go out of there way to save your ass?"

"Maybe that's just your guilt catching up with you," I say barely above a whisper.

His flinch is barely visible, but I know I've wounded him. Funny, it doesn't make me feel as good as I thought it would. He says nothing but turns away from me, removes his suit jacket, and starts checking the windows in search of one that's unlocked. I sit down on the front steps of the house that I hate so much, waiting, waiting for something to change, anything. I know it's me, my fault that my life has become such a piece of shit, but I can't seem to dig myself out. I don't know how to let go of the past, the guilt that is so engrained in who I've become. What I wouldn't give to get away from here, move out of this house, take a vacation, anything really. But any step I take toward a life away from what Tyler and I were trying to build—what we should have had—feels like a betrayal.

The front door opens up, and I look over my shoulder to see Luca standing there holding it open for me.

"You okay?" he questions, seemingly calmer than he was a few minutes ago.

"I'm fine thanks. You didn't break anything did you?"

He rolls his eyes and answers back sarcastically. "I got in through a side window, and everything is as you left it duchess. You're welcome."

I get up and making a point of ignoring him as I walk inside the house and toss my purse on the stairs. I turn around and look him straight in the eye.

"Get out."

He shakes his head in disgust. "You are a real piece of work you know that? Goodnight Everly," he says as he turns, walks away, and slams the door shut behind him, leaving me alone in my misery. I climb up the stairs and head straight to the master bathroom, draw myself a bubble bath and soak in the tub until I'm calm and my fingers are wrinkled up like little prunes.

I get ready for bed and walk over to Tyler's bookshelf before getting into bed. He was a collector of things— clothes, movies, photos, books—it was just his way and as much as I teased him about his hoarding ways, I always found it to be kind of endearing. I grab a criminal drama book and get into bed, preparing to read myself to sleep. I open to the first page and a paper falls out from between the pages. It's a ticket for a bet placed on a horse race four years ago, shortly before the time that he died. I've found things like this from time to time—ticket stubs, fantasy football charts, boxing bets—and it's funny because I never knew that he did this, that he would bet on sporting events for money. I guess it's just a guy thing to do, but it still surprises me that he never mentioned it. I put the ticket on the nightstand and shrug it off. It makes no difference now, it's not like I can ask him about it. I open up the book and begin to read the words on the page, never really taking any of them in, all the while silently praying for strength to break free from this pit I'm in. What I wouldn't give to find the girl who I used to be.

It's Sunday night and I'm lying on my couch watching the latest mind numbing reality TV sensation when I'm startled by the sound of the doorbell. My whole body tenses when I see Luca standing on the other side of the door.

"Hi Ev," he greets, hands in the pockets of his worn out jeans.

"What are you doing here?" I reply in a frostier tone than I intended.

"Can I come in?"

He looks unsure of himself, wary of my reaction toward him, but at the same time a little bit menacing. Luca is hot in every sense of the word, and if I didn't hate him so much I might actually get flustered by having him around. His dark hair is the perfect contrast to his green eyes, and his perfect features set him apart. I'm pretty sure he could have just about any girl that he wants. He's got to be at least six-foot-one, and it's clear even through his clothes that he's muscular, even more so than Tyler was. If he wasn't such an ass, he'd be beautiful. He tilts his head staring at me; he's probably expecting me to slam the door in his face. Part of me wants to, but part of me is curious to know what he's doing here. After what went down last time he was here with how I kicked him out after he'd helped me for a second time, I'm stunned that he'd even attempt to set foot on my property again. I guess he doesn't understand the concept of not being welcome. I hesitate for a moment before stepping out of the way allowing him entry. I close the front door and turn to face him.

"How are you?" he asks, trying to gage my mood.

"Did you really come back here to ask me how I am?"

"I came here because..."

"Because what?" I can't help but to be short with him. It's not just him, it's everyone, I hate how they all tiptoe around me as if though I might just have a psychotic break at any given moment. Well... Trust me, if I haven't lost my goddamn mind yet I'm not going to. I prefer drowning my sorrows in solitude, not random acts of craziness.

"I think we need to clear the air. I think we need to talk about what happened."

"I know what happened how could I ever forget? Talking about it doesn't help. It doesn't change anything, and if I were going to talk about it, you would be the last person I'd talk about it with."

"I think we both need the closure, I know I do and there are things that you just don't understand."

My voice drips with disdain. "You're not looking for closure, you're looking for forgiveness."

"Fuck forgiveness! I don't need your forgiveness or anyone else's for that matter. What I need is for you to understand, for you to see that I would never do anything to hurt Tyler."

He's practically yelling at me now, and fuck my life, but I didn't sign up for this shit. Hashing out the past is not on my list of things to do, not even close. I shrug my shoulders in defeat.

"Yeah, but you did! I get it, I understand that you didn't set out to hurt him, that you didn't directly hurt him, but your actions led to..." I sigh, unable to finish the thought, unable to continue with this draining conversation. I can't escape the past, no matter what I do, I can't hide from it. I can't seem to get away from any of it.

Luca runs his hand through his hair and averts his gaze. "I miss him too you know?" he says with a sigh.

"Don't," I warn. I don't want to hear about how much Luca misses Tyler. I don't need to hear about how we share the same grief, bond over the same pain, like we should be closer because of it.

What it really boils down to is the fact that he thinks I hate him and that I'm blaming him unfairly for Tyler's death. Maybe it is unfair, but the past few years of my life have been full of unfair and why should I have to be the only one who has to experience it. Screw him if he thinks he can walk in here and seek absolution for his sins; he'll be waiting forever as far as I'm concerned.

He looks up, eyes meeting mine again. "You don't know how many times I've wanted to reach out and tell you how sorry I am that you lost him."

"Luca, get out," I demand, my eyes filling up with tears that I refuse to let fall in front of him. He doesn't get the satisfaction of seeing my weakness, not ever.

He straightens his back and squares his shoulder as if he's preparing for battle. "I'm sorry Everly."

"Luca," I say, my voice faltering slightly.

"I'm sorry."

I turn my back to him and head back to the front door. "I want you to leave."

"I'm not done."

I spin back around. "What else is there to say?" It sounds almost like a plea. For what exactly, I'm not sure. "You came, you apologized, what more?"

44

"You need to know what really happened."

"I know what happened! My husband left me to help you and he got himself killed."

"That wasn't how it happened. It's time you hear the truth, it's been four years."

"I don't want to hear anything you have to say. There's nothing you could say that will make me change my mind about you. There's nothing you can say that would make me hate you any less."

"I don't need you to hate me Everly, I already hate myself. Don't think for one minute, for one fucking minute, that I don't blame myself, that I don't live with that every single day of my life. You think I wouldn't change it if I could? You think I don't know that he's dead because of my choices? I fucking know!"

We stare at each other each both of us winded, breathing heavy as if we just went twelve rounds in a boxing ring.

"Just stay away from me Luca. I will be professional at work and make sure that you have what you need in order to do your job, but that's as much as I can give you. I can't give you closure because this will never be done for me."

"Everly."

"I don't want your explanations, I don't want to hear the how and why of Tyler being gone, the end result is still the same."

"Everly…"

"It's the same! It's always the same, just leave it alone."

I know there's a reason he's here, I feel it deep down in my bones. I know he has something to say that I should hear, and I want to know what it is, but I can't hear it. I'm not strong enough for it; I don't think I can stand to hear anything else that comes from Luca's mouth. I'm terrified that whatever he tells me will make my pain that much worse.

"You're right." He sighs, his shoulders slump, and his head drops in defeat. "It wouldn't change a damn thing. I'll see you at work tomorrow," he says, giving me a parting glance before walking out the door.

I can't help but to notice the look of sorrow on his face as he leaves and it throws me off a bit. Makes me question myself because his pain makes me feel bad for a moment. It makes me almost feel awful for shutting him down. Why do I all of a sudden care about how he feels, or about his pain? And there is pain. It's obvious, I saw it there four years ago, and I see it still today. Is it possible that he's not over it, that maybe he still feels the loss as deeply as I do? Back then when it was too fresh, when the wound was still brand new, I didn't care about what he might be going through, but now... now I almost feel bad for the look of sadness hidden behind his features because I know that sadness all too well and I wouldn't wish it on anyone, not even Luca.

~ *Luca* ~

I don't know why I went there, what I'd hoped to accomplish by showing up at Everly's place. The house she lived in with Tyler, the fucking house that he built to make her happy. The house that cost him a fuck of a lot more than it should have. It's not that I was trying to get her to forgive me, I wasn't. I can live with her hatred if it makes her feel better, if it makes it easier for her to put one foot in front of the other and carry on. It's not about her forgiveness for me; I just thought she needed to know the truth. She needs to hear from me what very few people know, what those people have chosen to keep from her even now when the dust has settled. They allow her to live in her inner turmoil, and they allow her to walk in a clouded world where all she sees are glimpses of truth hidden behind a fucking mountain of lies.

Tyler was my best friend, my brother; I would have done and did try to do anything I could for him. Anything to keep him safe, to try and make him see his mistakes, but I couldn't make him see the things that he was blinded to. Tyler wanted what he wanted when he wanted it and there was never anything anyone could do to stop him. He'd been that way all his life with everything from a new pair of sneakers he didn't need, to a girl that I had seen and wanted first, to a house he couldn't afford. He wanted them so he took them; he had to have them, even if it meant hurting his best friend, even if it meant lying to his fiancée. Tyler West was a good man deep down. He cared about people, felt deeply, loved deeply, but when all was said and done, he was also a very selfish man.

Everly doesn't want to hear the truth, doesn't want to face what's always been right in front of her eyes. I can't force her to hear me out, so maybe it is better for her to live in oblivion. Maybe it's better for me too. Then I can stop pretending that I mean anything to her at all, I can let go of the idea that she might someday mean more to me. Her hate isn't totally unjustified, I played my part. From the moment I met her, I played my role, made her dislike me, made her think that I disliked her just as much — but really she was just a girl I could never have. I kept Tyler's secrets even when I knew it was the wrong thing to do, and if I'm guilty of anything, it's that...not getting him help sooner.

The clicking of heels tears my concentration from the stack of papers I'm going through; I look up to find Everly standing in my office. I mask my surprise before addressing her.

47

"Can I do something for you Everly?"

She looks nervous, unsure of herself, which she's never been with me before. She's never had a problem telling me exactly where to go. She never gave a shit about what I thought of her, not even for a minute.

"Here's the discovery you requested." She reaches out, offering me the file she's holding. I take it from her outstretched hand and give her my thanks not wanting to prolong this interaction. She's never come in here while I'm here before. Usually she waits till she knows I'm away from my desk at lunch or in with one of the partners before dropping anything off. She stares at me a few more seconds and then hesitantly speaks. "Luca, about the other night."

"There's nothing to say." I cut her off with a shake of my head. "You were right, I shouldn't have come by."

"Well that's just it, I was wondering." She looks away from me making sure that the hallways are empty before turning her gaze back to mine.

"What is it?"

"Did… Did Tyler ever gamble with you, bet on races or sporting events?"

I'm floored by her question, so much so that I have no idea how to respond. I stick with the simple truth but choose not to elaborate any further. "No, he never did that with me."

"Right. O…Okay."

"Why are you asking me this Ev?" I probe.

"It's just that every once in a while I'll find something around the house, hidden in random places, a book or a pocket, things that lead me to believe that he'd occasionally bet on things."

I let out a breath, nod my head and lie through my teeth. "Sounds harmless enough."

"Yeah. It's just weird that I didn't know about it that's all."

"I'm sure it was nothing," I say trying to reassure her even though I know better. She turns away and heads out the door before popping her head back in.

"Uh, thank you," she says quietly and then she's gone.

What the fuck did I just do? I just lied to her. This could have been the perfect time to tell her the truth, all of it. She already suspects it, probably for a long time even, but I couldn't do it. I couldn't look into her sad eyes and make them even sadder. *Fuck it*, I think, leaning back in my chair, *let her live the lie*.

~ *Everly* ~

After calling me several times and being sent straight to voicemail, I finally decided to call Morgan back. The fact that she still considers me her best friend is heartwarming because God knows that I don't deserve her loyalty. Four years is a long time to spend being blown off by someone who you consider to be a friend. As usual she invited me out to dinner so that we could catch up — only this time I didn't make up some lame excuse and turn her down. This time I said yes suggesting that I come to her house and have dinner with her there, giving us a quieter place to catch up.

I pull up to her building and park my car next to hers. Morgan is already waiting in the open doorway. She's hard to miss with her auburn hair and clear blue eyes. I get out of my car and walk up the drive stopping at the front door as she encases me into a tight hug.

"You look great."

"You too," I reply hugging her back. We hold on for a second longer before we part and she leads me inside.

"I'm so glad you came Ev. I haven't seen you in so long, I've really missed you," she says, her eyes tearing up.

Seeing her emotional makes me emotional, and I feel horrible for having shut her out for so long. I've only seen her a few times over the last four years, and each time I was short and unwelcoming.

"I'm sorry I haven't been a better friend Morgan," I say as I sit down next to her on an oversized couch. "It's just been a tough few years, but I know I've made it difficult for anyone to get close to me. It was just easier for me to keep to myself." I can't explain why I shut down the way I did or why I did it for so long. Of course I was grieving, but I should have let people support me.

"Why? All I ever wanted was to help you, to be there for you."

"It's easier to fall apart when there's no one there to witness it. Tyler was gone, and I guess a part of me went with him. I don't know, I just checked out."

"And now?"

"Now... I'm still checked out I guess but I'm getting a little bit better. I mean I'm here right?"

"Yes you are." She smiles.

We chat a bit longer and make our way into the dining room where she's served dinner. I'm surprised at how easy it is to pick up with her after all this time. We eat and chat as if though we've been doing it every week for the past four years. She was always the best person I knew — better than me, kinder, gentler.

We finish dinner, and Morgan pours us both a glass of wine. We sit back down in the living room and continue our nonstop chatter. It feels good being with her again.

"So have you heard that Luca is back in town?" she asks softly, almost as if she's afraid to tell me this piece of news.

"Yeah I know. He's an attorney at the firm where I work now."

Her eyes go wide with surprise. "Holy shit. I knew he was back, but I hadn't realized that you were working together. How's that going?"

"It's different." I shrug. "I still pretty much hate him, but I can at least tolerate being in the same room with him now."

"Well that's something at least." She looks down at her half empty glass and I can tell she wants to say something but she's afraid of how I might react.

"What Morgan?"

She looks back up and gives me a sad smile. "He's really not so bad you know?"

I think about it for a minute, my arm propped up on the back of the couch and my head resting on my hand.

"He came to see me the other day, because he said he wanted to tell me something. He said I needed to know the truth about what happened with Tyler."

"Oh my God Ev," she says on a breath. "What did he say?"

"Nothing," I reply, shaking my head. "I didn't want to hear it. I threw him out, but it's been bothering me ever since Morgan. I've thought about it, and I think I want to know."

"Everly…"

"Do you know?" I probe quietly, hesitantly. "Do you know what he was trying to tell me?"

She says nothing just stares at me debating whether to say what she wants to say.

"Please," I whisper. "If you know what happened…"

"I don't know all of it, just bits and pieces."

"Will you tell me?"

"All I know is Tyler was in trouble. I think that he got into something with some bad people. I know that Luca tried to help him."

I wipe a stream of tears off of my cheeks. I really didn't want to cry but how could I not. We're talking about Tyler and the possibility that... "It wasn't random was it? Was he murdered?" I ask already knowing the answer.

"I think so. I don't know for sure, I just know what Luca told me years ago. Right after Ty died, I went to see him to make sure he was okay. He got wasted, and he started talking but Ev, I don't know the whole story. I just know that Ty was in over his head."

"Why didn't you tell me?"

"Because I didn't know for sure, and you were so far gone. I could never reach you, you were so sad and broken, and so I just couldn't. I didn't know if telling you would make it any worse, and I was just scared for you. Then I thought over time you'd get better, that you'd want to go back to being normal."

"There is no normal after losing your husband the day after you got married."

"Oh God, No." She reaches out and grabs my hand. "I know. That's not what I meant. I just meant that I thought you'd eventually go back to school, I thought that you and I would go back to being friends like always. I thought you'd need me, and I wanted so badly to be there for you, but you wouldn't take help from anyone. After a while I just figured that maybe it was better that you didn't know. It was only speculation anyway. I had no proof, just the ramblings of a drunk guy who'd just lost his best friend."

"I need to know, I have to know what really happened."

"Luca's the only person who can fill in the blanks for you. He was closer to Tyler than anyone. If anyone knows the whole story it's him."

"Yeah." I nod my head in agreement. Luca is the only one who can tell me what really happened to my husband. I just hope that I'm strong enough to hear what he has to say.

❧

I got Luca's cell phone number from Morgan and debate whether or not to call him. Maybe I should sleep on this and call him in the morning, but I'm kidding myself if I think I'll be able to sleep after the bomb that was just dropped in my lap. I need to hear it all, not just random pieces that may or may not be true. I pull up his name on my cell and decide to text him instead.

Hey Luca it's Everly. I really need to talk to you are you busy?
I hold the phone staring at the screen until he responds.

Everly what's wrong? Are you okay?

I'm fine. I just need to see you, do you think you could come by my place.

It takes him a few minutes but he finally responds.

Gimme 30 mins.

I put the phone down on the coffee table and wait. Wait for Luca to deliver a truth that might just leave me more damaged than I was to begin with.

Forty-five minutes later I'm opening the front door for Luca. He looks dressed to go out in a pair of dark jeans and green button-down shirt. Why wouldn't he be going out, it's a Saturday night, and he actually has a life.

"Thanks for coming; did I take you away from something important?" I don't know why I'm asking, my nerves are getting the best of me. What he tells me tonight can change everything I thought I knew about my life.

"I was just out with some people from work when you called."

I nod as he passes through the open doorway. In the four years that I've worked there no one has ever asked me to hang out after work. Alright, that's a lie, they asked me a few times in the beginning, but I always turned them down. I'm sure that I come off as being unapproachable and even now I would have said no, but it may have been nice to get an invitation every once in a while.

"I'm sorry, I should have waited till tomorrow it's late."

He juts his chin out, nonverbally communicating that it's okay. "I was surprised to hear from you. Is everything alright?"

"I don't know." I reply walking back in the living room and tagging my wine off of the coffee table. "Can I get you a glass?" He's probably shocked by how polite I can actually be.

"No. I'm alright. What's going on?"

I take a sip of my wine before taking a seat back on the couch. "I need you to tell me the truth about Tyler."

He sits down across from me not saying a word. I can see an array of emotions playing across his strong features, and there's indecision there. I'm afraid he's going to get up and walk away leaving me with no answers at all.

"Look it wasn't easy for me to reach out to you, but you obviously know what happened and you're the only one I know who would actually tell me anything."

"Why do you want to know now? I came here before to talk to you about this and you shut me down."

I look down at my hands not wanting to show him any more vulnerability, not wanting him to see just how affected I still am. "I was scared. I didn't want to hear anything that might ruin my memory of Tyler and especially coming from you. But I can't go on like this, if there's more to the story then I need to know it."

I look back up, and he's scrubbing his face with the palm of his hands, likely trying to figure out what to do. When he looks back up at me, he seems to have made his decision. He takes another moment before finally speaking.

"Tyler liked to gamble, he liked to bet on sporting events, anything really. Baseball games, football, horse races, if you could place a bet on it he did. It started out innocently enough a game every now and then, a few hundred dollars here or there…but as time went on, as he got older, it got worse."

"Worse how?"

"Higher stakes, bigger bookies. In the beginning he'd find low-level college bets, but when he felt like he wanted larger winnings, he went off campus and found a real bookie, someone who takes it very seriously."

I close my eyes, resting my forehead in the palm of my hands. How didn't I know this, how didn't I see this happening? Was I really that oblivious, caught up in my own little fantasy world that I couldn't see that Tyler was living a double life right under my nose?"

"Ev."

"No," I say, lifting my head. "It's okay, go on."

"It got out of hand, he did well at first he won a lot of money and then he'd lose some big ones here and there. He'd bet on another game trying to dig himself out of the debt until it became too much, got out of control."

"Did you do it too?"

"No. I thought it was stupid, and I tried to get him to stop. I saw him getting in deeper and I tried, I swear to you I did, but he was obviously addicted to it."

"What was he doing with all the money he won?"

He lets out a sigh and shakes his head.

"Oh my God," I breathe out, realization dawning on me. "Was that how he paid for the construction of this house?"

"Yes most of it."

"He told me he'd used the money he inherited from his grandparent's deaths."

"He had some money, but not a lot; he gambled away a lot of that inheritance," he explains.

"Why? Why would he do that? The house could have waited, I never pushed him for it, I swear. It wouldn't have mattered to me."

"I believe you, but he wanted it for you, and when he wanted something he got it."

I look at him stunned, my body frozen, unmoving and more than anything sad. Sad for what Tyler felt he had to do to get ahead. I sit here wondering if I played a part in

56

that belief, wondering if I ever did anything or said anything to make him think I had to have whatever it was he was trying to provide me, when really all I ever needed was him.

"In the end he owed over a hundred thousand dollars Ev. He called me the morning after the wedding. He told me he was taking all of the cash you guys had received for wedding presents and he was meeting with the bookie to pay him something as a sign of good faith."

"He took our wedding money?" I question in disbelief. Would he really have done something like that? Did he think I wouldn't have questioned him about that at some point?

"Didn't you ever notice it was gone?"

"I never even thought about it Luca," I answer honestly. Money was the furthest thing from my mind at that point. "My husband was dead. I just assumed my parents or his went through it and took care of it. There was money in my bank account, I just assumed. I guess I just didn't care."

"I told him not to go," he tells me, leaning back in his seat. "That it was a bad idea, I told him to get on the plane with you, enjoy the honeymoon, and worry about it when he got back. But he was afraid it was going to somehow spill over onto you, that they were going to come looking for him and get to you. I couldn't convince him otherwise, and I'm not so sure that he was wrong. It got to the point that I was a little scared for your safety too."

Chills run through my body at the thought of how I could have possibly gotten caught in the crossfire. I might have been in danger too, and I guess I can understand why he felt like he had to at least try to go and smooth things over. I remember the conversation that we had that morning at the hotel.

"He told me you needed a ride home. That's what he said, we fought about it."

"Everly, I didn't stay at the hotel with the rest of the wedding party that night, I went home. He told you that so he could get away."

"I blamed you," I tell him softly, for the first time feeling badly for feeling that way toward him.

"You're right to blame me, I should have done something. I told him I'd meet him at the park, so that I could be there in case he got into any trouble. On my way there I called his dad, and I filled him in. He had known there was a problem but had refused to get involved until then; he thought it was just an immature game Tyler was playing until I told him just how serious it was. He said he'd give Tyler the money, the whole amount, he just asked that I get to him in time. Stop him from meeting with the bookie."

"But you didn't make it in time," I say softly, choking back tears.

His eyes are glassy when he shakes his head. "I didn't make it in time. I'm so sorry, if I had done something sooner, said something sooner then..."

"You don't know that. No one can know that."

"Mr. West would disagree. He blames me, says I should have come to him before it all went to hell."

I reach out and put my hand over his, and he looks shocked by the physical contact, by the fact that I'm actually touching him. "He was upset, I'm sure he doesn't feel that way now, Luca, he was your best friend." I can't believe what I'm doing right now, this is me comforting Luca, comforting the person I've focused on hating for years.

He nods and I pull my hand away from him. "I tried to get Ty to tell you, but he didn't want to hear it. He kept saying that everything was fine, that you didn't need to know, that it was safer for you if you didn't know."

I smile through the lump in my throat, the unshed tears that threaten. "He just kept lying to me. Everything was a lie wasn't it?"

"He loved you, that wasn't a lie. He wanted you, and he wanted to make you happy. He wanted to give you a great life. None of that was a lie."

"But he killed himself in the process. Did he really think so little of me that he believed I would rather have this stupid house instead of a simple apartment? I didn't care. As long as we were together, I didn't care. It could have been a shack, it could have been anything," I say in my defense, wondering if he's judged me all these years, thought that maybe I pushed him for more than I had.

"It wasn't about you. He had a problem that had nothing to do with you. This was about him and about what he wanted, and what he thought he needed. In his mind he had to have it—he wanted it all, and he couldn't see the bigger picture. He didn't realize the price he was paying until it was too late. Don't blame yourself for that. You had nothing to do with it."

I think back to all the times Tyler would act strange or moody out of nowhere, and I imagine those were the times he had lost a bet. I remember him taking phone calls at all hours, sometimes getting out of bed in the middle of the night and going to another room to talk...

"He'd take phone calls all the time and tell me it was you. It wasn't you was it?"

"No, probably not."

"What about when he'd leave and tell me he was meeting you, or bailing you out of some problem, picking you up, giving you rides."

"No Everly." He gives me a sad smile. "He wasn't with me. I guess it was easier for him to use me as an excuse than to tell you the truth."

"God I was so stupid, it was all right in front of my face and I didn't see it. I just believed every fucking lie he fed me. Every single one."

"You were in love."

"Yes. I was in love. I was also in denial," I say before taking another healthy sip of wine. "Who else knew?"

"His father, me, that's it I think. Ty wasn't big on sharing."

"Clearly not." I throw out one of my arms in disgust. "Not even with me."

"I'm sorry."

"I have a lot to process, there's so much for me to take in, and I'm grateful that you came here to tell me. I don't want to be rude to you, especially not now... but would you mind going? I want to be alone."

"Are you sure? I can stay, talk some more, listen...whatever I just don't know if you should be alone."

I shrug my shoulders. "I've been alone for four years, it's what I do. I need it."

"Of course." He gets up and looks down at me, and I can see the struggle playing behind his eyes. He doesn't want to leave, doesn't think I should be left alone, but he knows it's my choice and he has to respect it. "Call me if you need anything," he calls before showing himself out.

I put my wine glass down, settle into the cushions of my couch, and let the words sink into my head. The story of Tyler's death and how it really came to pass. I know it's true, every word Luca spoke was true. I know it is as surely as I know my own name, only now I don't know what to do with it. How do I move forward with what I know—will I be just as stuck now as I have been for the past four years? I give up on trying to find the answers tonight, choosing instead to close my eyes and allow sleep to come and take me away. Strangely enough never once shedding a tear.

~ Luca ~

It's been three days since I handed Everly the truth about what went down with Ty. Three days since I destroyed everything she thought to be true about her fucked-up life. I haven't seen or heard from her since. I've no clue if she's dealing with the news I've given her or just doing what she's been proven to do in the past, which is retreat. She called out sick from work yesterday and today—not surprising. I could imagine if I'd been given news like that I probably wouldn't want to get out of bed, but I would, I'd get out of bed and I'd move forward. This is the difference between me and Everly. I'd like to help her, I really would. God knows I care about the girl enough to want to make the whole shitty situation better for her, but she won't let me intervene. I know she won't let me anywhere near her and as much as I wish it wasn't the truth, it is, and I don't think there's anything I can do to change that.

So I do the only thing I can think of to get my mind off of Everly West. I drag my ass to the local bar down the street after work and I sit here, drinking away thoughts of her, admitting to myself that she'll never see me as anything other than her dead husband's best friend. She may not hate me anymore, but she'll never feel for me even an ounce of what I feel for her, what I always felt for her.

It's the weekend before school starts, and I'm at the campus bookstore trying to find the texts I need for my classes. The place is packed; I thought that if I waited till right before classes started I wouldn't have to deal with all the crowds. Apparently I was wrong; everyone had the same idea as me. I find the last book and head to the end of the line, cursing to myself because the way it looks I'm going to be in here for at least another hour.

The line ahead of me wraps around the entire book store, and if classes didn't start on Monday, I'd walk out of here and come back another day. But unfortunately I have no choice. My eyes land on the girl standing directly in front of me in line, she's struggling with holding on to all of the books in her hands. I roll my eyes at the sight of her wondering why she didn't just grab a shopping basket. The douche in me wants to let her fend for herself, but she looks as if though she's about to drop her load.

I reach out and grab the books that are about to fall and her breath catches, obviously startled at my intrusion. She looks up at me, eyes wide and I'm struck by her presence. This girl is stunning, long flowing dark hair, almond-shaped eyes, full lips – and that's just her face. I haven't even begun to admire the rest of her.

"You looked like you could use a little help."

"Uh yeah, thanks. There were no more baskets available when I came in."

Fuck she even sounds sexy; this girl is the total package. I look down at her and smile, all of a sudden not minding that I'm stuck in this line.

"Why don't you put your stuff in my basket? I have plenty of room."

"Oh, no it's okay."

"No seriously, I insist."

"You're sure you don't mind?" she asks hesitantly.

"Positive," I reply.

She gently places the remaining books in her hand in my basket and smiles up at me.

62

"Thanks," she says almost shyly. Fuck but she's beautiful.

I give her a nod and introduce myself. "I'm Luca."

"Nice to meet you, I'm Everly."

"Everly. That's a beautiful name."

"Thanks," she replies softly, tucking a loose strand of hair behind her ear.

I have the overwhelming urge to reach out and touch her — she's that type of girl. The kind where you know one time would never be enough, one taste would barely satisfy the urges you have toward her.

"Are you a freshman?" she questions looking up at me through impossibly long lashes.

"Yeah, how 'bout you?"

"Yup. Just got to campus yesterday."

"Living in the dorms?" I ask.

"Yeah, it would be an hour for me to commute. I didn't want to have to do that everyday, what about you?"

"I grew up around here, next town over. My buddy and I have an apartment just off campus."

"Cool."

We spend the duration of our time together talking about school, our schedules, and our majors; basically anything we can think of and when our time comes to an end I let her go. I let her walk away from me instead of getting her number, asking her to meet me for coffee or dinner, anything. I tell myself that there's time, I don't want to come on too strong and the campus isn't that big. I know I'll be seeing her again. That was my biggest mistake.

I make it back to the small two bedroom apartment I share with Tyler just off campus. His father insisted on renting it so that Tyler would be in a place where he could study and not be distracted by dorm life. I came along for the free rent. His dad never liked me much, always thought I wasn't good enough to hang around his son. Ty could do better in his choice of friends, and I know they fought about it, but Ty always took my back and his dad just learned to live with it.

"You get your books?" Ty questions as I walk into the apartment.

"Yeah, left them in my car."

"What's good for tonight? Last weekend before classes start."

Ty was always down for a party, always knew where the action would be. He liked to have a good time, even more so than me, and I could party with the best of them.

"You tell me," I call out, walking into the kitchen and grabbing a beer out of the fridge. Best part about living off campus is not having to hide your fucking alcohol.

"Big frat party tonight. First one of the year is supposed to be epic. You down?"

"Yeah." I grin before taking a pull of beer. "Met this girl at the bookstore man, fucking beautiful."

"You get her number?"

"Nah, I figured I'd see her around campus. Didn't want to come on too strong."

"Maybe you'll see her tonight."

"Hope so," I reply before walking away and heading off to my room.

We make it to the frat house just after midnight. It's a well-known fact that no college campus party starts to get good until after midnight. The music is pumping, and there are bodies everywhere; we can barely walk the place is so crowded. We make our rounds, grabbing a couple of beers and taking in the action as we walk around and mingle.

We settle into the action, Tyler placing bets on a game of beer pong, me enjoying the atmosphere and people watching. I glance up just in time to see Everly and some other chick making their way to the front door. I elbow Ty in the stomach grabbing his attention before pointing toward Everly and speaking.

"That's her, the girl from the bookstore earlier."

"Long brown hair by the door?"

"Yeah."

"Fuck. She's hot, go talk to her," he says, shoving me just as she walks out the door.

"Too late asshole, she's gone. I'll see her again, it's a small campus."

He nods before turning his attention back to the game. In those moments I considered her to be attainable, something I could strive for, hope to have one day. I should have gone after her, should have staked my claim. I had two chances, and I never got another.

The memories hit me like a ton of bricks, but I shake them off signaling the bartender for another beer. Tyler always got what he wanted, even the girl that I had my eye on, and I just let him have her. That's my truth, it's my fact, and I let her go without even trying to win her over. But to try to compete with someone like Ty was pointless—not because he had anything on me in the looks department but because he had everything on me in the ways that counted. Brains, money, status, charisma, confidence, all the things that I was lacking when it came to my ability to make a move on Everly.

"Luca? Is that you?" I turn in my stool and come face to face with a familiar face. One of Everly's old friends, a bridesmaid in her wedding.

"Janine, hey. How are you?"

"I'm good, really good. How about you? I had heard you were back in town working at a law firm right?"

News travels fast around here. "Yeah that's right."

"That's great. That's really great, I'm happy for you. Have you seen Everly?"

"I've run into her a few times," I confirm.

"Shit. How'd that go?" It's no secret that Everly and I never got along. I guess people think we might come to blows if we actually come face to face.

"Interesting."

65

"If it makes you feel any better, she doesn't talk to me either, doesn't talk to anyone. I tried to keep in touch for a while, but she wasn't having it so eventually I gave up. Can't help someone who doesn't want to be helped."

"Right," I mutter, taking another swig of beer.

"You look good, different all dressed up like that."

I look down at my dark gray suit then back up at her. "I guess even I can clean up huh?"

"Never thought you needed cleaning up. I always liked you just the way you were."

Fuck she's flirting with me. She was always a pretty girl, always hung around Everly and Morgan, but I never gave her a second thought. If memory serves, she had a bit of a reputation in college. Even now I'd rather be dealing with Ev's bullshit than sitting here with her, but the shit with Ev is never going to get me anywhere. Maybe a night with Janine will help me to fucking forget this shit I got going on. I signal the bartender again, this time getting his attention to get Janine a drink.

"So what have you been up to the last few years?" I could really care less what she's been up to. I'm lucky I even remembered the girl's name.

"Sales rep for a pharmaceutical company. Hours are good, money is great, can't complain."

"Yeah? Sounds interesting. You live nearby?" I question, getting closer to her, reaching over and grabbing a strand of her hair, letting it glide between my fingers. She gets what I'm asking; my voice is laced with a whole lot of insinuation.

"Yeah," she responds, in a breathy tone.

"Why don't you finish that drink up? You can show me where you live," I ask suggestively.

"I'd like that." She looks up at me, and I run my finger along the curve of her neck.

66

"Yeah? I'd like that too." I pull my hand back, grab my beer, and down it as fast as I can. She does the same with her drink. I throw some money on the bar, enough to cover us both, get to my feet, and put my suit jacket back on. She hops off the bar stool pulling her skirt down back to the point where it's semi decent. I grab her by the hand and give it a gentle tug. I lean down and whisper in her ear.

"You ready?"

"Yeah I'm ready," she replies, flashing me a sultry smile. I tighten my hold on her and guide us out of the bar. This is exactly what I need.

~ Everly ~

I go back to work on Wednesday, but I make it a point to avoid Luca at all costs. I don't want to deal with what he told me a few days ago, and I don't want to talk about it with anyone, I just want to forget it. Only problem with that is that the truth is oftentimes brutal, and the truth that I've learned delivered a heavy blow. I want to be angry at Tyler, I desperately want to hate him and curse him for putting himself in a situation where he ultimately got himself killed, but how can I be angry at him when he's already paid the ultimate price for his sins? How can I be angry at him when he was probably scared before he died, when being angry just feels so wrong. I vowed to stand by him, I promised to take his side, and even in death I feel like it's my duty to do that for him, to give that to him. Because even though he lied, even though he played a dangerous game, I can't forget about the fact that Tyler West loved me. He loved me the best he could, the only way he knew how, and yes he lied but he did it to protect me. I can't let myself twist that into something ugly when in my heart I know it wasn't.

Outside of my office I hear the usual five o'clock chatter, people getting ready to go home for the evening and saying goodnight to each other.

"Hey Luca, We're going to J&G to get some pizza, you want to come?" The invitation comes from Michelle, who works the front desk. I'm sure she'd love to be out with Luca, I've seen the way she looks at him.

"Yeah sure," he replies.

"Should we invite Everly?" Amber asks, and this shocks me. I thought she hated me, or maybe she's just trying to seem nice in front of Luca. She knows I'd say no if they did ask.

"Nah. She won't come anyway." His words hurt me for some inexplicable reason. They're true—he's right—I wouldn't have gone, and maybe that truth hurts the most. Years ago I wouldn't have said no, years ago I would have been all over an invite out for dinner.

There are times when I wonder what my life would have been like had I not ended up with Tyler, had things played out differently. It's funny because I met Luca before Ty, and when I did, I remember feeling that there were sparks there, a possible connection. He was nice to me, helpful, attentive, funny, and undeniably hot, but he wasn't interested in me like that. He let me walk away without as much as a second thought. He never asked for my number or offered to take me out. Oddly enough a few days later I met Ty and I liked him too. When I realized that they were roommates, I had hoped Luca and I could at least be friends but the more time I spent around them the less he seemed to want me there. Our relationship got progressively worse from there but I can't help to think what if... What if Luca had asked me out that day, what if he had wanted to get to know me that way? Would I have been with him instead of Ty, would I have been happier? I would probably not go around living my life day to day like I had nothing worth living for at all.

I wait till the coast is clear and everyone has gone for the day before locking up my office and head out. I get in my car and point it in the same direction it goes every day, to sit in solitary confinement in the jail I've created for myself. Home.

I call my mom after I've settled in for the night and fill her in on what Luca told me.

"Everly," she whispers through the receiver.

"Did you know Mom? Did you know what happened?"

"No. Of course not, I would never have been able to keep something like that from you, and I'm sorry honey, but I don't think your dad and I would have been okay with you marrying him if he was in that much trouble. We wouldn't have wanted to risk it."

I know this to be true. My parents doted on me growing up but they were also very protective. They would have never given me their blessing to start a life with Tyler if they knew what kind of trouble he was getting himself into. They would not have given me away to him so freely.

"I don't know what to think anymore Mom." I sigh, slumping my shoulders in defeat.

"Baby..."

"No, I just feel like I didn't know him, but I've been thinking about it, going back in my mind and there were definite signs there you know? Things I should have noticed but didn't."

"Why would you have noticed them? It's not like you were walking around looking for clues to unlock secrets and lies. You loved him, you trusted him, end of story. We all did."

70

"Because as a woman it is my job to know if my man is up to some seriously messed-up shit Mom, and I didn't know," I say, my voice getting louder with each passing second. "And the reason I didn't know is because I wasn't paying attention."

"You need to stop putting everything on you. I get that Ty's dead, I get that you loved him and miss him, but it is not okay for you to turn things around until you convince yourself that you were at fault. You didn't do anything wrong, and it's okay for you to be angry with him."

"I'm not angry."

"It's okay for you to be angry," she repeats.

"I don't even know if I have it in me to be angry at anyone else. I spent so much time being angry at the wrong person."

"Again, not your fault. You only reacted off of what you were led to believe, Luca must know that."

"I haven't really broached this topic with him."

"Well maybe you should. You need to make amends. It will make you feel better. Plus it will make working with him that much easier."

I know she's right, but my relationship with Luca has always been a slippery slope. Why bestow an apology on someone who probably doesn't even need it. He doesn't care if I hate him, because the thing is, he never really liked me all that much to begin with.

"I'll think about that," I say, having already made up my mind.

"Alright baby. Do you need me to get you some groceries?"

"Nope. Got them the other day."

"Good. I love you."

"I love you too Mom."

I disconnect the phone feeling just as lost as I felt before, feeling alone, unsure of what's next for me. The only thing I'm sure of is that I can't live the next fifty years of my life like this, existing in the world with no purpose and no destination. The thing of it is I've dug a hole so deep I don't even know how to begin to climb out of it. I turn off all of the lights, head upstairs, take a shower, and finally go to bed. I lay there for a long time trying to get comfortable, willing myself to relax even though I'm restless and anxious. Sleep evades me tonight, and it does for many nights after.

I get through the next few weeks without incident—no crazy revelations, unwanted run-ins, or arguments. I was finally able to get a full night's sleep last night. Luca has adhered to our work agreement, if he needs something he sends me an email and I take care of it without having to speak with him in person. It's a shitty way for me to act toward him, especially now that I know the truth, but I'm just not ready to mend fences with him.

I grab the nachos I just nuked out of the microwave, and I'm just about to settle into the couch to watch a movie when the doorbell rings. I put my plate on the coffee table and head to the foyer. I stop dead in my tracks when I see Luca standing on the front porch.

"Hey."

"What are you doing here?" I question, crowding the door with my body in order to keep him where he is.

"Can I come in?"

"No."

"Why not?"

I plant my hands on my hips and shift my weight to one side. "What do you mean why not? You just showed up here unannounced."

"It's not like I'm going to kill you Everly. I just want to talk to you."

I let out a frustrated sigh but move out of the way, allowing him entrance. He walks past me as I shut the door and turn to give him my attention.

"What's this about Luca?"

"I spoke to Morgan today, and she told me that she was worried about you. She says she thought you two had a breakthrough, she thought she was getting you back, and now you're refusing to talk to her. That you barely leave this house."

I can feel my cheeks flush in anger. I cross my arms over my chest, no doubt looking defensive as I do. "How is this any of your business?"

"He'd want you to be happy, he fucked a lot of shit up, but he would want you to be happy."

Happy? Happy? Really? I'll never understand why people throw that word around like it's so simple. As if I can just flip a switch and turn on the glee—well that's not possible, not for me. Short of amnesia, I don't know that there's anything in the world that could make me happy again.

"You don't know anything about what Tyler would want. Seems to me I didn't know very much about my husband at all."

"I know he wouldn't want you to stop living your life. You had plans for yourself, goals and dreams that you can still have."

"Not without him!" I yell throwing out my hands. "He was a part of my goals and dreams and now I know that it was all a lie, it was all wrong. And I'm sorry if I'm having a hard time dealing with that."

"I don't think it was a lie. He genuinely loved you, but he's not here."

"Just stop please."

"No, Everly he's not here. He's never going to be here again. It's time for you to let it go. Change your goals and dreams; make it so that they fit your new life. But don't just give up, don't just sit back and let the world pass you by when you have so much to live for."

"What! Huh? What do I have to live for? I lost everything, and I'm not sure I had it all to begin with."

"You have a family, you have your health, and you have a future. You get the future that he didn't get, and you're just wasting it. And for what? You think that he would thank you for putting your life on hold, for grieving for four years? He wouldn't."

I stand there breathing erratically, wanting so badly to pick something up and throw it across the room. I have the urge to watch something shatter and break into a million pieces the way that I've been broken; the way that Tyler has broken me.

Luca takes a step closer, I take one back in response. His frustration with me is visible, almost palpable. Why does he care so much about what I do with my life when he never actually gave a damn about me to begin with? He could have taken a chance that day we met, made a move and I would have gone for it, because I felt something, even then. But he didn't, he let me leave, and I ended up with Ty instead.

And now I'm pissed, pissed at him for not seeing me all those years ago, because if he had, maybe my destiny would have been different. So I'm pissed at him for thinking he can railroad me and tell me anything regarding how I choose to lead my life. And I'm frustrated, completely gutted, that he would use Tyler against me. Tyler who wanted to be the best at everything he did, Tyler who wanted me to be the best too and this… this life I'm living is not what he would have wanted for me. In fact he'd be disgusted by what I've become.

74

I shake my head and let out a sigh, "Really? And what would you have me do huh?"

"For starters get out of this fucking house every once in a while. It's a big world out there, start interacting with other human beings for a change."

"You're delusional if you think you can come here and tell me what to do with my life. How to fix *my* life! I'm perfectly fine the way I am."

"You're scared," he declares, as though it's a statement of fact instead of his jaded opinion. He says it as if he's absolutely certain that he's right, and that pisses me right off. I take four strides forward stopping inches away from his face, invading his personal space and not caring one bit.

"What am I scared of Luca? You think you're so goddamned smart, you know everything, you know me so fucking well? What am I scared of?"

He tilts his head to the side, making sure never to break eye contact. He's trying to make me uncomfortable, and I force myself to remain stone faced, never letting on that his tactics are working. "Living your life. Moving on."

"You're wrong," I reply defiantly, sounding like I mean it, even though I'm bluffing.

"Prove it."

I flinch at his words exposing a chink in my armor. "I'm not playing this game with you."

"Prove. It. Everly."

"How?"

"I want to get you out of this house, somewhere other than work and the grocery store."

He must be out of his mind. Yes. I'm pretty sure he's completely out of his mind if he thinks I would ever entertain the idea of going out with him.

"I'm not going anywhere with you. Seeing you at work everyday is plenty."

His hard face softens, and his lips tip up into a grin. "Are you afraid that you might actually like spending time with me? You might actually have some fun?"

I scowl at him. "Believe me that's not a concern, I can barely stand to look at you."

"Ah come on Ev, I'm not so bad, you might actually have a good time."

"That's doubtful." I roll my eyes and place my hands on my hips. "I don't want to go anywhere with you. Thank you for your offer but no thanks."

"You know it wouldn't be too hard to paint a picture of mental instability. The more and more you retreat, the easier it would be to convince people that you're capable of hurting yourself. What would your parents do if that seed was planted in their heads?"

"Are you threatening me?" I shriek in disbelief.

"It's not a threat. If they're scared enough for your safety, they would never leave you alone. They'd be breathing down your neck constantly, and maybe they'd insist that you move back in with them. Go to a therapist, take antidepressants, all the shit that you've been avoiding."

"You wouldn't do that. All it would do is scare them for no reason."

"Try me."

We glare at each other, venom in my eyes in what would appear to be a good ole fashioned standoff. Me with a death glare on my face and my hands on my hips, and Luca with a devilish grin and an heir of cockiness I'd like to slap right off of him. God only knows how long we stand there, but I break contact first.

"Fine, what am I supposed to do?"

The grin turns into a full-fledged smile. "Nothing, just be ready Saturday night at six o'clock," he says before walking past me and out the front door as abruptly as he arrived. I'm left standing there wondering why I just let Luca Jensen railroad me into getting exactly what he wanted.

The remainder of my week flies by a little too quickly for my liking. Once Friday morning arrives a sense of dread slips over my normally drab persona because I knew it was just a mere twenty-four hours away from my coerced outing with Luca. Seeing him at work is one thing, going out with him socially is totally different.

I couldn't be sure if he was bluffing about going to my parents, but I would do whatever I have to do to spare them any more pain. The stress of seeing me crumble took a toll on them, and they've spent so much time being afraid for me, worried that I'd do something to hurt myself after Tyler's passing and now that they know I'm having such a hard time dealing with the truth. I may be self-centered and selfish in my grief, but I'd like to think that even I wouldn't do anything to intentionally hurt the people that I love. If that means going out with Luca to shut him up then that's what I'll do.

I nearly jump out of my skin when the doorbell rings. I haven't been able to think of anything else but this all day long. I hate that I'm having this reaction to Luca; the fact that he has any effect on me at all makes me uneasy. Since I have no idea where we're going I've opted to wear a dark pair of jeans and a pretty blush top with scalloped edges. My brown hair is straight and falls freely down my back and my makeup is applied minimally. I don't want him to get the impression that I tried too hard to look good for this. As I walk to the doorway I'm hoping that I'm dressed appropriately for whatever he has in store for me. Regardless of how I felt about him personally, I always knew that Luca was a good looking guy. I knew it the first time I saw him in the bookstore, but when I open the door tonight, I realize just how good looking he is. His hair is styled in that just rolled out of bed way that guys pull off so well. His jeans are fitted to perfection paired with a grey button-down top.

I tear my gaze away, mentally chastising myself for noticing his looks. This is Luca for God's sake; my mind should *never* go there.

"Let me just get my bag," I throw over my shoulder as I head back into the living room. I grab my purse and a light jacket, take a breath, and head back to the open doorway.

"You look great," he states, once I'm in touching distance.

I say nothing in return, just put my jacket on and grab my keys off of the entryway table. I lock up the front door and follow Luca down the driveway to his car—a newer model black Dodge Charger. He holds the passenger door open for me, and I can hardly contain my eye roll as I slide into the soft leather seat. He closes the door behind me and rounds the car to take his seat in the driver's side.

"Where are we going?" I sigh, thinking of how bad of an idea this really is. Why am I letting myself get blackmailed into this stupid idea of his to get me out of the house more? What makes it worse is the fact that he's forcing me to spend time with *him* of all people. The person who I have spent years harboring the most sheer animosity for.

He smiles at me and pulls out onto the road. "We're going to get something to eat and catch a movie."

I stare at him with a disgusted look on my face. "Dinner and a movie? That's your big plan for getting me out of the house?"

He shrugs. "I figured we'd start small. I don't want to overwhelm you on your first outing."

"Being with you is overwhelming enough," I spit out. "It sounds more like a date than an outing."

A slow grin takes shape on his mouth. "It can be whatever you want it to be sweetheart."

"I'm not your sweetheart." I cross my arms over my chest almost defensively. What the hell is his problem? Did he just flirt with me? His dead best friend's wife? Maybe I'm overreacting; he's probably just trying to be nice. I'm not exactly the easiest person to talk to these days, I'm sure he's just trying to break the ice.

"Everly, just relax okay, we're just two people hanging out. I'm not going to hold your hand, or wrap my arm around you. I'm not even going to attempt to kiss you at the end of the night. At most I'm hoping we can get past the dislike you feel toward me and become friends."

"Yeah, that'll never happen," I mutter under my breath. I turn my head to look out the window; it's my nonverbal cue that I'm done talking. He gets the hint, turns up the radio, and drives us to our destination without saying another word. Just because he forced my hand to get me to come out with him doesn't mean I have to like it, and I definitely don't plan on making this easy on him.

We pull into the parking lot of a quaint Italian bistro I've driven by many times but have never eaten at. Once inside we're seated immediately and I can't help but to feel awkward about sitting across from Luca at a table for two. It feels too intimate. To the strangers sitting around us, we must look like a couple out on a dinner date. They'd never know how we really feel about one another.

We place our dinner orders and sit in silence for a while before I finally speak.

"This is weird," I say, averting my gaze.

"What?"

"Being here with you, it's just weird," I reply, shrugging my shoulders. "It's not like we ever got along not even before…"

Luca quickly cuts me off. "We got along alright."

"Maybe the first time we met! After that we barely tolerated each other."

"Tell me about work," he says, shifting to a more comfortable topic. What am I supposed to say about work? It's nothing to talk about, just a job I do because I can't be bothered with anything else.

"There's nothing to tell, you know what I do, and you know what it consists of."

"Do you like it?"

"It's alright, it's a job and it pays the bills."

He presses on. "But it's not what you wanted to do is it? I thought you wanted to be a lawyer, you wanted to open your own firm."

"How did you know that?" I'm surprised at his knowledge of my past plans, past as in plans that died right along with Tyler.

"There are a lot of things I know."

His cryptic answer leaves me with more questions than before. How does he know anything about me at all? Did he and Tyler have conversations about me at some point in time? And if they did… Why? What would make Luca interested in knowing anything about me? I push the questions out of my head and turn the tables on him.

"What about you? Last I heard you weren't sure if you wanted to be a lawyer."

He looks up at me, his eyes darker than usual, and something washes over his features some emotion he doesn't want me to see. "Eh... I finally made up my mind."

"Why?" I push, suddenly very interested in his answer.

He hesitates, looking at me with a cautious expression. Am I really that hard to talk to? What am I thinking, of course I am. I'm nothing but a bitch where he's concerned.

I ask again in a less abrasive tone. "Why Luca?"

"I wasn't sure what I was going to do when I left here. I was confused and a little out of it in all honesty. I had been accepted into law school in Chicago, so I went, ended up staying with my uncle there. I did a lot of security work for office complexes while I went to school."

I nod my head, taking it all in. I don't understand why all of a sudden I feel bad for this person, or more importantly, why I feel like a bad person for sending him away four years ago when he was so obviously hurting. Was my anger really worth it? The thing is, I was distraught, overcome with grief. I had just lost my husband. Had he approached me a few weeks later would I have dismissed him so quickly? I'd like to think that I'd have heard him out, but the truth is I was so fucked-up in the head that the end result would have likely been the same, and for the first time since it happened, I feel like I made a huge mistake.

"Are you happy with your choice now?"

"Yes, I am, because now I have a job that I really enjoy at a great firm. I'm learning a lot. "

Dinner comes just as I'm about to ask him for more details and before long the conversation is forgotten replaced instead with a more companionable silence. We get back in the car after dinner and I think to myself that spending time with Luca isn't quite as terrible as I thought it would be.

"What movie do you want to see Ev?"

"Would you mind if we call it a night? I'm really tired, I don't know if I'd stay awake during a movie."

He looks at me for a minute before speaking, probably trying to gage my mood, wondering if I'm actually tired or just full of shit. Truth is I'm a little of both.

"Alright, rain check?"

I don't answer him, don't even know what I would say. Do I want to hang out with Luca again? It certainly wasn't the worst experience in the world, but what would that mean for me and all of the time I've spent making him into my own personal villain?

He pulls out of the parking lot heading back in the direction of my house. "Come on, a night out with me wasn't so bad right?"

I unwittingly smile. "Why are you making it seem like I'm the mean one? You never liked me very much anyway."

I can see the smallest hint of a smile on his lips. "I liked you plenty. I just didn't think you were right for Ty."

"I loved Tyler!" I claim, preparing my defenses for battle.

"Of course you did," he remarks, gripping the steering wheel with both hands. "I never said you didn't."

As if on cue that all too familiar build-up of anger where Luca is concerned resurfaces. "Then what the fuck is that supposed to mean Luca?"

"Oh Everly come on...He gave in to everything you ever wanted, he tied himself up in knots trying to make sure that you were happy and you loved that shit. It was too easy, he never challenged you."

This! This is the Luca I know and loathe; this is very reminiscent of the old days where he would give me a hard time for even breathing in his direction.

"Who doesn't want a man who will do what he can to make his girl happy? How does that make me a bad person? And I didn't always get my way, not where you were concerned."

"I never said you were a bad person," he says, shaking his head. "You just needed someone who wouldn't let you walk all over them."

"What like you?"

"Not me exactly, just someone like me. But for argument's sake if you had been mine, you would never have gotten away with half of the shit you got away with."

I raise my hands in the air as if I were praising the Lord. "Thank God I wasn't yours then," I reply, unable to hide my disdain.

He laughs at my reaction, and I hate how the sound of it vibrates through me, making me feel something I most definitely don't want to feel.

"Ev," he calls out after the laughter dies. "A guy like me would have made you happy in many other ways. Someone like me is more than capable of making you happy, and not by breaking his back to buy you a house he can't afford, or a purse that costs more than the rent."

I glare at him unable to compute how we went from pleasant to this in a matter of minutes. "I hate you. I never asked for any of that shit."

"You wish you hated me," he says pulling up in front of my house.

"Can I go inside now? I'm pretty sure I've had more than enough of you."

His voice drops into a husky tone. "I like it that you ask me for permission." My heart races and he holds my stare for a beat before finally speaking again. "Yeah sure go inside. Have a goodnight Ev."

I recover quickly and open the door, but he grabs my hand before I can get out. I turn my head to look at him.

"Next Saturday, be ready, same time," he commands before releasing me. I get out of the car and rush inside locking the door behind me. What was that back there? All this talk about me being his—was he really talking hypothetically or was he serious? Was he just trying to prove a point? Did I really just agree to see Luca again? Fuck!

~ Luca ~

Being around Everly is bad for me; it's always been like that for me where she's concerned. She makes me want things I shouldn't want. Things that I was supposed to let go of a long time ago—the minute she began to date my best friend—but I'm coming to realize that maybe I never let it go. I masked my feelings by treating her badly, I allowed for her to see me as a villain, and I made her hate me. Even after Ty's death, it was easier for me to take the blame, to keep up the charade, even though I knew it was a lie. I have never been able to confront my emotions for her or come to terms with how I missed my opportunity with her.

How many times did I flirt with her tonight or drop stupid innuendos? How many times did I glance at her inappropriately or imagine that we were more than just two people having dinner. I felt people's eyes on us, admiring the young couple that we appeared to be, and I liked it. I liked that they thought it, I liked that it looked that way, and I didn't want it to end. I want more, I want a lot more moments like that, and I'm sure that makes me wrong, but I don't know if I care.

My intentions were good, I want her to let go of her grief, put it in her past and move on. I want her to look forward to getting up everyday knowing that she has something to look forward to—a purpose. The point was to get her out of her shell, not scare her off, but I can't seem to help myself around her. And me telling her how things would have been if she had been with a guy like me instead of Tyler… What kind of asshole am I?

I should stop, I know. I should leave her alone, but that one smile she gave me tonight… the one she was unaware she gave, that smile made it worth it, that smile sealed my fate. I'm going to keep forcing her hand, getting her out of that fucking tomb she lives in and at the very least I'm going to make her my friend. I can be her friend if she'll let me. I can put my feelings for her aside if it means that she can have her life back.

At the same time I can't help but to feel an unhealthy claim toward her. If I'm being honest with myself, I always felt that pull, and it's why I had to make sure she hated me when she was with Tyler. If she had given me any indication that she felt the same way for me as I did for her, I would have gone after her, and it would have killed my friendship with Ty. God knows I wasn't happy with him when he started seeing her.

I walk into the apartment focused mainly on grabbing a change of clothes and getting in the shower. I spent the majority of my morning shooting hoops at the gym, and I smell like shit. Ty's grabbing his car keys off the table just as I'm walking in.

"Yo," he says tipping his chin up in acknowledgement.

"You headed out?" I question, noticing he looks to be in a rush, and these days when Ty's in a rush, he's up to shit that I don't like.

"Got some shit to do." He picks up his cell, slides it in his pocket never looking up at me.

I nod, as I go into the kitchen and grab a water bottle. "I think everyone's getting together at Cal's tonight. You going?"

"No, not tonight. I have plans."

"You have plans that don't include going out and getting shit-faced or placing bets?"

He flinches but recovers quickly. He shrugs on a jacket and finally looks at me. "I have a date."

This gets my attention. "Wait what?" I say on a chuckle. Tyler hasn't been on a date in forever. He has his priorities straight (or his father does) and dating is not high on that list.

"I said I have a date, man. You heard me."

"Yeah I heard you, I just thought I heard wrong."

"Nope. Gotta learn how to make time for a little of everything right?"

"That's what I've been trying to tell you," I say, unable to hide the humor in my voice.

"Well I finally listened."

"Who's the girl? Is it the chick you were talking to at student union the other day?"

"No. It's uh… It's Everly."

I place my water bottle down in front of me and place my hands on the countertop, gripping it as hard as I can. "Excuse me?"

"I said it's Everly, she's in my Western civ class, sat next to me on the first day, and we got paired up for a project." His words hit me like a physical blow, he must be shitting me.

"Everly as in my Everly? The girl I met at the bookstore, the girl I pointed out to you? The girl I told you I was into? That Everly?" I try to control the fury in my voice, but I know I'm failing.

"Dude come on, you let her walk away from you, you never even made an effort to get her number. You talked to her one time, it's not like you wanted to marry her. You don't even know her."

"That's not the fucking point."

"Yes it is. It's exactly the point man, if she was yours I'd never go near her but she's not."

I have to get the hell away from him right now. I need to get my head on right, and I don't want to do something I might regret later.

"You know what, fuck it man, go out with her. It won't take long for her to realize what a dick you are," I spit out before grabbing my water bottle, walking away grabbing clean clothes out of my room and jumping in the shower. I hear the door slam shut a few minutes later, and I know he's gone.

I know I shouldn't be pissed, but I'm infuriated. If ever there was a time I wanted to punch the shit out of him this was it. Do I have a claim on Everly? I'm not delusional, and I'm not stupid, so no, technically I don't have a claim on her and that's my own fault, but he knew. He knew that she was on my radar, and he didn't give a shit. That didn't stop him from making his move. All of the fucking women on this campus, and he chose to go after her. I close my eyes and let out a breath letting the hot water release some of the tension in my muscles. I have to be the bigger man here, I need to let this shit go. I'm not going to let a girl I've only spoken to once come between me and Ty. He's like a brother to me, and I'm man enough to let this shit slide. It's just a date, they're not getting married. Tyler's priorities are set, he knows what he needs to do, what's expected of him, and he takes that very seriously. I just can't see him putting all of that in jeopardy for a girl. Even a girl as beautiful as Everly.

I thought that they'd go out on a date or two and be done with each other. I thought that Tyler's drive to impress his father and fulfill his legacy would be more important than having Everly. I was wrong. He fell for her fast, and she did the same with him. It was the most painful thing to witness because somewhere in my mind I knew that I had wanted that for me. I had wanted her for myself, but I bowed out gracefully so that my best friend could have what he wanted. I watched as he made her fall in love with him, never being completely honest with her about the things that he was doing behind her back, the chances he was taking that would one day cost him his life and her, her heart. Knowing the entire time that I could have done better, I would have done better, given her something that was real and honest, without the secrets that would leave her life in ruins.

But the time for thinking about what could have been is over. Now Tyler's gone, he's gone, and I hate it. I miss him, but Everly's alone and I'm done. I'm done burying what I feel, I'm done denying myself what I want, what I've always wanted. So I'm going to do whatever it takes to bring Everly back to herself and make her see me as something other than her dead husband's best friend.

~ Everly ~

I take a sip of my wine as I listen to Stella and Michael West go on and on about their latest charity functions. This after about a half hour of hearing Michael tell me all about the latest goings on at his firm. This he does in an attempt to woo me in hopes that I might just change my mind and come work for him, or better yet decide that I would like to reconvene my pursuit of a law degree. He believes that one day I'll wake up and realize that I should have been a lawyer all this time, that I should have gone to law school, taken the bar exam, and come work for him. This is something that I have no intention of doing. I have no desire to come work for him in any capacity. But I understand. I get why he feels the need to push me, why he wants me to accomplish what his son never would.

For Michael West failure was never an option where his only son was concerned, he expected and demanded the best of and for him. I've never doubted his love for Tyler, I never once believed that he didn't adore his son, but the amount of pressure he put on him was at times unbearable. I sit here and stare at Michael and wonder — now that I know the whole truth, now that I know the kind of problems Tyler was facing — about the pressure he felt to be the best. I can't help but wonder if his father's need for perfection in turn propelled his son to unravel.

Maybe I'm stretching theories here, making more out of it than there really was. I don't know, but I do know that had Michael been more understanding, less stringent, maybe Tyler would have gone to him when he started to run out of options. Maybe he'd still be here; maybe he'd have gotten help and turned things around. I know better than to live my life based on what if's… but I can't help but wonder.

It's done now, over, there's nothing that can be said and done, no reason to hold a grudge or blame this man. I'm sure he has enough guilt tucked away in the recesses of his own heart to last him a lifetime. For now, I'll do my part and give him what he needs, a living breathing connection to his lost son.

I turn my attention back to Stella whose gaze is locked with mine. It's an empty gaze, devoid of any real emotion. That died with her son, she's never been the same. No one can relate to that more than me.

"I was coming out of the bank this morning and I saw Luca Jensen coming out of the pharmacy. I had no idea he was back in town," she says softly. It sounds more like she's revealing a state secret than a statement of fact.

"Just stay away from him Stella. I don't want you anywhere near that boy, he'll only upset you. That goes for you too Everly, stay away from him."

I'm taken aback by his demand, telling us that we need to stay away from Luca when all the while he knows that Luca had nothing to do with Tyler's death. He also knows that Luca is the only other person in the world who knows the whole story and keeping Stella and I in the dark is more important than being honest.

"Unfortunately I can't do that," I declare, trying to keep an even demeanor. I don't want him to catch on to the fact that I know. "Luca and I work together now."

His face goes pale as his fist clenches the stem of his wine glass, and I'm surprised it hasn't actually shattered. "What do you mean you work with Luca now?"

"He came back from Chicago because he got a job offer here. He's an attorney at my firm."

"Did he even pass the bar?"

"According to his file, he's licensed to practice in Illinois and New Jersey."

"Has he said anything to you?"

"I'm not exactly the most approachable person Michael. He knows I hate him, and he keeps his distance. I do the same. It's not the ideal situation, but we're making it work. I don't think he is too keen on having a knock-down drag-out with me."

"Well I suppose it's good that the boy made something of himself after..."

"Don't go there Stella, do not bring up his involvement with Tyler."

"Of course you're right Michael, it's just, it's still hard to look at him and not think about it."

"Everly if he gives you any trouble, I mean anything, you let me know. I don't want that little shit anywhere near you. This is all the more reason you know? All the more reason for you to come and work for me."

"You know I appreciate your concern, I always have, but I'm fine where I am. I'm used to it there, and I like the people."

"Are you really fine? Are you fine knowing that that man is that close to you? Are you fine knowing that he never liked you and that he is the reason you are not living your life with my son right now?"

I bite my tongue so hard I swear I can almost taste blood. What the hell is wrong with him? Has he convinced himself that the lie he told everyone is real? Or is he just protecting Tyler's memory? I can understand that, I can understand wanting to keep his son's memory intact but at what cost? The cost being blaming it on someone who only ever tried to help Tyler.

Yes. Luca Jensen was never my biggest fan, he didn't care for me and I'll never forget that, but he did care about Tyler. He cared so much that he feels it's his duty to spend time with me now just to try and help me get on with my life. He cared so much that he let us believe that he was at fault for something that he didn't do and this just feels wrong to me. So I do the only thing I can do. I bite my tongue and pray for this dinner to end as quickly as possible.

I grab my bag off of the kitchen counter where I tossed it earlier, turn off the lights, and head outside to my front porch. I take a seat on the front steps and wait. I'm waiting for Luca to show up, the week flew by and now it's Saturday and because when he dropped me off last week he told me to be ready, I decided that it would be prudent to be ready. I am not geared up to have an argument with him about it, and if I'm being honest with myself, last week's dinner wasn't terrible. Now I find myself dressed in a deep navy blue top, white shorts with a brown chunky belt, my hair is brushed back into a tight ponytail, and I've finished off the look with brown earrings.

I hurry down the walkway a few minutes later when his car pulls up, throw open the passenger door and get in.

"Why were you sitting outside alone? I would have come in to get you."

"You coming to my door would indicate that this is a date, and this is not a date," I reply in a smartass tone.

"Jesus Everly who cares? I doubt anyone would alert the presses if I knocked on your door."

"I wouldn't want to take any chances."

He grins at me before finally putting the car into gear and pulling out onto the road. He looks good in a light pair of jeans and black t-shirt. He's leaning back in his seat looking relaxed and carefree, and I'm jealous for a second because I can't remember the last time I felt either of those things. I stare a little too long, long enough for him to catch me, but he's nice enough not to say anything.

"Where are we going?"

"State fair."

"Really?" I gasp, unable to hide my excitement. "That's an hour away."

"Yup."

"I've never been to the state fair."

"You haven't? Not even when you were a kid?"

I shake my head. "My parents took me to the small county fair a few times, but never to the state fair. I always wanted to go."

"Well then I'm glad I get to be the one who takes you."

I don't know how to handle sweet, thoughtful Luca. I'm used to jerky, asshole Luca. This is what I imagined he would be like when I first met him, back before I met Tyler, before he showed me the other side of his personality. I decide to leave it alone, and let it go. It was so long ago, and he's obviously changed for the better. He's seems to have lightened up toward me. I don't get the *I hate Everly* vibe from him anymore. Maybe we *can* be friends, maybe time apart and losing Tyler has given us some common ground.

I decide a change of subject is in order. "I had dinner with the Wests a few nights ago."

"Really? How are they?"

"They're okay but..." I hesitate.

"But what?"

"Mrs. West mentioned that she had seen you going into the pharmacy in town."

"What's so strange about that? Pharmacies are for everybody right?"

I can't help but giggle at his sarcasm, yes ME giggle. Unheard of in the last few years. "No it's not that, it's just Mr. West. He got very serious after that. Warned us both to stay away from you. When I told him that you and I worked together he looked like his head was about to explode."

"Interesting."

"I mean, I assumed that he's just afraid you're going to tell me the truth about Tyler. He doesn't realize that I already know."

"I'm sure, but it's complicated Ev."

"Why is it so complicated?" I prod.

"The police reports are wrong, they make it seem like Ty was just in the wrong place at the wrong time. The cops got there first, before anyone, before me or Mr. West. They knew it was no accident. Why would a guy like Ty, who had just gotten married, who was set to leave on his honeymoon in a few hours, be on that side of town? If he had dropped me off at home like he said he was going to do, why would he take that way back? That park is out of the way, it's the long route. They also found the cash that Ty had taken to pay off the debt. These are cops Ev, they're not stupid. They knew it was a homicide right off the bat."

Why hadn't I questioned any of these things before either? God I'm stupid. "Then how?"

"He paid them off. Your father-in-law is a very powerful man with a lot of connections in law enforcement. He called in some markers—he has the police chief in his pocket, did a big favor for him years ago—and asked him to return the favor. I wanted to tell the cops the truth, but he threatened to bury me if I did. He told me to stick with what Tyler had told you, that he was giving me a ride home from the hotel. By that time the police chief had already intervened so it wouldn't have done any good for me to say anything. He paid off Tyler's debt discretely which made you safe and once I knew that was done I left town."

"Oh my God. Why, why all the lies?"

"He wanted to protect you and Mrs. West I think, and to keep Tyler's image intact as well as his family name. How do you think it would look if a high powered lawyer's son was gunned down for illegal activities?"

"God, I hate this! I hate that this is all such a mess. I hate all of these lies."

"It's over Everly, why rehash the past? Tyler's gone, nothing we do or say is going to bring him back. Do I agree with his father's tactics? No. But at the very least my best friend died with his dignity intact. We don't need to mess with that."

I hate it even though I agree; it's not worth it to try and change what's already been done. What would it solve anyway, and he's right, it's not worth dragging Tyler's name through the mud. I wouldn't want to do that to him. I roll my eyes and let out a sigh. "I hate that you're being so rational."

"I'll take that as a compliment."

We drive for another 10 minutes before finally arriving at the fairgrounds. He opens my car door for me, and we walk in silence together to the ticket booth. He pays our entrance fee, and we walk the short distance to the entrance.

"Where to first?" I shrug looking up at him with a bit of giddy anticipation.

"You wanna hit a few rides first then grab something to eat or do you want to eat first?"

"Ummm rides first."

"Alright. Let's go." He grabs my hand and begins to walk toward the rides. I'm taken aback by his touch, flinching when our hands connect. If he notices, he doesn't say anything, and I keep my hand firmly wrapped in his. I don't know, I can't explain why I didn't pull away, snatch my hand out of his and break the connection, but I can feel it everywhere and it feels good.

Luca hands an attendant a bunch of tickets and pulls me through the gate leading to the swing ride. He picks a swing made for two and makes sure that I'm secured before sitting down next to me. My skin heats as I look down and realize our legs are touching. I don't think I've ever been this close to him, and I'm irritated with myself because I really, really don't hate it. In fact, I kind of like it. Maybe it's because I haven't been this close to anyone in four years or maybe it's because it's him. I can lie to myself and say that I felt nothing for Luca when I first met him, but I did, and I remember being disappointed when he didn't ask me for my number.

The swings start to lift and I jerk at the sensation, he places his hand on my knee in a way that's meant to soothe me and let me know that it's going to be okay. The ride starts to spin in a circular motion. I close my eyes and let the sensations take over. The fear is gone and replaced with a sense of exhilaration—his hand on my knee, us up in the air spinning and it feels like flying, like freedom. I'd forgotten what that feels like, and I never want it to end. I don't want it to stop, to go away like the promise of forever was taken away from me. It's strange to compare a ride to my life but in this moment it seems almost fitting.

When it does come to an end Luca makes sure to give it back to me, and we spend the next hour riding as many rides as we can. I purposely crash into him in bumper cars, and he lets me when I know that he could have easily rammed my car a time or two. He forces me to ride on the mini roller coaster even after I tell him that I hate roller coasters. I scream the whole time and when the ride is over, he makes me ride it again. Strangely enough the second time around I enjoy it more, so much so that I laugh as I scream.

"How's about a cliché bear?" he says heading over to the water gun game.

"Cliché?"

"Yeah, you know, no one can leave a fair without at least attempting to win a bear."

"Ohh, right. Okay, how 'bout I play against you?"

"I'm good with that. You aim your gun there," he points to the target. "Your light will start to go up, whoever gets to the top first wins."

I roll my eyes as I sit on the stool picking up my water gun and aiming it at the mouth of a very creepy clown. "I already knew all that but thanks for the recap."

"Alright smartass, just don't expect me to take it easy on you, I'm not the type of guy who would just let you win."

"I wouldn't expect you to."

The buzzer sounds alerting us that the game is starting, and my gun starts to shoot water. I adjust my aim and focus as my light starts to rise. My cheeks hurt, I'm smiling so hard and when the buzzer rings again signaling that someone has won, I look up to see that it's me.

"I won?" I squeal, looking over at Luca who's biting back a grin.

"You won."

"You let me win," I accuse, as I shove his shoulder.

His hands go up in surrender. "No, I didn't. You actually won, I can't fucking believe it either." I cross my arms over my chest, not sure if I actually believe him but his eyes never leave mine. "Pick your prize."

I turn away from him and look up at the row of bears, pointing toward a big fluffy brown one. The attendant gets him down and I thank her as she hands him to me. We begin to walk again and impulsively I shove the bear into Luca's hands.

He looks down on me in confusion. "What's this?"

"Well I won him, so I'm giving him to you."

"You're giving him to me?"

"Yeah, if you had won you would've given him to me right?"

"Right."

"Okay, so instead I'm giving him to you."

He stares at me for a beat before throwing his head back and laughing. The kind of laugh you feel going right through you warming you up from the inside out.

"Well thank you Ev. I'll make sure I take good care of him."

"You do that." I resume walking with a grin on my face and Luca falls in line right next to me.

"You ready to eat?"

"Yes. I'm starving now."

"Starving? We can't have that. What are you in the mood for?"

"Can we do cheese steaks?"

"Is that even a serious question? Do I look like the kind of guy that would say no to a cheese steak?"

I giggle before I reply, "No, you don't. I should have known better."

"But you didn't."

"Huh?"

"You didn't know better. You know it occurred to me, we've known each other for a long time, and we don't know anything about each other do we."

"We weren't exactly friends."

100

"I know, and that's my fault. I'm sorry that I didn't take the time to get to know you. It was just...it wasn't really anything to do with you, it was more me, my own issues."

"When I met you, I thought you were a nice guy."

"I am a nice guy," he declares using his thumb and his forefinger to tip my chin up. "Will you let me show you?"

My heart rate picks up as I try to catch my breath. I struggle to speak and instead nod my head in acceptance. There's a big part of me that does want to get to know him. I want to see who the real Luca is, and I'm suddenly all for him to show me. We take our food and find an empty picnic table to sit down at. We eat in silence, enjoying each other's company, and I don't think of anything other than this — this night, this fair, the company I'm keeping. I don't think about my job, my house, or my dead husband. The only thing I know is that being here tonight makes me happy, and I never thought it would happen, but I like being here with Luca. I like the time I've spent with him, because while I'm with him, even if only for a little while, I can forget that I'm not okay.

I did something immensely stupid when Luca dropped me off last night. He walked me to the door and instead of saying goodnight and being done with it, I asked him if he wanted to come over for dinner and a movie tonight. He didn't hesitate before saying yes, didn't even have to think about it. He agreed as if it were the best offer he'd ever received and that made me get that warm feeling I'd been experiencing throughout the night all over again.

I didn't dream of Tyler last night, I didn't even dream of Luca. I went through my nighttime routine, and when I hit the bed I fell asleep with no problems. It's been weeks since that happened; I was beginning to think I was never going to have a peaceful night again. I went to the grocery store and picked up all of the ingredients for my lasagna recipe and a loaf of Italian bread. On my way home I made an impromptu stop at the liquor store and picked up a bottle of Chianti, which I was told would be great paired with lasagna.

With all of that I had no time to question why I was going through all this effort for a night with Luca. I had no time to question why I took extra time to make sure the lasagna had three different types of cheese, or why I made it extra meaty. I didn't question why I made garlic bread from scratch instead of buying the pre-made kind. I especially didn't have the time to try and rationalize why I spent an hour making sure my hair was styled in perfectly loose waves or why I spent double the time on makeup, or why I chose to wear the pretty blush pink sundress I hadn't worn before instead of something more casual.

I stop myself from setting the table telling myself that this is something you would only do for a romantic evening with someone and this was most certainly not a romantic evening. I hear the doorbell ring just as I'm shutting the oven off, and I glance up at the hallway clock to see that Luca is here right on time.

"Hi," I greet opening the door for him to walk through. I take in the sight of him wearing a dark pair of jeans and grey button-down shirt and my mouth goes dry. I mentally chastise myself for ogling him and tell myself that I'll have to examine my reaction to him later.

"Hey, you look beautiful," he compliments me, striding inside and turning to hand me a bottle of wine. "I thought we could have some with dinner."

I tuck a loose strand of hair behind my ear all of a sudden feeling slightly shy. "Thanks. Ah, I actually got a bottle of wine too, but this is great, we can have yours."

"I'm sure either one will be fine." He looks toward the kitchen. "It smells amazing."

"Thanks. I hope you like lasagna."

"One of my faves."

"Great." I nod and start toward the kitchen, and he follows close behind. "I was just about to take it out of the oven."

"Can I help you with anything?"

God he's so nice, this is what I thought Luca would be like when I first met him. "You can help me set the table and open the wine if you want?"

"I can do that."

"The plates are already out on the island and the bottle opener is in the first drawer to your right."

He nods and grabs the plates, and together we make quick work of getting dinner on the table. I pull down a couple of wine glasses out of the cabinets and head into the dining room, placing one in front of his chair and one in front of mine. He trails behind me with the open bottle of the wine I bought earlier. He holds my chair out for me while I sit down and once I'm settled, pours me a glass. He sits and does the same, filling his wine glass up as well.

"This looks so good Ev, I don't even remember the last time I had a home cooked meal."

This makes me sad for him, in all the time I've known Luca I've never really seen him date. Whatever he does in his private life he always kept separate. It makes me wonder if he's ever had a girl to take care of him.

"What about your mom? I'm sure she's ecstatic that you're back home, hasn't she cooked for you?"

"Yeah when I first got back a few times, but it's been crazy with my schedule trying to settle into the new job, I haven't had much time for her in the last few weeks."

"I see. Well, dig in then," I say with a smile. I take a sip of wine as I watch him take a bite.

"Holy shit. What's in this?"

"Do you like it?"

"This might just be the best lasagna I've ever had."

"I'm glad you like it," I say, relieved that he's enjoying it. "Secret ingredient though, can't tell you what's in there."

"Hmmm. Alright, I can respect that as long as you promise you'll make it for me again."

"I can do that," I say quietly. For some unknown reason I'm happy that he's suggesting we spend more time together. I know these aren't the best circumstances, but

I'm starting to enjoy spending time with him, and I refuse to let myself feel guilty for that.

❖

After dinner we fill up our wine glasses and take them into the living room. I plop down on the couch and Luca sits down next to me.

He reaches over for the remote and looks my way. "What are you in the mood to watch?"

"Doesn't matter."

He starts skimming the active movie rentals and stops on a romantic comedy. "Let me guess, something like this?"

"No, I hate those, something with some action."

"Really?"

"Yup. I hate romantic comedies." I didn't always hate them; I used to love them actually, but having my own romance go up in a huge ball of flames kind of turned me off to them.

"Good to know," he says, continuing to scroll until we both agree on a new action-adventure release.

"Ev? How are you doing with everything that you've learned in the last few weeks?"

"I'm dealing with it, starting to process that things weren't always what they seemed."

"I am sorry you know."

"I know you are, and this helps. I was mad at you at first for forcing my hand, but I'm seeing that getting back to living is a good thing, otherwise what would be the point right?"

"Right."

"I just... Everyday I wake up and I hope to see something different. I hope that it was all just a bad dream and then I realize it's not and I can't help but wonder if I made a mistake."

"A mistake how?"

105

"A mistake in falling in love with the wrong man."

"Ev…"

"He loved me Luca. I know that, I have *never* doubted that not even once. But he also lied, and I deserved to know the truth and there are times when I think that I deserved more. I deserved someone who could be honest, someone who would love me enough to trust me. I would never have judged him, he had an addiction, and I can see that. I can rationalize it, and I would have stood by him. But I would have liked to do it with eyes wide open. I didn't deserve what I got."

"No you didn't"

"I've never said any of that shit before. I've been walking around for the last four years of my life, letting everyone believe that I was just mourning his loss, that I was so distraught that I couldn't get over it. And that wasn't a lie, I was, but I'm also pissed. I'm so fucking angry at him for putting himself out on the line, for lying to me, for being selfish, for getting himself killed."

"That's what's been holding you back, it's not the mourning, a part of you will mourn his loss forever, but the anger isn't good, you need to let it go."

"I don't know how, I didn't even realize I felt it until recently."

"I think you just let go of a shitload of it babe."

I choose to ignore the fact that he just called me babe, instead I think about what he said for a second before beaming up at him, "I did didn't I? It feels really good."

He holds his arm out in invitation. "Come here."

I don't question it, I just move closer to him, and he shifts me so that I'm leaning into his side, my legs tucked up behind me and his arm around my shoulder. I let my head rest on his shoulder and focus my attention on the movie, thinking that tonight I feel a whole lot lighter somehow.

I wake up feeling slightly dazed and more than a little confused. The house is dark except for the light coming from the television set. It dawns on me that I must have fallen asleep on the couch. I try to turn myself so that I'm on my back when I realize that I'm not alone, I look up to find Luca asleep behind me, one hand propped under his chin, the other resting on my hip. He must have sensed my movement because his eyes flutter open to reveal a soft dreamy look that I feel everywhere, his lip tips up slowly into a half smile before he speaks.

"Sorry, you fell asleep halfway into the movie, and I didn't want to wake you. I must have dozed at some point too."

I say nothing in response, just stare up at him, partly hazed, partly mesmerized by his sleepy features, and I can't explain why but I get the sense that this is right. A feeling of warmth and contentment pass through me making me feel almost like I'm in a dream. I reach up and gently run my fingertips across his cheek, they move down and around until my hand is firmly on the back of his neck and in what I can only describe as an out-of-body experience, I use that hand to pull him down to me. His eyes heat with something I've never seen before, making me melt even more. I tug harder, bringing his lips down to mine, and he comes willingly, making it so that I don't even have to think twice about it when I kiss him.

The hand that was resting on my knees snakes around my back, and he presses his torso down so that he can roll on top of me. My legs part, allowing him to settle in as I open my mouth and his tongue slides in. My other hand goes to his neck and before long they're in his hair, keeping him secured to me. I let myself go, taking what I want and giving it to him, in return letting myself enjoy the sensation of his tongue in my mouth.

I'm gone, completely lost in his touch and when I arch my back and his grip on my waist tightens, I snap out of the fog I'm in. I open my eyes, pull back, and push on his chest.

"Stop," I say, trying to catch my breath.

He looks down at me, his eyes still glazed over. "What's wrong?"

"I cant, I'm so sorry Luca I just can't do this," I say, feeling mortified.

I can feel his body over me get very tight. "You can't or you won't?"

"Both, it's just... I can't, this is wrong."

"What's so wrong about it? You're free, I'm free, you clearly feel something for me and I feel it too. What makes it wrong?"

"You're my dead husband's best friend, the best man in my wedding; do I even need to explain this to you?" I shove him hard, moving him just enough to allow me to sit up. He moves up the rest of the way pushing himself off of the couch. He stands up towering over me looking anything but happy, in fact he looks pretty infuriated.

"Who. The. Fuck. Cares. He's gone Everly, gone, never coming the fuck back. Do you really think that moving on with your life makes you a bad person?"

"No. I think moving on with you makes me a bad person," I shout. "Do you know how bad that would look?"

"No I don't know how bad it would look, and I also do not give a shit. I live my life for me Everly not anyone else."

"That's because you don't care about anyone but yourself."

He flinches at my words, his hands clench into fists. "Is that really what you think?"

"Who do you care about Luca?"

108

"Well until about five seconds ago I cared about you," he says, before turning around and leaving me sitting there alone. He slams the door on his way out, moments later I hear the car engine rev up, and he's gone. How the hell did I just get myself into this mess? What did I just do? A few hours ago Luca and I were on our way to becoming real friends and then I ruined it by kissing him. He said that he felt something for me and claimed that I did too. Am I so far gone that I can't even recognize my own emotions? Just look at all of the effort I put into making this a good night. He's right, totally right, and now he's gone and he's pissed at me and I don't know if I can fix it. What's more is that I don't know if I actually want to fix it.

~ Luca ~

I slam her door so hard I'm surprised I didn't shatter a window. I stalk down the driveway, get in my car, rev it up, and get the fuck out of there. I can't remember a time when I've been quite this furious, and I don't know if I'm angrier at her or myself. Being around Everly these last few days has been amazing, but I should have braced myself for something like this—prepared myself for her freak out—but I didn't, and now I feel like an asshole for blowing up on her. But I couldn't hold that shit in anymore. It's been building for years, and I can't bring myself to care anymore.

The logical thinker in me knows that I should have pushed her away when she kissed me; she was likely out of it, having just woken up, and she got carried away. I should have stopped her and explained that she needed more time to sort through her feelings, but I didn't do that. Instead I pushed her, took in further, climbed on top of her, and deepened the kiss.

I'm an asshole, I know that, but this is Everly, and I've been caught up in her web for far too long. Having her be the one to make the first move was too much. What man in his right mind would say no to that? Who would say no

110

to the woman of his dreams waking up in his arms and moving to kiss him? I'm only human and the way she made dinner, bought wine, and planned the whole night for us only made me want her more.

When she broke the kiss and pushed me off of her I snapped. I should have been kinder. I should have told her that I understood, that I knew she was dealing with a lot, and that I would wait. I didn't do that, instead I flipped out and walked out on her.

I'm at war with myself. Part of me wants to turn my car back around and go to her to make sure that she's alright. But the rest of me wants to leave it alone and go back to being a stranger in her life because it's safer that way. There's only one woman on this planet who can make me bleed, and it's her. I just can't do it anymore.

~ *Everly* ~

The tables have turned on me in a big way. I'm usually the one avoiding Luca at all costs while at work, but this week it's totally him doing the avoiding. He is going far out of his way to stay as far away from me as possible. He didn't even show for work on Thursday and by Friday I'm just pissed and confused. I even called and texted him a few times with no reply. I'd hoped that he'd at least be willing to talk to me about what happened last weekend, but I see that that's never going to happen.

I pick up my office phone and call Morgan. I've begun calling and texting her a few times a week, and I decide I need a little girl time this week. I need to take my mind off of Luca, and I do not want to go home to my lonely house tonight.

She answers on the second ring sounding her usual chipper self. "Hey girl."

"Hey, what are you up to tonight?"

"No plans, why what's up?"

"You want to get together?"

"Sure, your place or mine?"

"Neither," I respond shaking my head. "How about we go grab a drink somewhere?"

There's a long pause and for a minute there I think the call has been disconnected before she responds. "You actually want to go out?"

I smile, knowing what she's getting at. I never go out so for me to suggest it is probably shocking. "Yes."

"Who are you and what have you done with Everly?"

"I know. I'm just so sick of being home."

"You don't have to convince me babe, this makes me so happy. Why don't I meet you at your job and we can walk down to one of the bars on main."

"Sounds perfect."

I'm on my second Malibu bay breeze and stuffing my face with mozzarella sticks when Morgan finally brings him up.

"So how's Luca doing?"

I roll my eyes at her. "How am I supposed to know?"

"Don't you work with him?"

I sigh, and let out a deep breath before going into the details. "Yeah, I do, and we've actually hung out a few times."

She grabs hold of my wrist. "Wait what?"

"Yeah, after you called him telling him you were worried about me... thanks for that by the way. He came by and kind of bribed me into going out with him. He said I had to get out of the house."

"Well that was nice of him," she claims, her face getting soft.

"It's nice to bribe people?"

112

"No it's nice of him to care enough to want to bribe you to get out of the house."

"I don't even know how to respond to that."

"Just get on with the story."

"He took me out a few times and I was surprised but for the most part I had a good time. He was nice."

"He's always been nice."

"Not to me."

Now she rolls her eyes at me. "So what else?"

"I asked him to come by for dinner and a movie on Sunday."

"Oh. My. God!"

I shove my face in the palm of my hands and squeal. "I know. I know. I don't know what I was thinking."

"Everly! I'm so proud of you. Yay!"

"Wait, why are you proud of me?"

"Because you're making positive steps toward moving on and if it just so happens that you can move on with hottie Luca then that's just a bonus."

"You don't think me hooking up with Luca would be a bad thing?"

"Why would that be bad?"

"Morgan, he was my husband's best friend."

"Okay, honey, I hate to talk about this shit because I don't want to set you back or hurt you but Tyler's dead. You can move on with whoever you want. You wouldn't be wrong in doing that with Luca."

"Well I really screwed that up anyway. He won't even talk to me now."

"Ev what did you do?" It comes out as more of a warning than it does a question.

"I kissed him..."

"That's awesome," she squeals.

"It would have been awesome if I hadn't have pushed him away and freaked out."

113

"You didn't?"

"I did. I told him it was all wrong, and I tried to apologize, but he lost it and stormed out of my house. I haven't spoken to him since."

"Have you reached out to him?"

"Yeah, I've called and texted but nothing. He's avoiding me at work, and I'm not about to cause a scene there so...Done."

"Sooo not done. You bruised his ego, give him some time to get over it."

"You think?" I ask, more hopefully than I want to sound.

"Yup."

"Everly? Morgan?"

I look over my shoulder to see Janine standing there, looking at Morgan and I in awe. Janine was one of my best friends, one of my bridesmaids, and when Tyler died and I shut down, she tried to reach me a few times but she eventually gave up. Actually she was the first of my friends to give up. Morgan being the only one who *never* gave up.

"Hey Janine."

"Hi Janine." We both greet in unison.

"Gosh it's great to see you girls, especially you Everly. I haven't seen you in years."

I plaster a smile on my face. "It's good to see you too. You look great."

"Well thanks, you look great too. I ran into Luca the other day and I was telling him how worried I was about you."

This gets my immediate attention. "You ran into Luca?"

"Yeah, Oh wait... Don't tell me you still hate him do you?"

"Everly doesn't hate anyone Janine, she's not like that," Morgan pipes in.

Janine rolls her eyes in Morgan's direction and then comes back to me. "Well that's good, that boy is hot. We had a few drinks, hoofed it over to my place and let me tell you, the things that boy can do with his tongue."

I'm taken aback by her words. She's all but admitted to me that she and Luca hooked up. "I'm sorry, will you excuse me. I don't feel so well."

"Oh hon are you alright?" She couldn't be any faker if she tried.

"Yeah, sorry, too many drinks, not enough food," I say before hopping off the stool and rushing to the bathroom. Morgan is hot on my trail.

"Everly, don't freak out. You don't know that anything happened, Janine is a liar, and she always has been."

"I know," I reply, running the cold water and splashing my face. "I shouldn't even care."

"You like him, of course you care."

"How can you hate someone for so many years then like them all of a sudden? Is that even possible?" I question, as I grip the sink and lean down on it.

"There's a fine line between love and hate."

"Can we get out of here?" I ask, looking up at her.

"Sure, I paid the bill and grabbed your purse. We can leave through the back entrance."

"Thanks, I'll pay you back for my stuff."

"Don't worry about it."

We leave the bar and walk down the street to my law firm's parking lot where we left our cars. We say our goodbyes and I promise her that I'll give her a call this weekend. I watch her go and when I'm sure she's gone, I use my key to get back into the office. I head to filing cabinet where they keep all of the employee's personal information and I pull Luca's folder. I sift through until I

115

find his address, jot it down on a Post-it note and get the hell out of there.

12

I've lost my mind, I'm almost positive that I've gone completely postal but here I am, sitting in my car outside of Luca's apartment for the past twenty minutes trying to build up the nerve to go in. All of the lights are off and his car is out front which means he's likely sleeping. This is a really bad, really stupid idea. I move to turn the ignition back on in my car telling myself that I should just leave and then I think about how Janine all but admitted that she had sex with Luca, I think about how he walked out on me for not going any further than a kiss when clearly he's not lacking for attention and I think about how he's ignored me for five days, and I'm suddenly infuriated.

I angle out of the car, jog up his front steps and ring the doorbell. I wait about ten seconds before ringing it again, and again, and for good measure, again. I see a light go on in the upstairs window and then I hear footfalls and what I'm pretty sure are curse words. The door flies open and I'm met by Luca's angry glare but I can't focus on that— my eyes have traveled down to his bare chest. I assumed he had nice abs from the fit of his clothing, but I had no idea how perfect they really were. And the sexiest pair of pajama bottoms I've ever seen sit low on his hips. Jesus, why did he have to open up the door shirtless?

"Everly what the fuck?"

The boom of his angry voice snaps me out of my haze and helps me to remember why I'm here. I use all the force I can muster up, place both hands on his chest and shove him back. This allows me just enough room to slip past him and once I do I run up the staircase. I hear his heavy sigh and the door slamming followed by footsteps. I can sense him when he's right behind me, can feel his anger in the air like it has a physical presence. I turn to face him, place my hands on my hips and glare at him.

His eyes are trained on the ground seemingly trying to regain his patience, when he looks up again I can tell it didn't do any good, he looks just as angry. "Would you like to explain to me what the hell you're doing here?"

"I. Hate. You." I declare through clenched teeth.

"What else is new? You're not my favorite person either did you really have to come here after midnight to tell me this?"

"You slept with Janine!" I yell the accusation not caring if every person in a five mile radius can hear me.

His eyes narrow and flash with anger, and I can feel my heart hammering in my chest because he looks seriously pissed right now. His voice rumbles when he finally speaks. "What?"

I don't know if I'm stupid or just crazy but I straighten my spine, square my shoulders, tilt my head to the side and lock my eyes on his. "I said You. Slept. With. Janine."

"Who told you that?" I can sense that he's fighting for control, trying not to blow up on me.

"Morgan and I ran into Janine tonight. She was all too happy to fill us in. In fact she was singing your praises," I say in a whiny voice that a five-year-old would use to show their anger.

"Really?" He questions suddenly looking like he's enjoying this showdown. He crosses his arms over his chest and grins. "Why do you care if I slept with Janine?"

"Because you're not supposed to date my friends, you're especially not supposed to sleep with my friends; there's a code, there are rules that you're supposed to stick to."

He gives me a slow nod, before ripping my theory to shreds. "Those rules would only apply if you were my girlfriend. You *are not* my girlfriend, and you have never been my girlfriend. There is no code where we're concerned because the way we left it off pretty much says that we are nothing to each other."

His words hurt and I have no right to feel that way but none of this makes sense anyway so I carry on. "I never said that, I've been trying to talk to you for days," I yell throwing out my hands.

"What is there to say? You are not ready, and you will never be ready to move on."

"That's not true."

"It is."

"No."

"Yes. Yes. Everly, you refuse to let go." His hands are clenched at his side. He's angry at me, I get it, but this is going nowhere.

"I'm trying. I'm trying to let go, but I'm scared." I admit, doing my best to keep the tears away.

"What the hell could you possibly have to be scared of at this point?"

"This," I say motioning between him and me. "This thing with you. It terrifies me."

"Why?"

"Because for the first time in so long I wanted someone else. Someone other than him." It's as honest as I can possibly be with him. It's as honest as I've been with myself through all of this.

He stalks over to me and reaches out for my hand, but I pull away. "No," I say, turning away from him. "You slept with Janine."

He comes up behind me, pressing his chest to my back, his head rests on my shoulder, and his lips are close to my ear. I shudder at the feel of his breath on me. "You don't get to tell me it's wrong to be with someone else, because I'm not yours."

My body goes rigid, and I jerk my shoulder to get him off of me. Once I'm free, I whirl around, getting in his face. After what I've just admitted this is what he says to me? This is his attempt at smoothing things over? "You like this don't you? You get some sick satisfaction from messing with my head?"

There's a gleam in his eyes letting me know that he's absolutely enjoying this showdown "I don't care enough about you to mess with your head."

That's all it takes, the next thing I know I'm lunging at him, but instead of shoving him, punching him, or clawing his fucking eyes out, my hands grasp his hair, pull him down to me, and kiss him fiercely, savagely and a little possessively. I gasp when he grips my hair with his hand and wraps his free arm around my waist locking me to him. I melt into him when he deepens the kiss, lost to what he's making me feel, all rational thoughts left behind. I go up on my toes giving him better access and cling to him as if though my life depends on it. His hands move down my body grazing my ass, reaching the back of my thighs, and hauling me up. I wrap my legs around his hips never breaking the kiss, and the next thing I know we're on the move. Luca is walking through a doorway and then we're down on his bed, me on my back and him on top of me.

120

My hands are everywhere, desperately exploring the muscles of his back, his hips, his thighs, trying to make myself familiar with every part of him at the same time giving him permission to do the same. His hand rests on my stomach and slowly begins to slide up and underneath my shirt, his touch warming me all over. His thumb swipes at the swell of my breast making my back arch involuntarily, and a moan escapes my lips. His fingers graze my nipple causing a rush of wetness to gather between my legs. It's never been like this before, where I so recklessly abandon all self-control, where my only focus is on maximizing the sensations, nothing else. He breaks the kiss and I cry out at the loss of him, I don't want this to stop. He looks down at me, his face serious but the desire in his eyes is unmistakable. He wants me as much as I want him.

"Everly, I'm giving you two seconds to get up and walk out of here before I rip your clothes off and bury myself inside of you."

His mouth is so close all I can think of is getting it on me. I suck his lower lip gently nipping at it before letting go. He needs me to reassure him of my decision, he needs to know that I want him and I have no problem giving that to him. "I'm not going anywhere."

"Take your shirt off Ev. Show me that you want this."

His voice is hypnotic, soothing, making me want to give him what he wants. Without hesitation I sit up, grabbing the hem of my shirt, and pull it over my head. His eyes focus on the black lace of my bra, just the look of him filled with lust and hunger sends a jolt of electricity through me. He runs a finger over the scalloped edges of my bra before pulling the cups down exposing my breasts to him completely. There's no time to protest because his mouth is on me almost instantly, sucking on one breast while working the other one with his fingers, tugging and circling my nipples making me cry out in pleasure.

"Luca please," I whimper, not recognizing my own voice. I sound desperate and needy and at the moment that's exactly how I feel. I can't get him close enough; every touch just leaves me wanting more.

He responds by lifting his torso up and off of me, undoing the button on my pants and tugging them down my legs leaving me in only my underwear. I reach around my back undoing the clasp on my bra and shrug it off. I've only been this exposed for one other person and right now all thoughts of him are blurred by the man standing in front of me.

"You're so fucking beautiful," he says, eyes locked on mine.

I'm breathless now, panting for air as his hands go to the waist of his pajama pants. He has them down his legs and off before I can move and I barely make out the sound of them hitting the floor. I'm taken aback by the sight of him, his bare chest, broad shoulders, and the beautiful muscles that line his abs. My gaze travels down, and I swear I can feel my heart rate quicken. Luca is beautiful, from head to toe, completely and utterly blessed.

He leans down, placing a kiss on my lips, his hand down my panties causing me to whimper into his mouth. His finger slides through the folds of my wet pussy and my body convulses. The feeling of him on me is mind blowing, almost too much to handle, but I crave it, need more of him, as much as he can give.

"Fuck baby you're so wet for me."

"Condom," is all I can manage to get out of my mouth. He reaches over to his nightstand, pulls out a condom, and quickly takes care of putting it on.

"You're ready?" he asks looking down at me again.

"Yes."

He pulls my panties down and off in a split second, a gust of cold air hits my naked body before he's over me again covering me with his and he's kissing me again.

"Last chance baby."

"Please Luca," I beg, and he positions himself between my legs, his hard cock at my entrance making me want him all the more. I jut my hips up letting him know exactly what I want and Luca is in the mood to give me exactly what I want. He growls as he slides in filling me up making me cry out at the initial shock of him there.

"Fuck you're tight," he strains out.

It's been over four years since I've done this so the fullness of him leaves me with a mixture of both pleasure and pain but I don't care, I love it. I feel free, I feel alive, and moments like these are rare in my life.

He looks down at me assessing the situation, and I can feel the tension in his muscles, his need to move being overshadowed by his need to make sure I'm alright. "You okay?"

"Yes," I reply, on a breath. I relax my muscles allowing myself to acclimate to his size. I lift my head up to capture his lips with mine, tasting his tongue and gripping his shoulders, urging him to go on. Slowly, he begins to move his hips and I throw my head back, savoring every single sensation that travels through me. Every thrust is like a conduit, lighting me up, setting me on fire, making me beg for more.

I lift my legs and one by one wrap them around Luca's waist, deepening the connection even further. His cock feels impossibly large inside of me, stretching me to the max, enhancing the already intense sensations, passing though me. He kisses and suckles at my neck and starts to increase his pace, thrusting his cock harder and faster with every passing moment. I circle my hips, doing my best to meet his movements; I can barely register the sound of my own cries as my pleasure intensifies. I know it's coming, the buildup of pressure starting in my stomach and shooting out to my nerve endings. He groans in my ear, and I know he's close.

"Oh fuck Everly."

"Harder," I cry, and he complies, thrusting with a relentless rhythm making me delirious, I feel like I'm breaking apart into a million tiny pieces and I welcome it; needing him to shatter me in order to make me whole again. Our lips crash together again, tongues tangle, and with one final push of his hips I'm coming undone, falling down a spiral of bliss so huge I don't know if I'll ever recover. Luca collapses on top of me, and I hold tight to him as his release shoots into me. I hear his grunt of pleasure and can feel the pulse of his cock as he comes, leaving me sated and spent.

Luca nuzzles my nose with the tip of his. "Jesus Christ."

I close my eyes, enjoying the aftershocks of pleasure, his lips on my mouth, my chin, my neck. I hear him let out a sigh, and I whimper as he slides out of me. He kisses me one last time.

"I'll be right back." He moves out of the bed and walks into what I can only assume is a bathroom in order to discard the condom. The sound of water running telling me that I guessed right. I close my eyes letting myself relax, not allowing myself even a moment to think about or regret what just happened. A few minutes later the bed depresses, my eyes flutter open, and I'm looking up at Luca's beautiful face.

"Open your legs baby," he commands softly. My pussy spasms at the sound of his words, but I do as he asks and spread for him. He uses a warm rag to clean me up, tossing it on the floor once he's done. He climbs back into bed, settles into his pillows, wraps an arm around my waist and pulls me into his body. I like this, like how it feels to be in his arms, in his bed, so I rest my head on his chest, my arm around his waist and relax into him. I close my eyes and strangely enough it doesn't take long for me to let go and fall into a peaceful dreamless sleep.

13

The sun is beaming down on me, and I can feel it on my skin through my closed eyelids. Why didn't I shut the blinds? I'm feeling a little parched, overheated like I'm wrapped up in heavy blankets. I take a minute and open my eyes looking out the window... not my window. I look down on a sharp intake of breath to find that I'm completely naked. I'm about to freak when I feel movement behind me, an arm thrown over then tightening around my waist...Luca.

The events of last night come flooding back, being at the bar with Morgan and running into Janine, barging in on Luca, having an argument with him and finally throwing myself at him like a psychotic slut. I don't know whether to die of mortification or sneak out of here before he wakes up.

"I know you're awake Ev."

I catch my breath at the sound of his voice, then slowly turn around to face him. He looks unreal first thing in the morning, hair tousled, sleepy eyes, and a sexy grin. My heart flutters just looking at him. "Hi," I whisper.

He smiles at me sending a rush of warmth right through me. He looks happy that I'm here and that thought makes a little bit of my embarrassment fall away. "Hi." His lips come down to mine, and he gives me a chaste kiss.

I use his silence as my opening for a rapid-fire explanation. "Luca, I'm so sorry for showing up here like that last night."

He cuts me off with another kiss, this one deeper, hotter, just like that I want him again. I open my eyes when he breaks the kiss to find him smiling again. He clearly sees the humor in this situation.

"Babe, in case you missed it I'm very glad you showed up here last night."

"No, I know. It's just that..."

"Just what?" he probes, pushing a strand of hair behind my ear.

"I've never had a one-night stand before."

His entire body gets hard, his eyes guarded as he pushes slightly off of me, still hovering but now looking more dangerous than inviting. "Is that what you think this was?"

I stare at him for a moment, my eyes also guarded. "Wasn't it?"

"No," he answers immediately, no hesitation on his part. "Fuck no. You can't tell me you don't feel something for me and I know sure as shit that I feel something for you. This wasn't about one night, this was us breaking down a barrier, and now we can explore what's between us."

His reply scares me, at the same time making me happy. How do I reconcile the fact that a few weeks ago I HATED this man, hated him with such a passion and intensity that it almost consumed me? And now I'm here occupying his bed and wanting so badly for it to not end. "This is bad."

"What?" He questions, shaking his head.

"Oh shit." I'm panicking; there are so many obstacles that would stand in the way of Luca and me developing a relationship. I know that it shouldn't matter that he was my husband's best friend. He's gone, I'm free to move on with whoever I want, but I know how people talk and I don't want to deal with that. Then there are Tyler's parents, how would they handle news of Luca and me dating?

My family would likely be more accepting, but we also have to think about work. There's nothing written down about a no fraternization policy but I'm sure that it would still be frowned upon. Luca isn't my direct supervisor, but we would still need to be careful.

"Everly, don't go there."

"But..."

"No, wherever your mind is going don't let it go there. We did nothing wrong."

"Luca." It's a plea. I need him to untangle the mess in my head, to unravel the ball of knots in my stomach and tell me that everything is going to be alright, that we can get to know each other without worrying about what the potential for disaster is.

"We did nothing wrong," he says again. He cups my chin with his hand forcing me to look him in the eye. "I want you, you want me, there's nothing to stand in our way, we are both single available people, and there is nothing wrong with that."

"Okay." I breathe out, feeling slightly better.

"Are we good?"

We're as good as we can be right now but there's still the reason I came here in the first place last night. "I'm still pissed about you and Janine."

127

He buries his face in my neck and lets out a chuckle. "I didn't sleep with Janine."

"Luca."

"We kissed, nothing more." He wraps his hands around my waist, pulling me closer. "It was one time a few weeks ago, I was a little drunk but I ended shit before it got any further."

"Why didn't you tell me that last night?" Realizing that he didn't sleep with Janine makes a sense of relief wash over me, but I also feel foolish for coming over here the way that I did.

"I was too busy fucking you babe, plus you look cute all jealous and pissed at me."

I try to roll away from him "I wasn't jealous."

"Okay," he replies, grabbing hold of my waist and keeping me firmly in place, exactly where he wants me.

"I wasn't"

He grins and kisses my forehead. "I said okay."

"You didn't mean it, you're being sarcastic," I argue.

"Okay."

"Ugh," I say with a roll of my eyes. "I know it shouldn't matter to me."

"I like that it matters to you, it means that I matter to you."

He sends my heart aflutter again with his words. "I don't know how to reconcile that in my mind."

"Why do you have to try?"

"I guess I don't."

His forehead drops to mine, his eyes are heated and his voice is husky as his hand slips down my torso and cups my sex. "We don't have to figure anything out today." His fingers find my already swollen clit and start circling. Instinctively my hand comes up and I hold onto his neck, keeping him connected to me. "All that we need to do today is this. Enjoy what we have right now."

128

"Yes." I sigh, loving the feel of his hands on me.

His lips come down possessively taking mine in his and suddenly I'm all for his plan for the day. In fact his plan for the day is exactly what I want.

"We haven't left this bed all day." I stretch out my arms, thinking that I'd like to spend everyday like this.

"We got up for cereal."

"We stink."

"That sounds promising."

I giggle at his silliness. "How is our stinking promising?"

"We got that way together, it would be logical if we got clean together too."

"Ohh right, well I don't think I can handle any more of you right now, I'm overused, tired, and sore."

He hovers over me running the tip of his nose along my jawline. "You're sore?"

I sigh at the feel of his touch. "Yes, it's been a long time Luca, and even back then I don't think I ever spent the whole day doing it."

"Doing what?"

"You know what," I say shoving him lightly.

"Fucking Everly, you've never spent the whole day fucking."

"No," I confess, covering my eyes with my forearm.

He pulls my arm, forcing me to look at him and giving me a quick kiss. "We'll have to build your stamina," he says with a chuckle. He gets up and reaches out a hand for me. I take it, and he quickly pulls me up. "But for now we'll take a shower together, and then I'll make you dinner."

"Are you going to try to do things to me in the shower?"

"Not when you're sore baby," he says, tugging my hand. "Come on." He pulls me into the bathroom, lifts me up, and places me on the counter while he turns the shower on and grabs an extra towel for me. I use this time to examine him further; his slightly rounded ass is a sight to behold. I grabbed onto that ass many times today, and I loved every minute of it. He moves around fluidly, effortlessly with a certain air of confidence that I find increasingly attractive.

"Are you done ogling me now Ev? You think you might want to join me in here."

I was so caught up with inspecting him that I missed the fact that he had already gotten in the shower. My cheeks redden with embarrassment, and I suddenly feel shy, but I slide off of the counter anyway and head into the shower with him. He reaches out to tag an arm around my waist and pulls me to him. I know what he wants because I want the same. I rise to the tips of my toes and give him my mouth. My arms go around his neck, and we stand there in the middle of the shower making out for a long time.

We take turns soaping each other up and helping to rinse one another off. We kiss some more, hug, and touch, letting the water run over our bodies, enjoying this time in each other's company. It hits me that not once since my meltdown this morning have I thought of Tyler, and I'm grateful for it. Grateful that my mind is allowing me a reprieve from the constant sadness that comes with thoughts of him. Grateful that perhaps I can finally move on, that I'm finally *ready* to move on.

14

Luca's in the kitchen making dinner, and my ass is planted on his granite countertop watching him work and drinking a glass of wine. As I watch him move around, I notice that he seems perfectly relaxed, completely at home in the kitchen. I realize that I've never had a guy cook for me, not even once. Cooking was not in Tyler's repertoire — if it wasn't ready to serve or microwavable he couldn't hack it. I never minded cooking and taking care of him but this feels amazing too.

"Are you sure I can't do anything to help?" I question, feeling guilty about just sitting here doing nothing.

He chuckles and shakes his head at me. "You just can't sit still can you?"

I shrug but respond honestly. "I've just never had anyone cook for me before. I don't know what to do with myself."

He looks up at me with a hint of surprise in his eyes. "Never?"

"Well, I mean my parents obviously, Morgan too but other than that no."

He nods, and then goes back to seasoning the chicken he had defrosted earlier. "I like to cook."

I don't know why this surprises me but it does. "How'd you learn?"

He throws his head back and lets out a laugh. "Believe it or not my dad taught me how to cook."

"Seriously?"

"Yes, he said it was important for me to be able to fend for myself instead of ordering pizza every night when I was old enough to live on my own. And..." he drags out coming toward me. He places his hands on my knees and pushes them apart so he can position himself between my legs. I spasm down there again as he wraps his arms around my waist. "He also told me that the key to attracting a beautiful woman was to impress her with my culinary abilities."

"Is that so?"

"Yes, that's so. Are *you* impressed yet?" He chuckles.

"I don't know, I mean I have to taste this culinary masterpiece before I can answer that."

"Alright." He nods. "A challenge. I can handle that."

This all feels so surreal to me — being here with Luca, spending time with him, being involved intimately with him is something I never would have dreamed about. I guess that's not entirely true either, I did think of him that way after we first met, before Tyler became a part of my life.

I can't help but to wonder what would have happened if Luca had wanted me all those years ago, or if he would have made a play for me at some point. If there was a choice to be made between him and Tyler would I still have chosen Tyler? A few months ago I wouldn't have had to think twice about the answer to that question. Now I'm just not so sure. I cup his face in the palm of my hands and place a kiss on his forehead. "I'm glad you came home Luca."

He says nothing just looks at me, taking in my words. I've spent so long hating him for things that he never really had anything to do with, hating him for problems in my own relationship that I never knew existed. Then he came home and I certainly didn't make anything easier on him, I wasted no time in throwing around old accusations. But if he hadn't come back I wouldn't be here now—finally knowing the whole truth behind my husband's death—not feeling so confined by my existence, by my history, and not constantly feeling so alone.

"I know that I wasn't the nicest person to you when you came back," I admit.

"You thought I was responsible for Tyler's death. I understood your anger toward me."

My eyes are glassy with unshed tears, it's a struggle to contain them but I try. "Yeah, I know and I'm glad that you told me. I'm glad that I know the truth now but mostly I'm glad because when I'm with you I feel more like myself than I have in years. I never thought I'd get that back again."

"You deserve to be happy."

"I'm trying."

He squeezes my waist before letting me go and going back to the stove to continue cooking. He places his now seasoned and cut strips of chicken in a frying pan and adjusts the heat on the stove before looking up at me.

"Are you happy at work Ev? Is that what you want to do?"

"What's wrong with being a paralegal?" I ask defensively.

"Nothing."

I sigh and simultaneously roll my eyes "I'm just so sick of people telling me what to do about my career."

He walks over to me and grasps my chin, holding my face in place forcing me to look at him. "No babe, I don't

133

mean it like that. There's NOTHING wrong with what you do. It's a great job, it pays well, and I think it's amazing. But I also know you, and I remember that you wanted to be a lawyer."

"It just didn't seem all that important after everything that happened."

"And what about now?" he questions releasing his hold on me.

"Now, I don't know, I don't mind the work, I'm content there. I don't know if I'll ever really be ready for more. I don't know if I have the passion to pursue becoming a lawyer," I answer as honestly as I can.

"If you ever decide you want to go for it, I can help if you want."

"Thank you."

He nods and grins at me before returning his attention to his task. That conversation was easy, much easier than when Ty's father brings it up. He pushes, nags, and tells me what a mistake I'm making. He makes me feel like less of a person because I didn't do what was expected of me. I suspect that's what Ty often felt when dealing with his father, like he was constantly letting him down. It makes me sad for the boy I once knew, for the man I once loved.

⁂

"So? Did I pass?"

We're sitting at the dining room table in Luca's apartment having just finished a wonderful meal. He made chicken served over rigatoni with a sauce made out of crushed tomatoes, garlic, olive oil, and basil. It was seriously one of the best dishes I've ever tasted. The conversation over dinner was light, easy and free flowing. I can't believe how far we've come in the last twenty-four hours.

"Pass?" I question, pretending not to know exactly what he's asking.

"Yeah, did I impress you with my culinary skills?"

He looks boyish sitting there, waiting expectantly for my answer. Hopeful. I like this look on him. "I must admit this was great. I'm definitely impressed."

"Good," he states, looking pleased with himself. "I'm glad you liked it."

I nod then take a final sip of my wine. As I set the glass down on the table, I decide that I should probably end this for tonight. Too much of a good thing is probably not the best idea right now—we should probably ease into this slowly. Plus time alone might be good for me; it will allow me the space I need to process everything that's happened here. So... even though I really don't want to go, I decide it's what I'll do. "It's getting late. I should probably be getting home."

His eyes flicker with disappointment, and he makes no attempt at hiding it. "Do you have to go?"

"Well..."

"You should stay Ev. It's Saturday, and we don't have to be at work tomorrow. In fact, we don't have to be anywhere tomorrow. Stay, spend the night with me."

My heart flutters yet again, all I really want to do is melt into him—stay here and let this unfold however it may. "I don't have any clothes."

His eyes are full of mischief. "You don't need any clothes."

"Luca." I smile timidly at him.

"But if you insist I'll lend you a pair of sweats and a t-shirt."

"Okay."

"Okay."

I help him carry the dishes into the kitchen, and I rinse them while he arranges them in the dishwasher. It's a very domestic scene, one that I'm all too comfortable in with him. Maybe even a little too comfortable, but it feels good to be here like this. It feels strangely normal, and normal is just another thing on a long list of things that I haven't had in a very long time.

⁂

After dinner dishes Luca and I settle into the couch to watch a movie. I snuggle closely to him and dose off halfway through the film. When the movie ends, he wakes me up and leads me into his bedroom.

I stand in the middle of the room while he walks over to his dresser and rifles through the drawers.

"Here." He snatches up a black t-shirt and hands it to me. "You can put this on while I go turn off all the lights and set the alarm."

"Okay."

He moves to walk out of the room but I feel him come up behind me, and his fingers dig into my waist, his warm breath on my neck. "Ev, Just the shirt, nothing else." My breath catches at his command then he's gone, leaving me standing here a little vulnerable and severely aroused. It takes me a second to recover from his words but I eventually do. I walk into the bathroom and quickly change into the t-shirt Luca's provided. I contemplate his words for a moment wondering if I should do as he asks. He's already seen me naked; I'm not sure what my hang up is. Maybe I'm just a little embarrassed around him still, but I let that go and do as he asks, pushing my panties down my legs.

I wash my face with warm water and use the spare toothbrush that Luca gave me earlier to brush my teeth again. When I walk back into the bedroom Luca is already there wearing nothing but his pajama bottoms and pulling back the covers on the bed.

136

"Why do you look like that?" he asks with a hint of a smile playing on his lips.

"Like what?"

"Like you're terrified of me all of a sudden."

I wave him off like he's completely crazy. "I don't know what you're talking about," I tell him as I walk deeper into the room and casually hop into bed.

I can see the humor in his eyes, but he says nothing. He just turns off the lights and slides into bed next to me. I lay there motionless, staring at the ceiling unsure of what to do next.

"Everly?" he calls after a few moments.

"Yeah?"

"Are you still sore?"

I'm not sure what comes over me, but I break out in a fit of giggles. I can feel his eyes on me, but he says nothing as the giggling turns into full on laughter. He must find my hilarity amusing because I can almost make out a grin on his lips.

My laughter ends with a gasp when Luca grabs me, positions himself on top of me and pins my arms above my head.

"You think this is funny?" he questions maneuvering me so that he's holding both of my wrists with one hand now. He uses his free hand to push my t-shirt up leaving me exposed to him. He runs his hand down my bare skin slipping his fingers inside the lips of my already wet pussy. My breath hitches as he slips a finger inside.

"Not so funny anymore is it?" His eyes are dark, hungry, I can see the lust in them and I desperately want him to deliver on the promise that's hidden behind them. He crooks the finger that's inside of me in a come hither motion hitting me exactly where I need it.

"Is it?" he commands as he stops all movement, making me cry out for more.

"No," I whimper through shallow breath.

He removes his finger from inside of me and releases his grip on my hands while directing my next move. "Hold onto the headboard Everly, don't let go."

"Why?" I question him but still doing as he asks.

"This is your punishment for laughing, and if you let go, I'm not going to let you come."

Holy shit, no one has ever spoken to me like this before, I feel like I might just come hearing him say the words. I let my head fall back on the pillows, closing my eyes in order to get control of myself. Luca makes me feel almost delirious, needy in a way that I don't think I've ever been before.

He grabs my earlobe between his teeth, nipping at it, making me gasp in pleasure. "Do you understand Everly?"

"Yes," I respond, my eyes fluttering open.

"Good." His mouth is so close to mine now that I part my lips to invite him inside. The moment his tongue touches mine a blanket of warmth seeps through me and envelopes me with his scent. His lips begin a downward descent leaving a trail of heat in their wake. His tongue swirls around my belly button as he slides his finger inside of me again and resumes his movement there. I close my eyes, gasping for air, overcome with the sensations that his hands elicit from me. Just as I'm about to come undone his finger stills making me cry out.

"No."

"Shh. It's okay, just relax." He withdraws his fingers and uses his hand to push my legs apart. I keep my hands over my head as he asked, his command acting like an invisible bind preventing me from moving.

"You have a pretty little pussy Everly," he says running his fingers up and down my slit. I whimper at the sound of his voice, I swear he can make me orgasm just by talking to me. His finger swirls around my wetness, dipping inside of me then out again. My hips slowly rock, begging for more. He drops his finger lower, circling my anus, causing me to gasp at the feel of him there. He pushes through the barrier allowing just the tip of his finger inside.

"Luca," I cry, shocked by what he's doing to me, unsure if I want him to go any further."

"Shh," is his only reply as his mouth descends, lowering until he's close enough. He flicks out his tongue, lapping up my juices, swirling around my entrance, never removing his finger from my ass. I'm stunned by how good he feels there, everywhere, as if he knows exactly what to do to please me. He begins a slow assault on my clitoris, circling his tongue, pushing his finger deeper inside of me, while slipping another one inside my pussy.

"Fuck." I cry out at the invasion. I've never felt anything like this before, never *experienced* anything like this before. I'm completely filled up by him, consumed, unable to do anything but voice my cries of pleasure. He begins to speed up the rhythm, his attack on my clit now relentless, hard, and unmerciful. I'm loving it, every single moment of him in me, on me, is pushing me over the edge until I can't take any more. I feel the familiar explosion coming and right before it happens he pushes his fingers in me completely causing me to fall over the cliff, spiraling out of control in a sea of vibrant colors.

"Oh my God." I breathe out as my eyes flutter open.

He strokes my hair gently, and smiles down at me. "Hi."

"What the hell was that?" I question still struggling to catch my breath.

He chuckles in response, buries his face in my neck and wraps his arm around my waist. "That was me saying goodnight."

"Holy shit."

I feel his body shaking with laughter. "You like that huh?"

His question makes me shy. I'm not used to talking about what I do in the bedroom — it was never like that with Tyler. We just did our thing, we never discussed it. Luca is different, more open, clearly more adventurous, and I like that about him too. So I decide that it would go a long way in what we're building to give him an honest answer. "Yeah I liked that."

"I'm glad baby," he says, placing a kiss on my forehead and tightening his hold on me.

"What about you?" I wonder out loud.

"You're still sore."

"Luca."

"Go to sleep baby," he says, running his hand up and down my spine.

"Okay," I reply, moments before sleep takes hold of me.

15

We're standing in line at Niecy's, a small coffee house on Main Street waiting for the drinks we just ordered. When we woke up this morning Luca decided that we should spend the day together and I didn't put up much of a fight. We showered (separately), dressed, and then stopped here for a quick breakfast on the way to my house since I desperately need a change of clothes.

He stands behind me, arms wrapped around my waist as I lean back into him. I'm oddly aware of the people around me, but none of them paying attention to us. I can't help but to keep glancing at the door, waiting for the moment that someone I know will walk through the door. I'm not looking forward to facing judgment from anyone, but that doesn't stop me from being out in public with him. I look up when the front door opens again, and I freeze at what I see.

"Holy shit that's Victor Garza," I say, ogling the man walking in the shop with a beautiful little girl. First thing I notice is that he's tall, with thick dark brown hair and milk chocolate colored eyes. He's not necessarily my type, but God he's definitely gorgeous.

"You know who he is?"

"Everyone knows who he is around here. He was the hottest Latin singer in the world. He moved to town a few years ago and married a local girl."

"Elle, I know her. She's a really nice girl," he says, just as someone slams into my side. I look down and come face to face with the adorable little girl Victor just walked in with.

"Ava, be careful honey," he says to her as he reaches us. He grabs her hand before bringing his eyes back up to us. "Sorry, she's a bit of a tornado."

Luca gives him a nod, "It's no problem; she's adorable."

"Thanks, she takes after her mom."

"Yeah, tell Elle Luca says hi, she used to work with my mom."

He nods his head then bends down to pick Ava up. "I'll make sure to tell her. Nice meeting you, have a good day."

"You too," Luca replies.

I was pretty much stunned silent throughout that whole exchange, never uttering a single word. Luca's arms tighten around my waist, and I tip my head up to look at him. He's smiling from ear to ear.

"What?" I question with a glare.

"You were star struck."

"I was not," I huff.

"You went mute on me."

I roll my eyes and look away from him. "Shut up Luca."

"Relax babe, I think it's cute."

"Whatever."

We get our order and head out of the shop. I sip on my coffee as Luca drives and I begin to feel the all too familiar sense of dread I get every time I think of home.

142

Luca takes my hand in his and rests it on his thigh pulling my attention away from my thoughts and back to him. "What's wrong?"

I smile up at him, a smile that doesn't quite reach my eyes. "Nothing."

"Something is bothering you. You looked a million miles away just now."

I let out a sigh and turn my attention back out the window, watching the world drift by. "I just hate going home."

"Why?"

"Because it's a house that held so much promise and that promise was never fulfilled. It was where I was supposed to build my life with Tyler and now that he's gone it just doesn't feel right. It doesn't feel like a home."

"Then why are you still there?"

"Where else would I be?"

"If it's not where you want to be Everly then leave. Put the house on the market and get the hell out of there."

"It's not that easy."

"Okay. What makes this so hard?" he questions as he pulls into my driveway.

"He wanted me to have this." I motion toward the house. "His parents actually paid off what was left of the loan after I used his life insurance policy to pay off the majority of it. I just think it would disappoint them if I get rid of it."

"I get that, I know they lost their son, but you lost something too and it's unfair for you to be miserable here just because you don't want to upset them. I think a fresh start would be good for you. You don't have to make up your mind today Ev, just think about it."

"Okay."

I grab a change of clothes from my room and leave Luca lounging in my bed, heading into the bathroom to get dressed and put some makeup on.

"Luca, can you get me the black flat sandals in my closet?" I call from the bathroom.

"Sure."

He strolls in the bathroom a few minutes later, hands me the sandals and hops up on the counter. I turn back to the mirror and continue to apply my makeup.

"Can I ask you something?" he asks after a while.

"Of course."

"You still have all of his clothes in your closet."

I pause what I'm doing and look at him through the mirror. "That's not a question."

"Okay, why?"

I'm slightly annoyed and a little defensive. "I don't know why. I just do, I never got rid of it."

"I'm not judging you Ev, I'm just asking."

I throw my eye pencil down and let out a sigh. "I guess at first, I thought if they were there then I could pretend he wasn't really gone. After a while it just got too hard. I honestly block them out. I rarely even look at them."

"I'm sorry that this is so hard for you, but if you're going to move on, on your own, with me, with anyone, you have to start letting go."

"Another thing to add to the list of things I need to think about?"

"You don't have to do anything today."

"I know you're right. I just need to process it all okay?"

"Okay. You almost done in here? We should get going."

"Where are we going?"

"You'll see."

I don't push it, because I figure he probably wants to surprise me which is sweet. Tyler wasn't much for

144

surprises, not to say that he wasn't fun, because he was. What he wasn't was super spontaneous or romantic, that doesn't mean he still wasn't loving but just not in those ways. I'm beginning to see that Luca is a bit of both of those things and I like it a lot. I finish up in the bathroom, and we head out again.

I let my mind drift back to yesterday and how easy it was to be with him—to spend the day with him with no responsibilities, no expectations—just the two of us soaking up a day together. And then there was the sex...the sex was indescribable, crazy, adventurous, different from anything I'd ever experienced before. And if I'm being honest with myself, I have to admit that it is better—which is just another thing for me to feel guilty about. Sometimes I feel like I'm betraying Tyler, and when I admit to myself that there are things that Luca does differently or better than Tyler did, it makes me feel worse.

Tyler was my first love, my first lover, and I thought that it was going to last forever. I would have been blissfully happy had he lived, happy with what we had if we would have gotten the chance to live a life together. But now I know that there are things in my relationship with him that were just good when they could have been great, and when you add that to all of the secrets and lies he told, I wonder if a life with him would have been a mistake. This makes me feel guilty too; it actually breaks my heart because I don't want to feel this way, or think these things about someone that I invested so much of myself into. Someone who I vowed to love forever.

Luca's voice invades my thoughts. "You have that look again."

"What look?" I ask, scrunching up my nose in confusion.

"The one where I know something is wrong, but you don't want to tell me what it is."

"Oh, that look," I reply sarcastically.

"Yeah, that look."

I lean back in my seat and tilt my head up. I gaze out at the clouds through the sunroof for a second before bucking up and telling him the truth. "I think I'm just feeling a little bit guilty, and I know that I shouldn't, but I can't really help it."

"I understand."

"Do you?" I ask, shifting my gaze to him.

He smiles, never taking his eyes off the road. "I'm sleeping with my best friend's wife, what do you think?"

"It doesn't seem to be affecting you the same way."

"I don't let it," he declares with a shrug of his shoulders. "I'm not giving those thoughts any power over me because the truth is that he's gone and he would want us to be happy.

"You're right. I know you are, just keep reminding me okay?"

"I can do that."

We drive for another forty minutes before pulling into a large parking lot.

"Where are we?"

He pulls into an available spot and points to the building across the street. "Look over there."

I gasp when I look at the large building, I can't believe he actually brought me here. "The aquarium?" I ask staring at him a little dumbstruck.

"Yup. I thought it would be fun."

"I've always wanted to come here."

"I know."

"How did you know that?"

"I heard you tell him you wanted to come here once." He shrugs.

146

"He said it wasn't his cup of tea, that I should come with Morgan and make a girls day of it. I can't believe you remembered that."

"I remember lots of things Ev."

I place the palm of my hand on his cheek, and he responds by leaning into my hand. "You're a good guy. I'm sorry that I didn't see that."

"I didn't exactly make it easy." He takes hold of my neck and pulls me in for a quick kiss. "Enough with all the shit that happened in the past, let's get out of this car and go check this place out."

"Let's do it."

We exit the car, and Luca comes around to the passenger side, takes hold of my hand, and leads me to the aquarium. I'm still a little shocked that he would remember a conversation that likely happened more than six years ago, a conversation that I had long since forgotten. He's thoughtful, more so than I ever expected him to be, and I let myself believe that he was nothing more than a jerk that only cared about himself. But what I'm finding is that there's a lot more to Luca than anyone knows. He's exactly the kind of guy a girl would be lucky to fall for, exactly the kind of guy a girl like me could fall for. The question is, am I ready to let go of the past, to explore this with Luca without constantly comparing him or feeling guilty about Tyler.

Luca pays the entrance fee and hands me a map of the aquarium.

"Where to first?"

"You're letting me pick?"

"Yeah sure. You've always wanted to come here so you should pick what we see."

"That's easy... Penguins."

"I knew you were going to say that," he says, planting a kiss on my forehead. "Penguins it is."

We walk together hand in hand, and I watch the families together taking in all the exhibits—husbands and wives, parents with their children—and for the first time since Tyler's death I let myself hope that I can have that one day. That I can have a family of my own, one without the secrets and lies, one that will make all the pain I've been through worth it. Because if I ever get it, I know that I won't take it for granted.

We take in the penguin exhibit, watching as the trainers feed them and explain how they care for them. We spend the day walking around all of the exhibits, petting stingrays and baby sharks and watching sea turtles and sleeping hippos. We stop at the gift shop before we leave, where we pick up a bunch of souvenirs to take home. It might not be the most traditional date, but it's by far the best one I've ever had—one more day of me feeling like the girl I used to be.

16

It's late by the time Luca pulls into my driveway. We stopped for dinner on the way home, and after having been out all day, I think we're both pretty exhausted. His eyes are heavy, sleepy like mine, and all I really want to do is snuggle into him as I sleep.

"I can pick you up before work in the morning and take you to go get your car."

"Or you can stay here and we can pick it up in the morning," I suggest, hesitantly.

"You want me to stay?"

"Yes. I mean only if you want to."

"Of course I want to." I smile when he shuts the ignition off and exits the car. I open my door and he's there holding out an outstretched hand. I take it and he gently helps me out of the car. I hand him my house keys when we reach the porch standing closely behind him as he opens the front door.

We don't speak as he makes sure the front door is locked, and I turn the hallway light on in order to illuminate the stairs. I climb them first, him right behind me turning the light off when we reach the landing. My bedroom is flooded with the soft glow of moonlight giving the space a romantic feel; if I wasn't so tired I'd be turned on. I hear his clothes hit the floor as I kick my sandals off, I start to move toward the dresser but an arm wraps around my waist, keeping me where I am.

Luca grips the hem of my shirt, lifting it up and over until it's off of me. His fingers stealthily undo the clasp on my bra, pushing the straps down my arms until my torso is bare. Instinctively I cross my arms over my chest to cover up even though my back is to him. His fingers run along my bare back warming me up inside, and I can't help the little moan that escapes from my lips. He slips his hands in the waistband of my shorts and shoves, quickly discarding them along with my panties. I can feel just how naked he is behind me, and I anticipate his touch, but it never comes. Instead he throws back the covers on my tidy bed. I turn to face him dropping my arms allowing him to see the full view.

"Get in," he commands. His voice making me tremble a little.

I do as he asks, sliding into the king-size bed, watching his naked body as he does the same. His arm goes around my waist, pulling me to him, my head on his shoulder, hand resting on his chest and legs entwined.

"Why are we naked?" I finally asked confused by our lack of clothing.

"I wanted maximum contact and easy access for when we're both not so exhausted later."

I giggle but snuggle closer to him at the same time, letting my body melt into his. My mind drifts off to thoughts of how much fun we had today. Luca understands my past, he gets what the last four years have been like for me, and he doesn't run away from it or try to sweep it under the rug. He listens to me talk about my feelings and helps me to muddle through those murky waters, all the while making me face the things that I'd rather forget but doing it in a way that lets me know I'm safe with him. Luca makes me feel safe, yet I know that he's potentially very dangerous to my heart.

⁂

My skin prickles and I let out a long sigh, I'm trying to push it away, fight the sensations telling me that I need to wake up when all I want to do is sleep some more. The prickling sensation resides and I drift off again, so close to giving into my dreams when I'm hit with a wave of current. This time I moan and wriggle my hips before something pushes against me locking me in place. My breath hitches as my eyes flutter open, and I'm hit with another wave, this one stronger than the last, making me cry out and reach for the sheets. I grip them tightly and look down, heat flooding my body when I find Luca planted between my legs, eyes locked on mine, tongue working my pussy like his life depended on it. It doesn't take long for me to lose control as he expertly and swiftly takes me there, holding on tight as the orgasm rocks through me.

This makes going to sleep naked completely worth it, I think to myself as my body recovers. Before I can so much as move on my own, Luca grabs hold of one of my legs and uses it to flip me over onto my stomach. He spreads my legs apart, grabs my hips, and pulls them up, planting a hand on my spine so that my torso is still firmly on the mattress. He places a kiss on the small of my back, and his fingers begin to play within my wet folds quickly he pulls one in and out of me.

"Beautiful," he says, withdrawing his finger. His hands slowly circle my ass, massaging me, making me relax further into the mattress. I let out a sigh of contentment just before I feel the palm of his hand come down on my ass HARD.

"Luca," I yell out in shock just as he smacks me again, this time eliciting a cry from me.

"Shh," he says, slowly rubbing the spots where he hit me, making the stinging reside. He begins to play with me again, using his fingers to spread my juices over my clit, circling it with just the perfect amount of pressure. I'm shocked at how quickly he can build me up again bringing me so close to the brink of an orgasm. He gets me close, just within my reach, before he stops.

"No," I plead, wanting him to go on until I feel his hand come down on me again, slapping one cheek then the other. I don't cry this time, the mix of my body recovering from a near orgasm and the sting of his hand feels good. Too good. I have no idea what he's doing to me, but I push my ass out to him, silently indicating that I want more.

Luca likes to play—he plays in bed in a way that I've never experienced. But each time he leaves me hungry for more, wondering what else he can do to my body. His fingers resume their ministrations, skillfully taking me higher and higher till I'm on the brink again. Letting me fall flat only to strike out on me once again. This time when he smacks my ass, he slides his cock into my pussy making me cry out at the welcome invasion. I take what I can from him, as much as possible, because Luca feels phenomenal, makes me feel phenomenal.

He strikes my ass one more time before speaking. "My good girl deserves to come right?"

"Yes," I breathe out, not recognizing the tone of desperation in my voice.

"Yes what?"

"Yes Luca."

He uses one hand to grab hold of my hair, pulling so that I'm up on all fours. His other hand snakes around my waist, and he reaches down applying pressure to my clit.

152

"Is this mine, Everly?"

"Yes."

"Say it."

"It's yours Luca."

He releases my hair and thrusts harder, deeper, making me feel like I may come apart at the seams, all the while welcoming every exquisite second of it. His finger circles my clit one final time before I let go, letting the orgasm shatter me into a million tiny pieces. I feel him thrust, one, two, three more times before he's coming too, the familiar feel of his cock pulsing inside of me making me shiver.

We collapse onto the bed, still panting, coming down from the intensity of what just happened.

"Are you alright?" he asks, looking at me, I can see the question linger in his eyes.

"Yes."

"Did I hurt you, was it too much?"

"You didn't hurt me, it was different."

"I'm sorry."

"No, it was good different Luca. I like that you're creative in bed," I say with a smile.

He reaches over and runs his fingertips gently across my cheek. "I like to have fun but I never want to hurt you or scare you okay, you can tell me if it's ever too much."

"Are you like a dominant?"

"No," he replies with a chuckle. "I'm just a guy who likes a little adventure in bed. How I smacked your ass before…that's about as much as I'll ever do. I'm not into whips and chains or anything."

"I love how you make me feel."

"How do I make you feel?"

"Alive."

We shower together and Luca dresses in his clothes from yesterday then heads into the kitchen to make coffee while I get myself ready for work. He brings me a cup into the bathroom once it's done and then turns on the news, patiently waiting for me to finish. Once I'm done we drive back to his place where I hop in my car and drive to work, leaving Luca at home to change into his work clothes.

We both have busy days so even though it was nice to see his face around the office, we didn't actually interact. There's no clear cut rule about dating coworkers here, but it's best for everyone involved if we don't make our relationship public knowledge, so I'm fine with keeping our distance.

My office phone rings late in the afternoon, and I can tell by the caller ID that it's Morgan.

"Hey chickie," I say when I pick up the receiver.

"Hey, how was your weekend?"

"It was pretty good how 'bout yours?"

"It was bleh. Did you have time to think about the Luca and Janine situation? You're not still mad at him are you? Did you talk to him today?"

"I'm not mad. He told me he kissed her but that was it and I believe him."

"So you straight up asked him at work if he slept with Janine?"

"No. I asked him on Friday night when I confronted him like a crazy person at his house."

"Everly!" she says, clearly astonished by my insanity.

"I know."

"Oh. My. God."

"I know."

"Was he pissed?"

"Yes. Right up until the point that I threw myself bodily at him."

"WHAT?" she shrieks, making me think that I may have just blown an eardrum. "Tell me everything."

"I can't talk about it here. Come by my house after work, I'll make you dinner."

"I'll be there at six, and I want to know everything!"

"Okay, I'll see you later," I say just before disconnecting.

I glance at the clock on my computer screen, thankful that I only have a half hour longer to work. I catch movement out of the corner of my eye and look up to see Luca standing over my desk.

"Hi," he says, before taking a seat.

"Hi."

"How's your day been?"

"Productive. Yours?"

"Same."

"Is there something I can help you with Mr. Jensen?"

He slides a hand over his tie and grins at me. "I was hoping I could take you to dinner after work."

"I can't, Morgan's coming over to get all the sordid details of our weekend together."

"Ohhhh she is, is she?"

"Yes."

"Okay, it's good that you spend time with her. I know she's happy to have you back in her life."

God he's such a good guy. "Are you sure, I can cancel."

"No. Do your gossipy girl thing. I'll call you tonight."

"Okay."

"Alright seriously, I can't take it anymore. Please tell me what happened."

Morgan and I are halfway through dinner, and I've been putting off talking about me and Luca—partly because I want to torture her but also because I don't know what to say.

I look up from my plate, tilt my head, and avert my gaze focusing instead on the small window just over her shoulder. "Well you know I was obviously pissed off when Janine said what she did, and I felt the overwhelming need to confront him. I needed to know the truth."

I move my head back to look at her as she waves her hand around, indicating that I should get on with the story. "So what happened?"

I let out a sigh and slouch down in my chair, kind of wishing that I could disappear. "He was pissed and he got in my face. I got in his and then I threw myself at him. Literally."

Her eyes go wide with astonishment. "What did he do?"

"He carried me into his room, stripped me down, and screwed my brains out."

"You're lying," she challenges, shaking her head.

I take a sip of my wine. "No, I'm really not."

"*You* had sex with Luca?" she questions, not even trying to hide the disbelief in her voice.

I cover my face with the palms of my hands and peek at her through my fingers. "Multiple times."

"Oh. My. God."

"I know."

"Did you have to do the walk of shame?"

"No," I answer, dropping my hands back down to my lap. "I spent the night and then we hung out the next day, and then he asked me to spend the night again."

She smiles so wide I'm afraid her face might actually freeze. "So you spent two amazing nights at Luca's"

"Yes and one amazing night here."

"What?"

"He took me to the aquarium yesterday. He remembered that I'd always wanted to go," I say with a smile on my face. "By the time we got here it was late, sooo he spent the night."

"So are you guys like together now?" she probes.

"I don't know. I mean, yes. I guess so. Yes, totally," I stutter.

"Alright, you know I have to ask… How is he in bed?"

I laugh at her question, knowing that it was only a matter of time before she asked it. "Honestly? He's unbelievable," I reply dreamily.

"Eek… I wanted you to say that. You deserve unbelievable Ev."

"I'm a little scared."

"That's normal, you've been through hell and back, opening yourself up to anyone is going to be scary, but Ev, I think it's going to be worth it. You deserve the chance to move on and if Luca is the one that gives you that chance then so be it."

"It's just that sometimes I feel guilty, like I find myself comparing things that Luca does to Tyler."

She nods her understanding. "And what's the verdict?"

"I'm not saying that Luca is better, I'm not, I'm just saying that he's very different and the way he's different, I like a lot."

"If Tyler were still here, you'd never have explored those things. You'd never know that there are things that Luca does that you like more, so you have nothing to feel guilty about. This isn't cheating, it's not betrayal. You have been alone for a very long time, and it's natural for you to make those types of comparisons since you only ever knew Tyler, he was your only boyfriend. The comparisons will eventually stop."

This is a typical Morgan speech, always finding the positive, always telling you that things will work out the way they're supposed to, that everything happens for a reason, and right now that's exactly what I need to hear. "You're right."

"Always."

"Just don't let it get it your head," I say, and she smiles, making me so grateful that she waited around for me to stop being a bitch for the past four years.

I'm lounging in bed reading a magazine but not really reading it. I'm thinking about what Morgan said about moving on with Luca. About how amazing spending the weekend with him was—how natural it felt, how explosive it was. He's got a hold of me now, and I'm sensing that he would not let me go without a fight, not that I want to go. I don't. But the magnitude of how badly I want to be with him is a little bit frightening. I'm thinking about how no matter what I do, I can't stop thinking about him, when my phone rings. My stomach flutters, I don't even bother looking at the caller ID, knowing that it has to be Luca.

"Hello?"

I smile at the sound of his deep voice. "Hey. How was dinner with Morgan?"

"It was good," I answer honestly, unable to hide the excitement in my voice.

"Did you tell her all about our hot sexual exploits?" he questions with a chuckle.

I giggle and throw myself back against my pillows feeling more like a teenager than an adult. "I'm a little more discreet than that."

"Meaning?"

"Meaning that I told her all about it without giving her all the seedy details," I tease.

"Seedy? We're not seedy babe, our sex is hot."

"It is hot," I reply, my voice barely above a whisper, my body temperature spiking.

"What are you wearing?" he asks. I can tell by his tone that he's smiling.

I laugh. "No, no, no mister. I'm not falling for that trap."

"Aw, you're no fun."

"I'm way more fun in person."

His voice goes soft making my body melt at the sound of him. "Yes you are. So good in person, I wish you were here right now."

I wish I was there right now too but instead of admitting that I say, "I'm going to see you tomorrow."

"Work doesn't count."

"I guess you're right." I sigh, relaxing my body and closing my eyes.

"Meet me here after work. I'll order some dinner, we'll spend some time together, have some fun."

"Okay." I mentally chastise myself after realizing how quickly I agreed to see him. God maybe I could at least try to play a little hard to get.

"Bring your overnight bag, because I want to take my time with you."

"Okay." It comes out breathy. So much for playing hard to get.

"Goodnight Ev."

"Goodnight Luca."

※

I didn't see Luca all day, He was in and out of court and when he did finally make it in to the office, I was knee deep in work, and I couldn't sneak away to see him. By the time five o'clock rolled around, Luca was already gone. I make it to his house quickly, grab my purse and overnight bag out of my car, and ring the doorbell. I wait a few minutes and when he doesn't open I ring again. After a few more minutes of waiting I try the doorknob, as I turn it I realize that luckily it's unlocked. I climb the stairs that lead up into his living room, when I reach the top I can hear water running in the distance so I know he must be in the shower. I toss my keys and purse on the table and head to his bedroom to drop off my overnight bag.

I toss my bag just outside his closet door and kick off my sandals, deciding to go into the kitchen and rifle through his drawers for takeout menus. Luca walks out of the bathroom just as I turn to leave. My chest compresses as I take in the sight of him wearing nothing but a towel. His dark hair is wet and unruly, drops of water still glistening on his chest and abs.

"Hi baby," he says, his green eyes going soft. My heart melts a little when I look at them. They draw me into him, making me forget about everything else, making me want nothing else than to be close to him. I walk across the room to where he stands, getting as close as I can without physically touching him. I go up on my tiptoes, throw my arms around his neck, and hop up. Luca's arms catch me just in time, hoisting me up as I wrap my legs around his waist, my face in his neck inhaling his scent.

"Hi," I murmur into his neck.

His arms go tighter around me and I revel in the feel of them on me, enveloping me. "What's this?" he questions softly, placing a kiss on my hair.

"I'm happy to see you," I say, with just a hint of vulnerability that I'm sure he doesn't miss. He doesn't miss much. I breathe him in one last time before lifting my head to look at him. The look on his face is my undoing, this draw I feel to him is undeniable, unmistakable, unlike

160

anything I've ever experienced. It excites me as much as it terrifies the hell out of me.

He places a kiss on my forehead. "I'm happy to see you too."

I bend my head, running my nose up and down his cheek, nuzzling into him, making my own desire grow with each passing moment, feeling him grow beneath me.

"What do you want baby?" he questions, his eyes going from soft to liquid, his voice getting husky and I know what he wants me to say, I know that the air in the room is changing going from sweet to heated.

"You," I reply, nipping his ear between my teeth, letting him know that I'm on board for the ride.

He walks me over to the bed and throws me down. I reach up and take hold of his towel, but he grabs my wrists and pins them down over my head before I can pull it off.

He runs his tongue along the base of my neck, I moan tilting my head to the side giving him more access. "You want me?"

"Yes Luca."

"What do you want me to do to you?" he asks, grinding his hips into mine. I whimper at the feel of him there. "You want me to play with your pretty little pussy again?" he asks on another swirl of his hips, driving me crazy with the mix of his movements and his dirty words. "Or should I play with your ass? Hmm? I can spank you till its red... Would you like that Everly?" he asks just as he bites my shoulder.

"Oh God," I say on a breath. How does he do this to me every single time? He has the ability to make me lose all self-control; he makes it so that I would do just about anything he asks, so that I *want* to do everything he asks.

"You like it a little dirty hmm baby?" he asks with a grin.

"Yes," I cry out. I could come just listening to him speak to me like this.

"Should I tie you up Ev? Make you use your mouth on me? Play with your clit until you're so close and then take it away?"

"Luca."

"No?" he asks, teasing me with his words. "You just need me to fuck you hmm?"

"Yes."

"I can do that for my girl," he says with a sexy grin before stripping me out of my clothing painfully slow and finally ditching his towel. When the barriers are finally gone, when it's just him and me there naked and needy, he buries himself inside of me taking me slowly, uninhibited. Taking his time, giving me exactly what I need, exactly how I want it. It's heaven.

17

The last few months have passed by in a blur. Things between Luca and I have progressed quicker than I anticipated they would. We've been spending as much time as we can together, which is pretty much every waking hour outside of work. If I'm not spending the night at Luca's place, he's spending the night here in mine, and that's exactly what happened last night.

I'd gone out for my now weekly Friday night drinking date with Morgan and I'd texted Luca before I left the bar and asked him to meet me at my house, letting him know where the spare key was and that he should feel free to let himself in.

When I finally made it home, he was waiting for me in my room—eyes hooded, chest heaving, and more than ready for me. He wasted no time in pulling me inside and stripping me down where he proceeded to tie my wrists to the headboard and do all the things that he had mentioned he'd do to me if he got the chance to tie me up a few weeks ago.

The sex with Luca is wild, uninhibited, and naughty in the best possible way. Not to say that we don't have normal sex too, we do... A lot, but when Luca wants to play, he always takes me to new heights. I never imagined I'd like it as much as I do; in fact there are often times when I downright crave it. Crave the feel of his hand on my backside or his particularly drawn out method of foreplay.

This morning is no different. Luca is hovering over me, his hands between my legs, his mouth at my ear telling me what a good girl I am for spreading wide for him, and me on the brink of an orgasm. All he ever really has to do is call me his good girl, and I'll do anything he wants — it's like flipping a switch. This is what's happening before the moment that I die of sheer embarrassment. This is because right before Luca sends me over the edge, my bedroom door thrusts open.

"Everly, are you awake?"

I shriek in horror and Luca throws himself on top of me to shield my naked body from my mother.

"Mom," I cry out in a mix of surprise, mortification, and annoyance. I thank the stars for the fact that most of our bodies are still covered by the down comforter draped over my bed.

"Oh my God," my mom says, quickly shielding her eyes from the show that we're giving her. "I didn't realize you had company, I just stopped by with some groceries."

"Shit," whispers Luca, his head now shoved in the crook of my neck as he fights laughter.

"Well...Um... Hello Luca."

He averts his gaze, choosing instead to look at my face. "Hi Mrs. Phillips."

"Mom, would you mind waiting downstairs while we get dressed."

"Oh right, of course," she says, turning away from us. Her eyes likely burning at what she just witnessed. "I'll just put your groceries away and make some coffee. Take your time," she says before closing the door.

"Oh. My. God," I whisper as Luca silently laughs. "This isn't funny," I hiss, smacking him on his bare shoulder. "We just got caught by my mom having sex."

"We weren't having sex babe, I was playing with your pussy. There's a difference."

"Get off of me right now," I demand, doing my best to not to pummel him.

"Ev, we're two consenting adults."

"I know that but no parent should ever walk in on their child doing what we were doing and no child should ever have to deal with this level of humiliation."

"Alright, relax, let's go down there and talk to her."

"No!" I shriek. "You stay here, take a shower, and I will go talk to her, explain how things are and smooth things over before you go down there. I can't deal with a confrontation right now."

"I don't want you to face her alone."

"Baby please, please just let me handle this my way."

His eyes go soft, maybe because I've never called him baby before, until now he's always just been Luca, but the term of endearment just feels right, natural even.

"Alright ten minutes though," he concedes.

"Ten minutes," I agree. "I can work with that."

He rolls off of me allowing me to get out of the bed; I throw on a pair of yoga pants and a tank top and head for the door.

"Ev," he calls, still lounging on the bed.

I come to a stop and look back at him. "Yeah?"

His lips go up into a small grin. "Did you just call me baby to get your way?"

I change my trajectory, walking away from the door and heading back to the bed instead. I put one knee on the mattress stretch out and place a kiss on his lips.

"I called you baby because it felt so right that it just came out of my mouth. I didn't even have to think about it."

He stares at me through hooded eyes for a moment "Go before I throw you back down on this bed and have my way with you."

I give him a bright smile and do as he asks, I leave the room and head downstairs to the kitchen where not only can I smell fresh coffee brewing, but there's also the distinct smell of bacon being fried.

"Mom," I say hesitantly as I grab onto the edge of the countertop.

She turns away from the frying pan she's currently hovering over and faces me. "Everly, I'm so sorry, I should have called and I know you said you've been doing your own shopping but I brought you some anyway because I really wanted to see you."

I shake my head, "It's okay Mom. I'm just sorry you had to walk in on that."

"I am too," she says giving me a smile that's full of humor. "It won't go down in my top ten favorite moments but honey, I'm also glad."

"You're glad?" I repeat, making sure I heard her correctly.

"Yes. I'm glad because finally, *finally* you're moving on," she states, placing her hands on my upper arms and squeezing. "You've been getting out more and more, starting to take care of yourself better, seeing your friends again, and clearly you're dating again."

I tilt my head and ask in hesitation, "And it doesn't bother you that the person I'm dating is Luca?"

"Why would that bother me?" She lets go of my arms and shakes her head. "Luca's a good man, and you know now that he had nothing to do with Tyler's death."

"But that's just it Mom, he's my husband's best friend," I say, stating the obvious. I walk over to the coffee pot and prepare myself a cup of coffee listening to my mom spew her wisdom.

"He *was* your husband's best friend, but your husband is no longer here, and I think that relieves Luca from his duty to stay away from you."

"Mom!"

"What, am I wrong? She moves to the frying pan and starts removing the cooked bacon. "Who cares who you move on with as long as you move on, and do it with a good guy?"

"That's what he says."

She opens the refrigerator and pulls out a carton of eggs. "He's right."

"So you're really okay with this?" I ask skeptically.

"I'm okay with whatever makes my baby happy again."

I think of the hell I've put her through the last few years, of course I didn't mean to but I know it took a toll. I give her a shy smile and tell her the honest truth. "He makes me happy."

She stares at me, her eyes wet with unshed tears and nods at me. "You love him."

I shake my head, in order to squash whatever ideas she's having right now. "No, it's only been a few months, we're not there yet, and I don't know if we'll ever be."

"You're there, you just don't realize it yet," she declares as if though it's fact instead of her own personal misguided opinion.

"Mom," I groan.

"I'm making you breakfast."

"I see that," I reply sarcastically just as Luca makes his appearance in the kitchen. I give him an "everything's okay" smile, he smiles back his "I told you so" smile. He walks over to me slides an arm around my waist pulling me into his side and places a kiss on my forehead. I can sense my mom watching us out of the corner of my eye.

"Luca, I hope you like eggs, bacon, and toast."

He gives me a squeeze before releasing me and moving to the coffee pot to pour himself a cup of coffee. "I do Mrs. Phillips, thank you."

"Please, call me Jill."

He nods at her as he adds cream and sugar to his mug while I sit there in the middle of my kitchen replaying my mother's words over and over in my head. "You love him." How did she get that from talking to me for ten minutes, from walking in on us in bed together? Sex and love don't always go hand in hand so if she's basing her statement on that she's dead wrong. Or is she?

I push these thoughts out of my head, choosing instead to focus on the relationship we're building right now. I'll enjoy what we have and take it one day at a time. No one needs to profess his or her love just yet, what we're doing is good enough as it is.

I go to the cupboard, grab the sliced bread, and start making toast for everyone. I listen in as my mom asks Luca about work and he explains in detail how he's finally settling in and feeling good about his work. They go back and forth, and I'm content to just sit here and watch the two of them find an easy rhythm with each other. Tyler had to work harder at getting comfortable with my mom than Luca does aaanndd...There I go comparing them again. I suppose Morgan was right, it's going to take time for me to stop doing that and things are going to come up which would naturally make me want to compare the two, but I'm not sitting here willing Luca to change, to turn him more into the kind of man Tyler was. No...I am more than happy with everything Luca does.

"I think it's about time for you to start sorting through some of Tyler's and your old things," I hear Luca say. I take a minute to process his words before putting down the magazine I was sifting through as he looked through some case files.

"You do?"

"Yes, I do because I think you and I both know that you don't need them, most of it is just old clothes and things that you never even look at anymore. "

"That's a big step. I just don't..."

"What?"

"I just don't even know where I would start."

"Follow me."

"Luca," I call watching him grab a garbage bag from the kitchen and jog upstairs.

"What are you doing?"

"I'm helping you purge the past," he says grabbing hold of the garment bag that sits in the back of my closet silently taunting me for the last four years. Just another memory of a shattered dream.

"That's my wedding dress Luca," I say with steel in my voice.

"I know," he says tossing it on the bed mercilessly. "Why do you still have it?"

"Because it's my wedding dress."

"And what? Are you saving it for the daughter you and he will never have?"

I gasp, shocked by his cruel words, and tears immediately filling my eyes. "Oh my God, how dare you say that?"

I see a flicker of remorse right before he continues his verbal assault. "You're no longer married Everly."

"Yes I am."

"To what? A dead man? Is that the fucking life you want? You want to live in this fucking shrine of the life you never got?"

"That's not what I'm doing."

"No?" He questions me almost as if it's a challenge. He stares at me for a beat before unzipping the bag, opening it to reveal my beautiful custom wedding gown. I close my eyes, because it's almost too much for me to take in the sight of it now."

"Look at it," he says, his voice full of determination. "I want you to open your eyes and look at it."

I take a moment to gather up strength and courage, it's just an article of clothing for God's sake, a dress, nothing more. I open my eyes taking it in. I can still remember the excitement I felt when I tried it on for the first time. My mom and Morgan and I cried tears of joy—we knew instantly that this would be the dress I'd wear when I married Tyler.

Luca rifles through one of my drawers, grabs something, and comes back to the bed. He unhooks and then picks up the gown—in his hands I spot a black pair of scissors.

"Luca," I warn, my eyes going wide, a bit of panic setting in. *He wouldn't fucking dare,* I think to myself.

"It means nothing," he says, taking the scissors to the bodice and cutting in a straight line.

"No!" I scream, lunging for him, but he takes several steps back as he continues with his calculated destruction. He looks up at me, tosses the scissors on the floor, and uses his hands to rip the rest of the dress in half. He pushes the dress into my hands and I clutch it as I fall to the ground and begin to sob uncontrollably.

"There's a garbage bag on your bed. Have your cry and then throw it out. You'll feel better once it's gone," he says, walking out of the room and leaving me holding the tattered shreds of something that once meant so much. I fucking hate Luca.

I'm not sure how long I sit here, holding the dress close to me. Letting the facts dance around in my head. My husband is dead, has been dead, and this is a dress, a dress that has been sitting in a bag in my closet for four years. I shouldn't be crying about getting rid of it, it's just one more thing that I've held on to for far too long. I compose myself, picking myself off of the floor and carefully put the dress in the garbage bag. As completely out of line Luca was for pulling this shit, a part of me thinks that maybe it was for the best, a first step in letting go of what once was and will never be again.

I sit on my bed a long time, thinking about the choices that I've made, and the choices that I need to make in the near future. It's daunting, but this was a start. A difficult start, yes, and also not by choice, but it's a start nonetheless.

"Everly?" I look up and see Luca standing in the doorway arms and feet crossed, leaning against the frame. His posture is guarded as if he's preparing himself for my wrath. "I'm sorry. I was really out of line."

"Yeah you were."

He nods and pushes off from the doorframe crossing the distance between us before coming to sit on the edge of the bed with me. "It seemed like a good plan at the time. The last thing I wanted to do was hurt you."

"You went about it all wrong but I know your intentions were good. It was just a hard thing to let go of." I shrug.

"I know."

"I know it can't be easy for you, coming to this house, my house with Tyler, and seeing his things everywhere, but up until now you've been amazing about it and...I don't know, maybe we can start off slow, get rid of some of his books and knick-knacks first and work our way up?"

He wraps his arm around my waist, drags me over to him, and places me in his lap. "I'll help you however you want and you can take as much time as you need."

"I just don't want you to think that I'm holding on to him—because I still wish he was here—or that I'm not over it."

"Everly, he was your first love, your husband. I know that there's always going to be a part of you that loves him… But are you over it?"

"Every day that I spend with you, it gets a little easier, it hurts less and less and I think maybe part of my problem was that I was lonely, I surrounded myself with his things, his memory, and I shut everyone out. Every day I feel more like the old me."

"I'm glad that you let me in."

I snuggle into him, reveling the feel of his arms wrapped around me. Hoping that this will last, that I won't lose Luca too, because I don't think I'd be able to handle that kind of loss again. I place a soft kiss on his neck.

"Will you throw the bag out for me?"

He tugs at a strand of my hair. "Of course. I made some dinner."

"You did?" I love that he can be so thoughtful; taking care of me even when I don't know that he's doing it.

"Yeah, I thought you might be hungry, and I wanted to give you some time alone."

"Thanks." I smile, coming to stand on my feet and putting this scene behind me. A trashed wedding dress and a decision to purge the past in hopes of a better future. *I can do this*, I tell myself, and for the first time I truly believe it.

I lay snuggled up in Luca's arms the way I love to be. My head on his chest, his arm curled around my waist, our legs intertwined.

"Why do you like me now?" I question, needing to hear what changed for him after all of these years.

He tilts his head to mine, "What do you mean by now?"

"Come on Luca, you always hated me."

He shakes his head, "You're wrong, I never hated you."

I roll my eyes. "You were mean to me. You were sarcastic, you'd make fun of me all the time, and it was weird because you were so nice to me the first time we met."

"Being a jerk was easier than admitting what I really felt, or worse, letting anyone else see how I really felt."

I suck in a sharp intake of breath. "How did you feel?"

"The same way I feel now," he says, positioning himself on top of me. "Like you're mine. Like you should have always been with me."

"Luca," I whisper, my heart racing.

"I saw you in that bookstore, and I wanted you from that moment on. I hated that you were with him, but even though you were, in my mind I always felt like I had this fucked-up claim on you, and he knew how I felt about you, and he went after you anyway."

"Wait what? How? Luca, I met Tyler a few days after you. I never saw you after the bookstore, how could he have known?"

"You didn't see me, but I saw you Ev. My biggest mistake was not making my move when I first met you. I thought I'd get another chance, and I didn't want to come on too strong."

"You liked me?" I question in disbelief.

173

"Baby, I went home afterward and told Ty about you, told him how I met this girl, the most beautiful girl. That night we went to a frat party, it was crazy and crowded, but I spotted you again. I pointed you out to him just as you were leaving. He told me I should go after you but I told him no, you had already left. I figured it was a small campus I'd see you again once classes started."

"Oh my God."

"I never thought you'd have a class with him, and he'd make a move on you. I never thought he'd take you knowing how I felt."

"Luca," I whisper, tears swimming in my eyes. "I didn't know. I swear to you, I liked you too. I wanted you to ask me for my number, I wanted you first. I just thought...and then I met him, and he was sweet, charismatic, it was hard not to like him. I was shocked that first time I went to your place and I saw you there, but I thought at least we could be friends. Well you know how well that worked out."

"I should have been better to you. It wasn't your fault, but if you would have shown me just once while you were with him that you cared about me, even a little, I would have gone after you, and it would have fucked my friendship with Ty up."

"I get it now," I say stroking his cheek. "I'm sorry it happened, I'm sorry he did that to you."

"All's fair in love and war, but I'll tell you right now," He pushes a strand of hair from my face. "I'm not letting you go again."

"I don't want you to let me go," I answer honestly.

His eyes heat when he looks at me. "Tell me you're mine Everly."

"I'm yours"

"I love you Ev," he says, breaking down the walls, irrevocably changing the trajectory of my life, making me want to replace everything that once was with something even sweeter.

"I love you too," I say, unafraid of what that means, of how it changes everything, how it makes this relationship even scarier but I can't bring myself to care.

When he makes love to me tonight, it's different, slower, sweeter; there's an apology in his eyes for the hurt he caused me earlier. It's an unnecessary apology because I've already let it go. All I can see now is the jade in his eyes shining through like a beacon signaling me home. I think of Tyler and what he did to his best friend, what he did to me, I think of all of the unspeakable truths I've learned about Tyler West, and I'm through with living it, wading through the waters of a life that wasn't what I thought it would be.

18

I stare at my reflection in the mirror, not hating the person staring back at me. I actually kind of like her again. Luca pulled me into his office earlier and asked me if I could reschedule Friday drinks with Morgan so that he could take me out to dinner. He said he had a shitty day in court and really just wanted to be with me tonight. How could I possibly say no to that? Morgan is so in love with the idea of Luca and me being in love that she was totally fine with my bailing on her, especially since I got a double dose of her last weekend when she dragged me to the mall on Sunday for some much needed shopping (her words not mine). The one good thing that came out of that shopping trip is the sexy lingerie and the little black dress I have on tonight. My hair falls in curly tendrils around my face and though I normally gear myself toward more natural makeup, tonight I upped the ante by applying a more dramatic smoky eye.

Ever since Luca told me he loved me it's like the part of me that I was constantly keeping at bay has broken free. I think that deep down I saw myself as unlovable—I taught myself to believe that no one would ever really love me again. I've also learned to start letting go of some of the guilt I felt for taking up with my husband's best friend, hearing the story from Luca's point of view, how Tyler knew how he felt about me but asked me out anyway, really helped me to let a lot of those feelings go. I think that maybe wherever Tyler is right now, he's looking down and can take peace in the fact that Luca is finally with the girl that he wanted for himself.

"Jesus Christ babe." I smile at his words, looking up and seeing him standing in the doorway. He began his day with a suit and tie but has long since lost the jacket, but the gray shirt with the black tie compliment his green eyes nicely.

"You got here fast."

"That last meeting didn't take as long as I thought," he says, walking in the bathroom. Our eyes are locked as he approaches and only when his chest touches my back do I close my eyes and lean against his frame. "You look beautiful." I smile, eyes still closed, flourishing under him, his compliments, his love breathing life back into me.

My eyes open with a flutter and meet his in the mirror again. I stare for just a beat before replying. "You look pretty good too."

"You ready to get out of here? I'm actually kind of starved."

"For food?" I chastise.

"No, but the sooner I get you fed the sooner I can get you home and have my main course."

"What's on your menu for tonight?"

"I don't know, maybe a blindfold."

"Let's go," I say, sounding very breathy all of a sudden.

He chuckles, kisses the side of my head then leads me out of the house to his awaiting car.

It only takes about fifteen minutes to get to the steak house we decided to go to. Luca was able to call ahead and have a table waiting for us. The restaurant is packed, as it is every Friday and Saturday night, and we're seated at a corner table, which overlooks the ocean. I almost wonder if Luca requested this table to minimize the chances of us being spotted together. Though I've gotten better about being out with him, I still tend to look over my shoulder out of habit. I guess the idea of someone we know spotting us together is still a real fear of mine. I'm not sure that they would really understand. I want to let it go, but I need to know if my assumption is correct.

I put down my menu and ask, "Did you request this table specifically?"

He closes his menu, setting it on the table before giving me a soft smile. "I did."

"Why this table?"

"Because it's private."

"Because you thought I wouldn't want people seeing us together?"

He reaches across the table and takes hold of my hand. "Ev, I know you still worry about people seeing us out together. You think they're going to judge us, and I am just trying to make it easier for you."

"I know you are. I love you for it, I'm just sorry that you feel you have to go through all this trouble for me. If people see us and judge us, we'll deal with it. We can't hide forever and I'm grateful that you love me enough to try even though you probably hate it."

The waiter arrives to take our orders before Luca can respond but I'm sensing that clearing the air was a good thing. He looks more relaxed, happier even, and I'm glad that I was able to give him that. He needs to know that I'm in it for as long as he'll have me, and if that means dealing with uncomfortable situations, then so be it.

We're halfway through dinner when I decide to broach another subject with Luca.

I spear a piece of broccoli and chew it before I speak. "I wanted to talk to you about something."

178

He puts his fork down and looks at me, giving me his undivided attention. "What's up?"

"I've been thinking a lot, ever since I got rid of the wedding dress and we cleared out some of his belongings."

"You can say his name babe it's alright."

He's right. I'm avoiding using Tyler's name, not because I want to forget Tyler, but because I'm tired of my life revolving around him. I'm tired of obsessing over every little part of my history and constantly dragging him into the present.

"I'm just trying to be considerate. This is our relationship, and we need to start living it without dragging Tyler into it."

"I agree." He nods. "But there's been a lot of things we've needed to work through and the majority of those things involved him. We can't pretend he didn't exist, and I don't want you to have to do that. It'll get better with time."

"That's what I'm getting it; I'm never going to get better if I keep holding on to it all. I have to let it go Luca and I'm never going to be able to do that if I stay in that house."

"Okay..." he says with obvious curiosity.

"I think I want to put the house on the market."

"That's a very big decision."

"I know, that's why I wanted to talk to you about it. I wanted your opinion."

"You're not happy there?"

"I hate it. After he died I wanted to get rid of it, but his parents paid off the mortgage and it seemed important to them, so I stayed. But it's felt more like a prison than it has like a home for years; it's suffocating and the only time I'm happy there at all is when you're there with me."

"Then get rid of it Everly, I had no idea you hated it that much. You shouldn't have to be there at all."

"I just have to figure out where I'm going to move. I don't know if I really want to buy another house right now. I don't want to have to worry about the upkeep, that's something that my family has always taken care of for me. I was thinking of maybe looking for a condo or a townhouse."

"You can move in with me Ev."

"What?"

"Move in with me."

"Luca, I think it's too soon for that don't you?"

"I'm not going to pressure you, but I love you, you love me who cares how long we've been together if we're happy."

"Can I think about it?"

"Yes. You can take all the time you need."

"Everly? Luca?" My skin crawls at the sound of Janine's voice; I look up to see her standing at our table with a stunned look on her face.

"Janine." Luca greets his voice deep with just a hint of annoyance.

"What are you two doing here...together?"

"We're having dinner," he answers shortly. "What are you doing here?"

"Here with a friend."

"It's good to see you getting out and about again Everly."

Luca appears to be done with this conversation when he speaks up. "Is there something we can do for you Janine?"

"You never called Luca."

"I don't remember promising that I would."

"I just thought."

"We kissed once, I didn't make you any promises, I didn't put a ring on your finger, in fact I'm in a relationship right now, and I'm *very* happy."

I see the exact moment when it clicks in her mind, when what he's just said has registered.

"Wait, are you telling me that you and Everly are together now?"

"Yeah, that's exactly what I'm telling you."

I want to turn away from her, to not have to see the look of disbelief and disgust on her perfect face, but I don't. I steel my nerves, square my shoulders and tell myself that she doesn't matter.

"I'm sorry, I don't understand."

I tilt my head toward her and snap, "What's there to understand?"

"For starters, I though you hated Luca."

"Well not that it's any of your business, but you were wrong."

"This is the man who led your husband away to his death on the morning after your wedding. You've blamed him for years."

"How would you know? Up until recently, I haven't seen you in years."

"You made it perfectly clear that you wanted to be left alone Everly."

"And you all too conveniently accepted that one of your best friends wanted to be left alone after her husband died. It was so easy for you to walk away from me? I was in mourning, I couldn't think straight, I couldn't see straight, I was in pain and you chose then to listen to me?"

"It wasn't my job to be your keeper."

"No it was your job to be my friend, and you didn't do a very good job of that."

"Friends? What like Luca was to Tyler, great fucking friend, leading him to his death and to add insult to injury screwing around with his widow?"

I hear a chair skid violently across the floor and Luca comes to his feet. I'm up in a flash positioning myself

181

between him and Janine, because even though she's a malicious bitch who deserves nothing more than whatever he's fixing to give her, this is my fight.

"Everly, get out of my way." His fists are clenched, his posture rigid. I look up at him and place my hands on his chest.

"It's okay, she's not worth it."

I turn to face Janine but make sure to lean back into Luca, firstly, to show her that we're a united front, and secondly to stop him from hitting the bitch.

"What upsets you more that he's screwing me or that he wouldn't screw you?"

Her eyes go wide, face pales, and she looks as if though she's been struck. Luca's arm slides around my waist pulling me closer into him.

"Why would I be upset, if you want to whore yourself out to the worst possible person, be my guest. It's you who looks like trash not me."

"I'd rather be his whore than be anything like you, opening your legs to anyone with a dick."

"Ev," Luca mumurs, trying to stop me before I lose all control. Luckily for him, I'm not quite there yet. I tilt my head back to look at him.

"What, it's the truth, everyone knows how she is and everyone's had a turn. I however stood by her when everyone was talking crap about her," I say to him before turning back to her. "Why don't you run along and take your judgmental ass back to wherever you came from."

She takes a step back in retreat, her face distorted in anger.

"Oh and Janine," I call before delivering my parting blow, "If I hear from anyone that you're out and about gossiping about me and Luca, I'll be more than happy to show you exactly how trashy I can be."

She moves quickly, getting the hell out of there, I can see that we've garnered the attention of a few surrounding tables, but I fight to keep my composure as Luca spins me to face him. He's fighting back a smile but he looks at me with pride in his eyes.

"So much for a corner table," I say with a roll of my eyes.

"Babe you were fucking vicious."

"She deserved it, and now I'm mortified."

"Don't be, it's already forgotten. Do you want to get out of here?"

"No. I'm not letting her run us off."

I pull away from him and take my seat, he follows suit. "Are you going to use this as a way to pull back from me?"

It breaks my heart that he thinks that, but I can't really blame him. It's not like I've done anything to reassure him that I'm not going to bolt at any second. "No Luca, I'm not going anywhere."

"Good," he says, reaching across the table and claiming my hand. "I know you were scared that this would happen Ev, so if you want to go it's okay."

"I was scared that it would happen, but now that it has it's done with and I'm fine. It was bound to happen at some point. Well, maybe without the claws being drawn, but it's fine. I'm okay."

Amazingly enough, I am okay with what went down, with being seen with Luca by someone who knows our past, and what's even more shocking is that I truly don't care as much as I thought I would. If I have to deal with people's judgment of me and my choices then so be it, it's worth it if I have Luca in the end. My life as I've known it for the last four years is officially over.

~ Luca ~

I have no idea what the hell happened or how I got to this point in my life. One minute I'm done with Everly, pissed at her for shutting me out again, not caring if I ever see her again, and the next she's knocking on my door in the middle of the night. She was prepared for a battle, but when the tables turned and it was me pushing her away she let go, and what I got when she did...Magnificent. Her coming to me was completely unexpected but damn if it didn't only make me want her more. And now...well now we're in a relationship and that's probably the hardest thing for me to believe. This time with her has been unreal and intense, because I'm finally living the life I wanted with the woman who I always wanted. I never thought that would happen, I didn't think it was a possibility.

To hear her tell me that she loves me is surreal. For so long I thought that my feelings for her would go unreturned. I can't believe how lucky I am. I sound like a girl, I know, but shit, when you care about someone for over eight years and finally get them it's kind of hard not to be fucking thrilled. She's everything that I knew she would be and more, sweet, kind, beautiful, and every day she gets more and more fierce. She's coming into her own again, and I'm happy I get to witness it. The way she laid into Janine last week shit… I've never wanted her more than I did in that moment and our sex life is already indescribable.

The knock on my office door brings me back to reality, and I look up to find my dad standing there.

"Dad," I say, not hiding the surprise in my voice. "What are you doing here, is everything okay?"

My dad and I are cool, we've never been super close like my mom and I are, but we have a decent relationship. He's there when I need him and stands by my side when it counts. He's not a show affection type of guy, but he's a good dad nonetheless.

"Yeah everything's fine. I was down at the home store picking up some things and I thought I'd stop by, is that okay?"

I lean back in my chair and grin. "Of course it's okay, you can stop by anytime you want."

He strides into my office and takes a seat in one of the available chairs in front of my desk.

"You haven't been by to see your mom in a while. She's trying to give you your space, but she's worried."

"Why is she worried?" I question, cocking my head to the side.

"The way things went for you last time you were here, hard for her not to worry about you. I worry too. You weren't exactly the man of the year around here."

"I get that, and I'm sorry that you guys were worried. I'm settling in, I like this job, like my place, but I'll do better to make time for you."

He sees his opportunity and doesn't hesitate to strike. "How about coming by for dinner on Saturday. Mom would love to see you and I could use some help fixing the garage door."

I bite back the laughter, my dad has never been the handiest of men, but he must really be in the dark about his latest project if he's asking me for help. This is new. "What you're really saying is that you want me to fix the garage door right?"

"The least you could do for your old man," he declares with a jut of his chin.

"I'll be there on Saturday Dad."

He grabs on to the armrests preparing to stand. "Good, I'll let your mom know."

I don't think before I ask. "It alright if I bring someone?"

"You dating?" he probes, letting go of the armrests and settling into the chair again.

"I'm seeing someone yeah, I would really like to bring her if that's alright."

"Of course."

They need to know about Everly because as far as I'm concerned she's permanent. I'm not letting her go, they need to understand and accept that.

"I'll call Mom and tell her myself but I'm telling you now, it's Everly West."

"Fuck." My father's face goes dark as he leans forward resting his forearms on my desk. "Are you kidding me? That girl hated you, blamed you for her husband's death, and now you're telling me you're seeing her."

I let out a sigh. I don't blame him for not being thrilled. If I was in his shoes I'd probably be a bit leery too, but the last thing I want to do is have a walk down memory lane and rehash the past with my dad.

"I let her think what Ty led her to believe was true. I didn't want her to have to deal with the reality of what got him killed."

"And now she's just fine with you?" he bellows, getting up and beginning to pace my office, the way he used to pace in front of me in the living room and lecture me when I was in trouble as a kid.

I lean back in my chair again, try to keep my calm. I don't want this to escalate into an argument. I just need him to know the facts and accept my choices. "Now she knows the truth Dad, she knows what happened and she's okay with it now. She's with me, and we're happy."

"Forgive me, but I just don't want to see you get hurt. You know I don't involve myself in your personal business often, but I have to tell you I'm worried for you. You've paid for far too long for sins you did not commit."

"I love her."

He sighs, knowing that there's nothing much he can say at this point, I've never declared my love for anyone, so he knows that if I'm saying it it's true.

"You love her… she love you?" he asks, pinching his nose between his thumb and forefinger. Ten minutes in my office and I'm already giving him a headache. This wasn't how I planned for this conversation to go but I can tell by his stance that he's going to let it go.

"She loves me."

He makes no attempt to convince me that I'm making a mistake, offers me no advice on how to end things with Ev, says nothing further, he simply nods his head.

"I'll see you both on Saturday," he says before walking out of my office. I wait till he's gone then waste no time in picking up the phone and calling my mom. She reacts much the same way as my dad did when I tell her about Everly, but when I explain to her how things have changed she's at least a little more open to the idea of me and Everly together.

~❧~

Everly was understandably anxious when I told her we were having dinner at my parents' house. Given our history, she was worried about what they might think of us together and was not thrilled with having to face them just yet. I can see the hesitation on her face as I open the front door to my parents' house. I grab on to her hand and give it a squeeze.

"It's going to be fine," I say, hoping to comfort her. She still looks nervous, but she squeezes my hand in return and gives me a small smile and a nod.

I walk with her hand in hand through the house leading her into the kitchen where I know my mom is cooking.

"Hey mom," I call, releasing Ev's hand and coming around the center island to give her a hug.

Her face lights up when she sees me, making me feel like a shit son for not making more time for her. "Hi sweetie."

I detach myself from her embrace with a smile and claim my girl's hand again, wanting to keep her close. "Mom, you remember Everly."

"Of course, Everly, it's very nice to see you," she greets warmly, though I notice she doesn't move to give her a hug or a kiss which is unlike my mother. She's one of the most affectionate people I know.

"It's nice to see you too," she replies, sounding a little too timid for my liking. "It smells really good in here, is there anything I can help you with?"

I can tell my mom senses Ev's apprehension, and she softens her gaze and gives her a more genuine smile. "I've got it all under control, why don't you pull up a chair. I'll get you a drink and we can chat."

"That sounds great."

I pull the counter height chair out for Ev, which earns me a smile and a soft "thank you."

"Luca, your father's down in the man cave, let him know you're here so you can install the garage door opener and be done with it."

Everly looks up at me, the thought of me leaving her alone with my mother makes her anxious, but she doesn't say a word. I take a seat in the stool next to her and turn my attention back to my mother.

"Mom, we just got here, can I spend some time with you first. There's plenty of time for you and dad to put me to work."

She gives me a knowing look before moving to the wine rack, grabbing a bottle and glasses.

"So how long have you two been seeing each other?"

"Not long."

"A few months," I amend her answer not wanting my mom to think this is a flash in the pan type of thing. She needs to understand the seriousness of this relationship. I see shock register in her delicate features, the fact that it's been months and I haven't said anything to her isn't going over well.

"It was my fault he didn't tell you. I was just afraid of how everyone was going to react, and I wasn't ready to deal with it. He wanted to say something; he just wanted to give me the time I needed."

This seems to pacify her, her face going soft again. She knows me well enough to know that if I really had wanted to tell her about my relationship with Ev, I would have. Which means Mom is reacting to the fact that Ev put the blame on herself for my own decision, so she's also figuring out that Ev has my back and she likes that. She would want that for me, someone who's not afraid to step into the line of fire for me.

"I know you must be worried for Luca, because given our history we haven't always seen eye to eye or been the

190

best of friends, but I realize now that I was wrong about him, and I wouldn't do anything to hurt him."

I want to bang on my chest and drag her out of here caveman style. I know she's anxious to make a good impression on my mom, but she also hasn't hesitated to stick up for us, to defend our relationship and I love her even more for it. She's getting through to my mom too—I can tell by her less guarded stance, and the way she looks at us with less hesitation.

"I'm glad that you understand why I would be a little apprehensive, but I'm not here to judge you or your relationship. Luca's an adult, and I'm happy as long as he's happy."

"Well then be happy Mom," I say doing my best to reassure her.

She looks at me a moment longer before turning away. I'm pretty sure she's going to go easy on Ev now so when I finish my glass of wine, I excuse myself and go off to help my dad with the garage door repair. Everly seems a little bit more at ease as I go, and I'm satisfied that she'll be able to get through this evening just fine.

~ Everly ~

I thought I was going to have a panic attack when Luca left to go help his dad but thankfully I held my shit together. This is important, this is me and Luca proving to his parents…his mom specifically, that we're the real deal. It might be the only chance I get to prove to her that I'm worthy of his love, and I can't let him down. He would stand by me regardless, whether his mom loved me or hated me I know he'd still stay with me. He'd deal with that kind of tension in order for us to be together, but I don't want him to have to do that. Especially when he's already sacrificed so much for me.

"So how are you doing now that you know the whole truth?"

"I'm alright, but it was hard to hear the truth. I felt like all of that time I spent with Tyler was a lie, and I didn't know how to come to terms with that."

"And now?" she asks thoughtfully.

"Now it's better, I'm learning how to let it go, accept it for what it was, understand that he loved me the best way that he knew how but also that he was severely flawed. I didn't have a perfect relationship, and his lies cost us all a lot."

"That sounds about right."

"Luca's helped me a lot."

"He has a good heart."

I nod in agreement and give her a timid smile. "It's more than that, he loves me, and from the beginning he made sacrifices for me that I didn't even know he was making, and I don't know how I can ever repay him for that."

"Is that why you're with him? Gratitude?"

"No, it's not about gratitude. I cared about him too in the beginning, I wanted him to like me, and I thought that he was mean to me because he hated me. But really it was the opposite and when he told me the truth about what really happened, that knowledge allowed me to slowly move on, and it allowed me to explore feelings that I had for Luca that were just hidden beneath the surface for a long time."

"So you really care about him."

"I really love him. I really do, and I didn't think that would happen for me again, and it's scary that it had to happen with Tyler's best friend, but more and more I'm starting to believe that it was just meant to be."

"He deserves that, someone to believe in his love like that."

"I agree. I know I'm probably not what you would want for him."

She tilts her head giving me a confused look. "Why would you say that?"

"Because ultimately you lost your son for four years, and now he's back and he's telling you that he's in love with the one person who you probably blame for him leaving in the first place. He was blamed for things he never did, and I was in the center of all of that."

"But you weren't the real reason right? I mean who dragged him nto the lies? Was it you?"

"No. It was Tyler."

"Yes it was Tyler, and Tyler is gone; he's not here to blame so I had to let that go. I never blamed you, and when I found out you were with Luca I was worried because I didn't know where you were emotionally, but now I see you've got a hold on things. You know what's right and real, and if you tell me you love my son then I believe you and I'm happy for you both."

I breathe a sigh of relief. For the first time since I set foot in this house, I feel like Luca's mother accepts me, accepts us together, and that's all I really wanted. Dinner goes off without a

hitch not at all as uncomfortable as I thought it would be and though I was really nervous about coming tonight I'm really happy that I'm here.

Luca gives my neck a squeeze with his free hand as he drives us to his apartment. I turn to face him and even though it's dark I can easily tell that he's happy and relieved. "You won my parents over tonight."

"They're really great baby, you're very lucky to have them, I'm just glad that they don't hate me."

"No one could ever hate you."

"I don't know about that, but I was really scared that they would."

"Nothing that happened in the past was your fault. You were left in the dark on a lot of things. We can all wish that things would have happened differently, but we still can't change anything."

This is something that I've thought about a lot in the last few weeks. "I don't know that I would change it if I could, it all happened for a reason right? And we're together now. Who's to say we would have lasted had we gotten together so young, maybe it just wasn't our time."

"When did you get so smart and philosophical on me?" he questions making me laugh. "I love it when you laugh."

"There was a time not so long ago when I was afraid that I might never laugh again. You gave that back to me."

"You do the same for me. I never thought I'd have that from you."

"I love you Luca."

"I love you too Ev."

⁂

Luca came by this morning to help me box up the remainder of Tyler's things. Actually, Luca came by to box up Tyler's things on his own because he knew that I wouldn't be able to ever do it without having a minor breakdown. Not because I'm still madly in love with him but because getting rid of those things signifies that I'm finally letting him go and I can't help but to carry a little bit of guilt in that. I don't know why I kept everything for so long but I realize that it's not healthy for me to keep hold of the personal belongings of a man who's no longer here. There are a few pictures and things that I'll keep as a reminder and a lot of things that I'll give to Tyler's parents. I'm sure they'd like to have some of it.

I finally got around to meeting with a realtor and after doing a walk through and appraisal she finally came by a couple of days ago and put a for sale sign on the front lawn. I know that I shouldn't be but I'm shocked at how relieved I feel every time I look outside and see that sign out there. I've hated living here for so long, but I really thought that I'd be stuck here forever—that sign in my lawn is like being one step closer to freedom, one step closer to ridding myself of a house that has been like a prison to me since Tyler ceased to exist. I hate that I feel this way about a house that at one time held so much

195

hope, a house that at one time contained all of my dreams for the future, but all of those dreams died with Tyler. It took some time, but I finally believe that I deserve to have a life beyond the pain, that I can have happiness again despite all of the heartbreak and as difficult as it's been, I have Luca to thank for that.

I'm finishing up loading the dishwasher after clearing all of the breakfast dishes when I hear the doorbell ring. For a minute I think that it might just me my mom dropping by unannounced again but I'm surprised to see Tyler's parents standing on my front porch when I open the door. I haven't seen them since having dinner with them a while back and by the looks on their faces, they are not happy with me.

I look back and forth between them and greet, "Stella, Michael. How are you?"

Stella's posture is impeccable, her frame rigid and I can tell it costs her, but she gives me a tight smile nonetheless, "May we come in?"

"Of course," I say opening the door wider to allow them access inside. If I couldn't tell it before I can tell it now just by their demeanor and the expressions on their faces that this isn't going to be a friendly visit.

Michael turns to face me and clears his throat before hitting me with it. "Everly we got a disturbing phone call last night from one of your neighbors."

I jerk my head not even bothering to try and hide the surprise on my face or the hint of hostility in my voice, "Excuse me? You got a phone call from one of *my* neighbors? Why would my neighbors be calling you?"

He holds his hand up in an attempt to placate me, stop me from going off the rails. "Well we were obviously concerned for your well being, living here all on your own, a young widow never knowing from one day to the next if you'd be alright, so we asked them to keep an eye on you."

I cross my arms along my chest holding them like a shield to protect me from the bullshit I know that they're about to hit me with. I can not believe that they've had people watching me all this time. "I see and what disturbing news did the *neighbors* give you?"

"Well for starters dear we were stunned when they mentioned that there's been a man coming in and out of your house at all hours but we knew we had to get right over here when we heard about the sale sign on the lawn. Everly what are you thinking? We're honestly concerned about you."

Oh this is rich, this is un-frickin-believable that anyone would have the audacity to try and question what I do with my life. "With all due respect Michael, I'm an adult. Who I have coming in and out of *my* house is really none of your business. I've been on my own for four years, and if I feel like it's time for me to date, I have every right to do that. And I have the right to sell *my* house it if I want to. I don't think this is the best place for me anymore."

His face is red with ire—he actually thinks that he gets a choice here, that he has a right to dictate what I do and with whom I chose to move forward with. Or perhaps he'd rather just see me live my life alone forever, that's the price I'm supposed to pay for loving and losing Tyler.

"This is the house that my son built for you. *You* because you wanted it and now what? Now it's not good enough for you? All of a sudden you're beyond this, you'd rather leave it behind?"

I take a deep breath trying to calm my emotions while at the same time steeling myself against the guilt trip that he's throwing at me. I've spent way too long feeling guilty for every little thing where Tyler was concerned, I'll be damned if I allow him to put me right back there, not after all of the progress I've made, not after what I've learned about the past about how this man pulled peoples strings like a puppet master weaving a story based on nothing but lies.

"I did want this house. I wanted it so that I could live here with Tyler, I wanted to build a life here, a family, and I'm never going to get to do that! I'm never going to get any of those things with him. It's a dream that cannot come true... ever...and I'm sorry if that upsets you, but it's how I feel. I need to live my life, and I don't want to do it in a house that reminds me of all of the things that will never be."

I glare at Michael whose expression matches mine. Stella places a hand on his shoulder, likely trying to calm him down. She doesn't look quite as upset as he does—I think she gets what I'm saying. If there was any hope of me breaking through to them it all goes to shit when they see Luca come waltzing down the stairs and into the foyer as if he owns the place.

"Babe, what's going on, I heard voices from upstairs."

Stella's eyes open up in shock as she lets out a gasp. "You? What are you doing in my son's house?"

Luca lets out a sigh; he knows what this is about for the most part. He also knows things are about to get ugly. "Hello Mrs. West, Mr. West."

I swear I can see a blood vessel burst as Michael turns red. He has no control over his anger, it's written all over his face plain as day. "Answer the question young man, what are you doing here?"

Luca doesn't react to Michael, he shows no emotion at all but stands his ground nonetheless. "I'm here to help Everly pack up the house."

"I want you out of this house this instant, you don't belong here," demands Michael, as if he had any right to allow or decline anyone access to my house. I knew he was a borderline control freak, but I had no idea just how bad he was. Well screw him if he thinks he can decide any part of my life for me. It's just not going to happen, not anymore.

I walk over to Luca who now looks like he's trying to hold on to his patience and grab his hand. It's a very calculated move on my part, a statement that they can't miss. I watch as both of their gazes drop to take in the sight of us conjoined. I'd be lying if I said a tiny piece of me wasn't enjoying this.

"He's here for me," I declare calmly, "because I want him here. I don't know what makes you think that you have the right to kick anybody out of my house. I'm sorry Stella and Michael, but Tyler is gone, and it's about time that we all stop acting like he's coming back. He's never coming back, and I'm tired of living my life as if though he is. I can't stay here anymore. I don't want to pretend that this is our house, mine and Tyler's, when it's not. It's a shrine to someone who's not here anymore, and I'm sorry for that, every day I'm sorry for that, but it's time for me to move on."

Stella is frozen solid, stuck in place. The shock of it all might have just been too much for her but Michael... Michael is seconds away from exploding. "What, with him? This is who you want to move on with, the man who killed your husband, our son?"

"You know as well as I do that Luca didn't kill anyone. Some stupid asshole shot Tyler in broad daylight for God knows what reason. That is who you need to blame, that is who killed Tyler. We can go around blaming everyone, but it's never going to change the fact that he's gone. Tyler made the choice to leave me that morning to *take Luca home*," I say that last part with a bit too much sarcasm, I don't give a fuck if he figures out that I know the truth, I've had more than enough of this conversation.

"He could have told Luca to call a cab, he could have *chosen* to stay with me, to get ready to catch a flight to our honeymoon, but he didn't, he chose to get in that car and that is on him. Why don't we ever blame Tyler for his choices huh? Why don't we ever make him responsible for his part in it all? Let's just blame everyone else instead, let's blame totally innocent people because that's so much better than accepting the truth." I'm screaming now, barely keeping it together, barely managing to hold the tears at bay.

I soften my voice. "It was meant to be that way, it was meant to play out the way it did and no one can change it. I'm tired of blaming people for things that they can't control. No one controls life and death. Not Luca, not me, not you. So to answer your question, yes. This is the man who I chose to move on with."

This is when Stella comes unstuck, looks at me then turns her gaze to Luca and speaks. "Your best friend's wife? Stealing his wife, is that really how you want to honor Tyler's memory?"

Luca squeezes my hand then lets it go. He takes a step forward and addresses Stella, "I'm sorry that you feel that way, but I loved Tyler like a brother, I'd never have done anything to hurt him. I'm sorry every single day that he's gone. I miss him too, I wish things would have turned out differently for him, and I played my part in his death. I'll carry that with me forever."

I hate that he's still living this lie, allowing her to believe that he had anything to do with Tyler's death, but I say nothing.

"I'll never stop feeling guilty for that," he continues. "What I won't feel guilty for is caring about Everly. Tyler would want her to be happy. He would want both of us to be happy, and we can be that together."

"How dare you speak for my son? You have the audacity to look at my wife and tell her you know what Tyler would want?"

"Yes, I believe he would be okay with this. But even if he weren't, it doesn't matter, we're not doing anything wrong. We're not having an affair behind anyone's back, we're both free to be with whoever we want and what we want is to be together. You don't get to make that decision or make Everly feel guilty about it."

Stella tilts her head and looks at me. "You promised to love my son."

"And I did, with all my heart, and a part of me always will but loving him doesn't get me loved in return and that's a very lonely place to be. It's a lonely life. I'm still young Stella, I want to have that chance again, I want to have a family, and I want children of my own. Would you really deny me that? Would you really rather see me living in this house all alone, with no one to ever feel about me the way I once felt about your son? Don't you think I deserve to have that again?"

I watch as a tear escapes from her eyes, falling to her face, she reaches up to wipe it away and takes a breath. "Yes you're right, you should have that, all of that, and no one deserves happiness more than you. It was a shock that's all; I guess as long as I had you I still had a little piece of him too. He was my baby, and it's hard to let go of that."

"You don't have to lose me Stella, I'm not going anywhere really, it's not like I'm leaving the country, you can call me whenever you need to, and we can still have dinner together. It doesn't have to change."

"Well then I guess there's nothing left to say."

"Like hell there isn't, you want to throw your life, your reputation, away on a man like this then you're right, it's none of our business but this house. My son's house."

"Everly's house. She owns this house outright, and she's free to do whatever she wants with it."

"She owns this house outright thanks to our generosity."

"I never asked you to pay off the loan, not once did I ask you for anything, if it's the money you're worried about I'll be more than happy to cut you a check for what you so graciously gave me."

Stella grabs Michael's arm, forcing him to give her his attention, she gives him a look that I've never seen from her before but I can tell she's silently warning him to back off. He lets out a sigh — message received — and once she's done with him she turns her gaze back to me. "You'll do no such thing Everly. That money was a gift, it was never something that we wanted you to pay us back for, and it wasn't something that we gave you in order to keep you tied to us. We did it because Tyler wanted you to have this house, and if you no longer want to live here then that's your choice too."

"Thank you."

"Let's go Michael, let's leave Everly to enjoy the rest of her day." She completely ignores Luca in all of this. I guess I should be thankful for her help, and I can't imagine that it's easy for her to be around Luca. *Baby steps*, I think to myself as they say their goodbyes and after a draining confrontation finally see fit to leave.

"That was brutal."

"You handled that as well as you could. Proud of you babe."

"Thanks. I'm glad you were here."

"Baby, I swear it on my life, I'm here. I'm not going anywhere, nobody, nothing will ever come between us. I won't let that happen, I'll do anything I have to do to keep you with me."

21

"Where are we going?" I question for the third time in five minutes.

"It's a surprise."

"What is it with you and surprises?"

He shrugs his shoulder and smiles. "You make it too easy."

"Oh okay," I say with a laugh. I look outside the window, watching as we enter a little lazy town. It's the town where I had originally wanted to live with Tyler, but it was outside of our budget at the time. It's only about fifteen minutes away from work so I've been looking at apartments here since I put the house on the market. I haven't quite made up my mind on moving in with Luca yet. "I love it here. It's so pretty, and the beach is right down the street."

"I think I knew that."

We continue on, driving through town for a few more minutes enjoying the scenery and finally turning off on one of the residential side streets. He pulls onto a picturesque street and drives up to the end of a cul-de-sac.

"Whoa, nice house," I say taking in the two story country style house before me. It has a huge wraparound porch, windows everywhere, and beautiful landscaping. It's pretty much perfection. "What are we doing here?"

"You like this house?"

"It's beautiful."

"Your house is bigger."

"My house is too big, that's just another one of the reasons I'm looking forward to being rid of it."

"This house belongs to a friend of my mom's; she's divorced and the house is just too big for her. She's looking to downsize so she wants to sell this house. I was thinking about buying it."

"Holy shit Luca," I say in excitement. "This is amazing; this is like a dream house. You should definitely buy it."

"I want to...for us."

My breath hitches as I come to terms what he's just said.

"Luca..."

"Don't tell me it's too soon Ev because it's not, we've known each other forever, we've been through every emotion together that two people could go through, and now we love each other."

"I know but..."

"But, if you still feel like it's too soon for you at least do this for me, come inside, take a look around, tell me if you love it as much as I think you're going to, and if you don't want to move in right away, I'll live in it first and you can move in when you're ready."

"You would do that?"

"Yes babe." He grins, wraps his hand around the back of my neck, and pulls me in for a kiss. "I'll do that as long as you don't take forever to move in."

"Okay, then let's go look at it."

The house is straight out of storybook; it's perfection from top to bottom with a stunning mix of hardwood and stone floors throughout and vaulted ceilings. The kitchen is fit for a chef with state of the art appliances, granite countertops, and beautiful white cabinets. I never want to leave this place.

We walk throughout the entire house together, taking in all four bedrooms, the two full bathrooms upstairs, an adorably manicured backyard, and fully finished basement. By the time we're done with the tour I'm totally in love with it.

"What'd you think?" he probes as we walk back out to the car.

I stop in front of the passenger side door and smile up at him. "I love it."

"How much do you love it?" he questions, wrapping his arms around my waist and pulling me closer.

I take the opportunity to get closer to him and wrap my arms around his neck. "So much that I think we should buy it."

"Yeah?"

I hear the surprise in his voice and giggle. "Yes, have a little faith in me would you, and I'm not waiting to move in with you, I'm just going to do it."

He brings his forehead down to mine. "I have faith in you. I just want to make sure that you're sure."

"I'm tired of putting my life on hold baby, I want to be with you, and I want to live with you in this house. We practically live together anyway."

"Okay, I'll call the owner and let her know. If she's serious about selling, I'll start on the paperwork."

I pull back from him slightly and place my hands on his chest. "Don't we need to go get approved for a mortgage too?"

"I'm already approved," he says in his most nonchalant tone.

I nod trying to figure it out in my head based on the price he told me, "Well, I mean my credit is good too and when I sell the house I'll have money to put toward this one."

"Ev, I was just going to buy it for us."

"What?" I question and shake my head. "No, Luca. No way."

"Why not?"

"Because, if we're talking about living a life together, starting a life together, then we need to be a team. I don't want to live off of you, and I wouldn't want you to live off of me. If it's meant to be our house then it should be in both of our names, and we should both be financially responsible for it."

"You're serious."

"Very."

"All in? No backing out?"

"I'm all in. I love you."

"I love you too. We'll go in it together."

I spent some time visiting with my mom and dad today, I haven't gone to see them in a long time, and I thought it would be nice to surprise them. Plus I wanted to let them know about my plans for selling the house, though I left out the part where I plan to buy another house with Luca. I think one shock a day is enough for them, but they were so happy with what I did tell them. All they care about is that I'm finally starting to make decisions about my life again, that I'm making plans for a future instead of wilting away. I can't imagine what they must have felt, what they must have gone through the last four years—having me but not having me all the same. I hate that I put them through that. I hate the thought of having caused them that kind of pain.

After leaving their house I decide to drop by Luca's apartment with some rented DVDs; a night holed up with him snuggling on the couch is exactly what I need. As I pull up to his street, I catch sight of Michael walking into the apartment. I manage to park, shut the ignition, and rush out of the car and up the sidewalk in just a manner of seconds. If he's here to give Luca a hard time I want to put an end to it immediately, he needs to understand once and for all that this is my choice. Thankfully the door is unlocked allowing me access inside the apartment quickly and with very little noise. I remain at the bottom of the stairs hoping to get he reason for his visit before I come up.

I lean up against the wall as Luca starts talking. "Can we just stop with the small talk and get to the part about why you dropped by my place unannounced?"

"Well I see your manners haven't improved over the years." I never realized just how snide Michael can be. I suppose Tyler kept me as sheltered as he could from his father's darker side.

"My manners are fine; I just don't take kindly to people trying to rule everyone around them."

"Is that how you see it? Well you're wrong, I'm protecting my family."

"Just like you protected Tyler?" Luca questions, likely adding fuel to the already raging fire. His words are true, but I'm scared that he's going to set Michael off. "If you would have had a different kind of relationship with your son, he might have come to you before he got himself in so deep that he got himself killed."

"And you were better? You waited too long to tell me, it was too late to help him."

"It wasn't my place to tell you anything, I saw how hard you rode him. You made it impossible for him to come to you. At least I was there for him, at least I tried. I will carry guilt every day for the rest of my life that I couldn't do more, that I couldn't save him, but he was *your* son. I paid my penance, four years away from my family, all this time being made out to be a villain when I wasn't even there, and I took it, I did that for him. I did it because you asked me to."

"Everly would never believe any of that," Michael states, pissing me off because he sounds a little too sure of himself. I contemplate making my presence known, knocking him off his high horse. He thinks he has me so far down in my grief that I can't see straight anymore, that I'm not capable of distinguishing the difference between fact and fiction.

"Oh but she does, she knows." I catch myself before I make a move, Luca's words causing me to stay frozen in my spot. "Everly knows everything, she's known for months, and she's finally moving on with me."

"What? You told her?" Michael booms. I can almost hear his carefully guarded patience snapping.

"She knew something was off, she just asked me to verify, and I was done lying to her."

"You little shit. How you dare say anything to her, you swore."

"Get your fucking hands off of me," Luca demands, very slowly, very deliberately, very scarily. "She deserved to know the truth."

"And you just had to be the one to give it to her? No Luca let's be honest, you told her so you could make it easier on yourself to get closer to her."

"I told her because she was dying, she was trapped in a shell of a life that you created, and I couldn't stand to see her like that. I love her; I want her to be happy, to be free from the past. And if you loved her, if you really considered her family, you would want that for her too."

Michael doesn't respond, he says nothing at all. It's eerily quiet; the only sound I can hear is the sound of my own accelerated heartbeat. I almost move to go upstairs again when Luca finally speaks again.

"If it's not me it's going to be someone else. She'll fall in love again someday, she will not stay alone forever. Even you can't be that delusional to believe that she's going to live her entire life alone in remembrance of Tyler, that's never going to happen."

"Then let her move on with someone other than you, anyone other than you. You were never good enough to be friends with my boy and you are not good enough for his wife. I will not allow it. Do you know what people would say? It's outrageous."

The sound of something, likely a fist slamming down on the table makes me jump. I'm assuming it came from Michael.

"And there you have it, it always comes back to you doesn't it? Always back to you and your reputation, God forbid your life should seem anything less than perfect. You let your son's killers get away, paid them off, and tampered with evidence so that it wouldn't ruin your squeaky clean reputation."

"You shut your mouth you know nothing. He was my son, my only child—I wanted him to die in peace with his good name intact. What's so wrong with that?"

"Why don't you ask Everly what's wrong with that? Or better yet why don't you ask your wife what she thinks? Ohhh right," he draws out sarcastically, "she doesn't know does she?"

"I came here to tell you to stay away from Everly. Do what you have to do to let her down easily and break it off now."

My hearts racing a mile a minute now. I'm furious at the nerve of him. How he thinks that he has any power over my life at all is beyond me. I'm angrier at myself for letting the guilt that they made me feel keep me stuck in a place that was so dark I could barely pull myself out.

"Or what?" Luca asks, his tone is menacing, powerful, and I'm thrilled he's not backing down.

"Or I use all of my pull and resources to ruin your career. When I'm through with you, you will never practice law in this state again."

Oh my God, I think to myself as the tears start to well up in my eyes. How the hell did this conversation deteriorate so rapidly?

"Go for it, run me out of the state again, but just know this time before I leave, I'll return the favor, maybe I'll have a little informational chat with your wife. And if I ever do leave, I'm doing it with Everly, so be my guest, do your worst."

"You may have been able to convince Everly of your story but you won't be able to convince my wife, she'll think you're crazy. She knows I'd never lie to her. Think about it a day or two but don't take too long to make a decision. I'm very motivated; I will not hesitate to destroy you."

"I don't need any time to think, I'd never chose a job over the woman I love. I'd never choose to have status over a family. The answer is no."

"I'm giving you the time anyway."

I can tell that the conversation is over and move quickly, letting myself out of the door as quietly as possible wanting to remain undetected. I run around the side of the building and hide until I'm sure that Michael is gone. I jog to my car, get in and get the hell out of there, driving home as fast as I can. I can't face Luca right now. I can't bring myself to see him, not when I'm so torn about what to do. Can I let him give up his career just to be with me? What kind of person would that make me, I'd be no better than Michael. It's not like I can plead the fifth, not when I know the truth. Being with me means having to sacrifice everything, and I don't know that I can live with that.

I've waited a few days, waited to see if Luca would call things off or break up with me, but the longer I wait, the more evident it is that he's not ever going to do it. He loves me no matter what, no matter what obstacles arise — above his own career — and that makes me love him even more, more than I ever thought possible. Maybe even more than I loved Tyler, but none of that matters now, none of it helps when I know that us being together is hurting him.

Happily ever after doesn't exist. It's a myth, and if it does exist it's not for me, was never meant to be for me. I thought I had it once, thought I held it in my grasp but just like that, love slipped through my fingers. Now here I am again, with that old familiar pit of emptiness in my stomach, the air thick with sorrow and sadness. I know I'm doing the right thing, I can't stand the thought of anymore sacrifices being made on my behalf; I can't stomach the idea that the man I love would give up something that he's worked so hard for just for me — not after all that he's been through, all that I put him through over the years.

I place the flowers down at the foot of the gravestone. I don't know what brought me back here today, but it seemed like a good place to start. My life as I know it has to end today, and it starts with this goodbye.

"I need to tell you how angry I am at you. How hurt I am that you didn't trust me, that you didn't love me enough to tell me the truth. I would have stayed by your side, I would have tried to help you, but you kept me in the dark for so long about so many things and it hurts."

I lower myself down and sit on the grass, wrapping my arms around my legs and hugging them to my body.

"I think I understand though. I get that maybe you didn't want me to think any less of you, I get that you were scared that you might lose me, and I realize that you were trying to protect me, but shit Tyler, you built our whole relationship on lies. Sometimes I don't even know which parts were true. Like how you knew how Luca felt about me and you went after me anyway, it was a shitty thing to do. I'm not saying I regret our relationship, I'm not even saying that I'd change it, any of it, but I wish you would have been honest. I wish that the foundation of our relationship was more stable, but I guess I can't really blame you for lying huh? What kind of hypocrite would that make me? I'm about to lie to Luca, I'm about to break our relationship apart in order to protect him... so I guess in the end I'm no better than you are, am I?"

I rest my head on my knees and let out a breath. I try to keep the tears that threaten at bay, try to tell myself that it's all for the best.

"I love him you know. I do, and I'm sorry if that means that I've betrayed you in some way. It was never my intention, but I think that everything happens for a reason. I think Luca was meant to pull me kicking and screaming out of the dark, he was meant to help me find myself again. I had hoped that he would be a permanent figure in my life, but your father has seen to it that that will never happen. I'm not sure where this need to interfere in everyone's lives comes from; you'd think he'd have learned his lesson by now, but clearly that's not the case. What else can I do Ty, I have to leave him right? If I don't he loses his career, how could I do that to him after he gave up so much because of me already?"

I swipe at my face, wiping away the tears that have fallen. "I can't do it to him, I can't. I have to let him go, and the thing is Ty, I have to let you go too. I wanted to tell you that I forgive you for the mistakes you made, for the secrets that you kept, and for the lies you told. How can I not, when I loved you so much, when a part of me will always love you," I sob.

"This is so hard. It feels like I'm losing you all over again, but I need to close this door. I need to let you go."

Hesitantly, I push myself off the ground and stand up, running my hand on the tombstone like I've done so many times before. Maybe I'll come back one day, maybe I won't, but I know that if I do, it won't be for a very long time. I can love Tyler from afar, loving the memory of him without holding on to the same level of devotion. It's my time.

"Goodbye Tyler," I call out as I walk away from my first love.

I told Luca I'd meet him at his apartment. I thought it would be easier for me to do this in his space, where it's me who makes a quick departure when all is said and done, leaving him to his life. I can't shake the sick feeling in my stomach as I jog up the stairs to his apartment. I find Luca in the kitchen cooking what's most likely a meal that he intended to share with me.

"Hey babe," he calls making my heart do a little flip. God I love him so much, I don't know how I'm going to get through this without tears.

"Hey."

"Where's your stuff? I thought you were spending the night?"

"I can't stay actually."

"Why?" he asks, looking confused. "Are you alright?"

"Yes. I'm okay, I just wanted to talk to you about some things."

He turns the flame on the stovetop off and walks over to me.

"What's up?"

"I've been doing a lot of thinking over the last few days and I've...I think that this thing between us is just moving way too fast."

"Okay. We've known each other for a long time, it's not like we had to start from scratch. We've been together a few months now, but if you think it's too fast for you then we can slow it down a bit, just tell me what you need."

"That's just it, I don't know what I need or how I even feel about any of it anymore. I just need to make it stop."

"What do you want to stop?" I can tell his patience is waning. "Is this because of the house? I told you I'd buy the house on my own. It's not a big deal, you know that. You can move in if and when you're ready, not a moment sooner. I'm not trying to pressure you."

"I think the house is great Luca, I do. I think you're right though, if you want it you should have it but don't buy it for me, or because you think I'll eventually move in. Buy it because you want to live there."

"Alone... Is that what you're trying to say? Are you trying to break up with me Everly?"

"Yes."

"No." He shakes his head. "You would not do that. You love me; you want this as much as I do. Did someone say something to you?"

"What? No… this has nothing to do with anyone but me. It's too much too soon and it's overwhelming. I can't handle it all, and I need to be on my own. The timing is just off."

"Bullshit."

"It's true."

"Bullshit," he says again, grabbing hold of my arms. "You love me."

"Luca."

His grasp on me tightens as he shakes me. "Tell me you don't."

"Luca."

"Tell me you don't love me Everly."

"I don't love you."

"You're full of shit." He releases his hold on me, taking a step back.

"I'm telling you the truth. I never meant to hurt you, you have to believe that. I went to the grave before I came here and it all became so clear to me but I don't love you. I was in love with the idea of you, what you represent in my life, and I'll always be grateful to you Luca, always, because without you I'd still be stuck in my sad little life. You brought me back to life, you did that, and that's huge but I think I confused my gratitude for love."

"You really believe that?"

"I love Tyler West. I will always love him, and I can move on now, get out of that house, find a place to live that I love, figure out what I want to do with my life and not be afraid of living it, but when I think of love, of who I love, and it's still him. I'm not over it as much as I'd like to believe I am. Being with you made it easy for me to pretend that I'm okay, that my heart is healed when it's

217

not. It's not, and I'm not sure if that part of me will every truly be healed."

He stares me down and runs a hand through his hair. "You're a piece of work you know that. You come here with all this talk of gratitude, and I know it's bullshit. You're still running scared and I love you Everly. I swear to God I do, I'd do anything for you, I'd do anything to keep you but this is just too fucking much for me. If this is what you want, then go... leave, I'm not going to try and stop you, but this bullshit card you're playing is weak and at the very least I deserve the truth."

"I gave it to you," I say, steeling my spine.

"You're a liar."

"No that's you, and Tyler, and Michael, you're the liars. I'm just the girl who got caught up in all of the lies. I'm the one who got broken down by it all, so don't you stand there like a hypocrite and call me a liar when you lied to me for years."

"That was not my choice."

"You had a choice! We always have choices."

"What, like you're making a fucking choice now? Taking the easy way out instead of staying with me and working out whatever it is that's pushing you away, instead of fighting for something that you know could be great."

"I'm doing what's best for me right now. This decision is best for me, and I need you to understand and accept it."

"I don't. I won't. If you go, go now because I'm done with this stupid conversation. If this is the game you want to play then you'll be doing it without me."

"Goodbye Luca."

Squaring my shoulders, I turn on my heel and make a quick exit. I don't crumble down to the ground outside his door, I don't sit and cry in my car, I don't drive home and sit in a lonely dark house by myself or wait for him to come after me. The damage is done and now I have to deal with it head-on like an adult. I can't go through another four years like the last four. At least Luca is alive, he's free to live his life, to meet another woman, have a family. I should be grateful for that, be grateful that he gets to live a life, have a great career, and I can be proud of myself for giving him that. For not making the easy choice, the selfish choice, to stay with him pretending like I don't know what the consequences of that are for him. No... this is the best thing for him, and I have to honor him by living my life the best way I can.

I hit the Bluetooth button on my steering wheel and scroll through the numbers until I reach the one I'm looking for and hit go.

"Everly dear? Is that you?" His voice makes my skin crawl, I hate that I have to talk to him at all.

"Yes, it's me," I return, icily.

He hesitates but only for a moment. "Is everything alright?"

"No. It isn't Michael, not when you insist on playing God with people's lives."

I hear his sharp intake of breath. "Everly I'm not sure what you're referring to."

"I overheard your conversation with Luca the other day, I know that you threatened him," I say bluntly, there's no use in beating around the bush with someone like Michael, he'd chew me up and spit me out.

"I think..."

"It's done."

"Pardon me?"

"I just ended it with him Michael, I told him it was over and that I didn't love him, he won't bother me again."

"I see."

"You have to leave him alone now," I demand. "You have to keep your end of that bargain and stay away from him, let him live his life, let him have his career without any interference from you."

"Of course."

I grip the steering wheel as tight as I can and take a deep breath. Who would have thought that one person could cause so much havoc in my life? "There's one more thing I need you to do for me."

"What's that?" I can hear the curiosity in his voice. I wanted to believe he would tell me to forget all about it; that once he heard how angry and upset I was he would back off and tell me to go back to Luca, but I know now that that's not the case. He's too self-centered of a man for that, to care about what anyone else wants or needs. None of it matters unless it suits his purposes.

"Stay away from me too."

"I'm afraid I can't do that. I do care a great deal for you Everly even though you might not think that at the moment but it's true, and then of course there's Stella. She'd never understand why we were no longer in contact."

I knew he'd throw his wife into the mix, use her to make me feel guilty to get what he wants. "I'll continue to see Stella regularly. I would just prefer that you not be there. If I schedule dinner with her make sure you're working late those nights, tell her something came up. I don't care what you tell her, just don't be there."

"Perhaps if I give you a bit of time."

"No," I cut in, not wanting to go into negotiations with him. He can take them and shove them for all I care. "This is it, this is the only deal you're getting from me. You got what you wanted, and now it's only fair that I get something too."

220

"Very well then Everly." He sighs. Funny, for a moment there I almost think he cares about me, but then I remember all the hurt he's inflicted on those he claims to care about, and I let that notion go.

"Goodbye."

"Goodbye," is the last thing I say to him before I disconnect the call, funny... I feel like I've said nothing but goodbye today. As for Michael, I honestly hope I never have to see his face again.

Morgan can sense the agony on my face when she opens the front door. This is the only place I could think of to come after the day I've had. She's the only one I can really be honest with about all of this.

"Everly? What's wrong? What are you doing here?"

I smile at her shakily. "Can I come in?"

"Of course," she says, moving out of the way so that I can pass through the doorway. "Are you okay?"

I shake my head as I drop my purse and keys on her entryway table. "I broke up with Luca tonight."

"Everly!" she calls out in disbelief. "Why would you do that? Did he do something to you? I swear to God I'll kill him."

"He didn't do anything, he's perfect."

"Then why?"

I take a moment to gather my thoughts as I walk past her into the living room and lower myself onto her couch. I close my eyes and focus on my breathing, trying to get my emotions under control before I break apart or worse. "I overheard Michael threatening him."

"What!" she shrieks. Her eyes go wide, and her cheeks flame up with a scary amount of anger as she sits across from me.

"He threatened to use his clout to get Luca fired, to make sure he never practiced law again if he didn't leave me," I tell her, as I begin to pull at the hair band around my wrist, the sting it gives me when it snaps back is scarily comforting.

"What did Luca say?"

"He told him that he wasn't leaving me. That he loved me and having love was more important to him than having a job."

"Everly that's great." She smiles. "That's more than great, why would you break up with him?"

"I just..."

"You just what? He has the right to make that choice; you actually broke up with him so that he wouldn't lose his job?"

"Morgan, it was the right thing to do."

"For who? For you or him?" She shakes her head at me. "Everly! He loves you, and you love him. What are you doing? You of all people should understand how precious love is, how it can be gone in the blink of an eye—and instead of cherishing it, you're throwing it away?"

"I'm doing it for him," I half yell. "Why should he be stuck in a life he didn't want? I know how that feels! Four years of living a life that I never signed up for, I don't want to do that to him."

"Yes but you didn't have a choice, he did. He was given a choice and he chose you, and then you turned around and you took that choice away from him. Do you not see the irony in that?"

"I'm a hypocrite, I already know that, but I'm doing this because I love him."

"Or maybe you're doing this because you'd rather lose him on your own terms than lose him in a cruel twist of fate. This way you can manage the hurt and contain the pain."

Her words sting — they hit home in a way that nothing ever has before. God, she's right, this is the only way I could lose him and control it, control how it went down, how I dealt with it afterward. I really am fucked-up but what's done is done and now I need to own it. "It's over now, it doesn't really matter."

"Ev."

"Can I stay with you for a while?" I ask, needing to change the subject. I can't talk about this one more minute.

"Umm, yes, of course you know that. Why though?"

I give her a bright smile. It's fake, but it's all I have to give right now. "I have an offer on the house. I'm accepting it, and I really need to start over. I need to leave the past behind and that house is one of the things I'm saying goodbye to. I have all of my things boxed up and ready to go."

"The spare bedroom is all set up Ev, you can have your clothes brought here and you can stay as long as you need."

"Just until I find an apartment okay?"

She nods her acceptance. "What about work? You have to see him on Monday."

"I handed in my resignation today. I waited for Luca to leave and handed it to my supervisor. I apologized for not giving notice, he asked me to stay, but when he saw how determined I was he accepted it. All in all I think he took it okay."

I watch the worry pass through her features. She's such a good friend, I'm lucky I didn't lose her with how badly I treated her over the last four years. "What are you going to do for money?"

"I have some money saved up for now, and with the sale of the house, I'll be okay until I figure out what I want to do. I'll pay you for the room."

"No you won't, it'll be nice to have someone around here for a little while; living alone can be lonely."

I sigh, giving her a sad smile. "I know the feeling."

"You don't have to be alone Ev." She grabs hold of my hand and gives it a squeeze.

I nod, suddenly feeling overcome with exhaustion. The emotions of the day are weighing down on me so heavily and all I really want to do is sleep it away. "Would you mind if I just call it a night?"

"No."

"I'll just go get my stuff out of the car and grab a shower first."

"Take your shower," she says coming to her feet. "I'll get your bag for you."

"Thanks Morgan."

"Anytime babe."

I stay in the shower for a long time, reliving the events of the past few hours and letting the hot stream of water wash over me. It is scalding my skin, helping me to remember that I'm alive. I'm alive, this isn't the end for me—I don't have to go back to being that sad, lonely girl just because Luca is lost to me now. I can still find ways to be happy. I can be alone and lead a good life. Maybe I'll go back to school, get the law degree like I planned in the first place. I can keep the important people to me close, like Morgan and my parents. I've always loved to travel, and I haven't done that in years. I can take a trip, maybe go to London, I've always wanted to do that. This doesn't have to be that bad; I can do all of those things. Happiness isn't something that should be wrapped up in one person. So maybe I'll never have happiness in love, maybe I'll never have that kind of happily ever after, but I can still live happily on my own terms.

I rifle through my bag, which Morgan slipped into the bathroom during my shower and pull out some comfortable sweatpants and a t-shirt. Luca's t-shirt, one of the many he's left lying around my place over the last few months. I can't help but to wonder what he's doing right now, how he's doing. How he's handling our confrontation earlier, is he as devastated as I am? I hate that I hurt him; the look on his face will haunt me forever. He let me into his life so willingly, so openly giving me everything that was him, and I acted like it meant nothing to me, when really it meant everything. His love is everything to me, and I treated it like it was useless, like it hadn't changed me for the better. By the time I finally crawl into bed, my body has given out on me, my brain is fried, and I'm grateful that I'm able to fall asleep easily.

~ Luca ~

I had the weekend from hell. Everly coming to me to break things off claiming that she didn't love me knocked me on my ass. I was not expecting her to do that, she seemed happy, I know she was happy. Something had to have happened to make her have such a change of heart, but I don't know what, she gave me nothing. At first I thought Michael had something to do with it, but that would ruin his relationship with Everly, and he wouldn't do that. It took every ounce of control I had to let her walk out of my apartment, I think I gave it a whole fifteen minutes before I got in my car and went looking for her. I ended up at her house but she wasn't there, which means she's either at her parents' house or Morgan's place. I decided against going to look for her, she made her choice and I decided to give her some space. That decision nearly killed me and ultimately led to me drinking myself into a stupor for the rest of the weekend. I told myself I'd never let myself feel this way again for her, let her hurt me this way. I can't blame her for the past, she didn't know how I'd felt about her all those years ago, but she knows now. She knows, and she still screwed me over.

I chug the rest of my coffee, willing the remnants of my hangover away and rise from my chair, grabbing my notepad and pen before I make my way into the conference room for yet another Monday morning meeting. The thought of seeing her is both nerve wracking and exciting to me. I'm nothing but a glutton for punishment. I can't help but hope that she's changed her mind, that she'll smile up at me and let me know that everything is okay between us. When I walk in the door and take a look around, she's nowhere to be found. Maybe she called out today so that she wouldn't have to face me. I wouldn't put that past her, she's done it before. Maybe this has affected her after all.

It doesn't take long for old Mr. Harvey to call for attention. "I called this meeting because we're going to have to figure out a way to redistribute some of the workload for now. As of today Everly West is no longer with the firm."

I drop my pen on the table and look up, likely unable to hide the shock on my face. She fucking quit her job so that she wouldn't have to deal with me. I guess I shouldn't be floored, but I am, I'm stunned silent. Everly West just never ceases to shock the shit out of me.

If this is what she wants then so be it. Let her live her life however she sees fit, if that means she remains alone forever then fine, that's her choice. If she ends up moving on with someone else, I'm sure it will sting but eventually I'll get over it. I have a life to lead and clearly Everly doesn't want to be a part of that. I'm not about to beg. I tried to show her a different way, God only knows I tried to give her more but when push comes to shove it always goes back to Tyler for her. I thought I'd broken through the walls, but I was just a distraction to her, a way to forget for a little while, not really who she wanted at all.

~ Everly ~

I had all of the contents of my house moved into a storage unit in town a few days ago. The majority of Tyler's things, which Luca packed up before I broke up with him, went to Goodwill, except for a few things that I had boxed up and sent to his parents. I kept some of his favorite books for myself because letting go doesn't mean having to forget. It's been almost a month since I last saw Luca. I thought that it would get easier with time, not having him around, but I was mistaken. It's just as hard today as it was that first day, that first night without him. I closed on the house last week and made a really good profit on the deal. I was able to pay a full year of rent up front on a one-bedroom condo downtown and not even make a dent into the money, I move in next week. I also traded my car in for a new car, a car that doesn't remind me of Tyler—it was my last act of defiance against my past.

I finally decided that it was time to at least try to do something with my chosen career, so I submitted my application to law school. I thought the process would take longer but because I had already been accepted and chose not to go after Tyler's death, they re-accepted me almost immediately. I'm still not a hundred percent sure that it's what I really want, but I figure it's worth a shot, and I start in a few months. When I met with my academic counselor a few days ago to go over my schedule and tuition, she told me that my tuition had been covered by an anonymous benefactor. It didn't take me long to figure out that this was Michael's parting gift, but how he found out I had gotten into school is beyond me. I'm sure he has connections in admissions, because he seems to have connections everywhere.

I was angry at first, so angry that I almost went to his office to tell him to shove his stupid gift because I no longer needed anything from him. But the more I thought about it, the less angry I got. If he wants to throw his money away on me then let him, it's the least he could do for not helping Tyler and for costing me Luca. What he won't get is a thank you from me...Ever! It may make me no better than he is, it might even make me a bitch, but whatever, I can live with that.

So there you have it, life goes on, with or without Luca. I can see the beauty of everything that I've accomplished in the last few weeks on my own. In the end I guess I didn't need him holding my hand and walking me through it all. It felt good to be independent; to take these steps forward on my own. That doesn't mean that I didn't wish every single day that he was still here. It doesn't mean that I don't miss him with everything that I have, because I do. There are times that I feel like I might just go crazy without him, times where I have my cell phone in hand set to his name and the only thing standing between me and hearing his voice again is the push of a stupid button. Why I can't push it is beyond me, why I can't just call him and explain what happened, let him make up his own mind, choose for himself whether he wants me or a career. That would be the smart thing to do, because the more I think about it, the more I think that I acted rashly, that maybe Morgan was right and my own fear of losing him got in the way of my rational thoughts. Only now so much time has passed that I don't know how to make the first move, I don't know if I could stand his rejection even though I know it's what I deserve. Luca Jensen probably hates me, and I can't blame him, not even a little bit. I can only hope that mixed in with the hate is just a little bit of the love he once felt for me.

"How are you doing?"

I look up from my spot on the couch where my eyes were trained on one of those fixer-upper shows on the home channel to see Morgan hovering over me with a bottle of wine and two glasses.

"Hey, I'm okay. What's up?"

She plops down next to me, hands me a glass, and pours us both drinks. She takes a generous gulp and I follow suit.

"Are you all set with the move? How are you getting everything from the storage unit into the apartment next weekend? I can help."

I love that she's always willing to help out; she's honestly one of the best people I know. "I hired a moving company but I can definitely use some help unpacking and decorating."

"Cool, I'll be there. I'll bring some pizza."

"Morgan, I don't know what I would have done without you the last few weeks. I know I didn't deserve anything from you after the way I treated you the last few years."

"Everly."

"No, seriously it's true. I went through a really horrible time when I lost Tyler and I pushed everyone away. My family didn't give up on me because they couldn't, I'm their daughter. But out of all of my friends, all of the people I considered to be close to me, you were the only one who stuck around, you were the only one to try consistently to get through to me. I shouldn't have shut you out like that." Pushing her away is one of the things that I regret most about the last few years. If I could change it I would.

"I'll never give up on you Ev, you're my best friend. You're the sister I never had."

"Oh shit, you're going to make me cry."

"I'm sorry. I don't want to make you cry and I know that you don't want to hear this babe but I hate to see you so sad."

"What are you talking about?" I play the dumb card and take a drink of wine.

"I'm talking about how unhappy you've been these last few weeks, and that doesn't mean that you aren't doing great, you are. You've accomplished so much and all on your own, and I think that's important. I'm so proud of you, but the sadness is there, it's unmistakable."

"What do you expect me to say, I'm not going to deny that I'm sad, or that it hurts that Luca isn't around, but I made my choice and if I've learned anything it's that you shouldn't let sadness drag you down. You have to fight for pieces of happiness and that's what I'm trying to do."

"You shouldn't have to fight for pieces of happiness, you should just be happy."

There's that happy word again. Happiness is an ideal that I've never really managed to master. "How do you suggest I get happy?"

"Talk to him, tell him the truth, that you're an idiot and you thought you were doing the right thing but you regret it."

"Don't sugarcoat it or anything."

"You don't need anyone to sugarcoat crap for you, you need someone who can be honest with you, and that's me."

"It's too late Morgan. I can't go back now and tell him that I made a mistake, besides I'm not so sure that it was a mistake."

"You know it was mistake," she says with a scowl. "If it was a great choice you wouldn't be miserable now. You can't take matters into your own hands and play god with people's future."

"I'll think about it okay?"

"Okay."

It's not a lie, I will think about it—I've been thinking about it since it happened. I'm just not sure thinking on it will change my mind, the damage is already done. I sit here and continue drinking my wine, my eyes fixed on the TV screen but my mind on Luca and all the reasons why I should just leave him alone, the only problem is that I don't believe any of them.

~ Morgan ~

I heard Everly crying a few nights ago. She probably thought I was sleeping but I'm sort of an insomniac, it takes me forever to fall asleep. I've heard her cry herself to sleep most nights since she went through with her stupid idea about leaving Luca. Now that she's all moved into her new apartment, I can't be there to make sure that she's alright. I'm not around to keep her company, and I'm terrified that she's going to fall into that old familiar pattern of retreating into herself and shutting people out. She's come so far in the last few months, she's become the old Everly again, and I don't want to lose her.

I'm a firm believer in everything happening for a reason, that our lives will eventually lead us where we're meant to be but I'm not naïve enough not to realize that sometimes we have to give fate a shove in the right direction. Everly is so screwed up that she needs more of a tow. I'm about to make shit happen for her, I only hope she doesn't hate me for it, and if she does well then... at least I tried.

I sit across the street sipping a latte and wait for the car to pull out of the driveway. I watch it disappear down the street before getting out of my car, jogging across the street, and ringing the doorbell. The door opens just a few seconds later and I'm greeted by a woman. She looks exactly as I remember her, Stella West, Tyler's mother.

"Hello, may I help you?" she questions cautiously yet politely.

"Hi Mrs. West, you may not remember me. I'm Morgan, Everly's best friend."

"Oh My. Of course Morgan, it's been a long time. Won't you come in? Is everything alright with Everly?"

"Yes Everly is fine," I answer quickly in order to reassure her. I walk into her massive home, every bit as grand as I thought it would be. "I'm so sorry to interrupt you but I was hoping that you would be able to help me with something."

"Well I'm not sure I'd be the most suited but I'll certainly try."

"That's all I ask, thank you."

"Can I get you something to drink?"

I smile but shake my head, trying to remain polite and hide my anxiety. "No, I can't stay, I just... Mrs. West, I know you know that Everly is trying to move on with her life, and part of that is falling in love again, and she's done that with Luca Jensen."

She nods her head, giving me a soft smile as well. "I know this dear, I saw them together not so long ago. It came as a shock at first, but I realize that the heart wants what it wants and I would never stand in the way of her happiness. I believe she's suffered enough."

"I'm glad to hear you say that, because there are people that don't want to let her be happy. There are people who would rather see her miserable and alone than end up with someone like Luca."

She tilts her head, a look of concern in her eyes. "To which people are you referring?"

"I'm referring to your husband Mrs. West."

Her voice gets tight and I pray that this doesn't all go downhill from here. "I'm sure you must be mistaken."

"I'm not. Your husband went to see Luca, he warned him that if he didn't stay away from Everly he would destroy his career, and he would make it so that he would never be able to practice law here again. Luca said no but Everly overheard the conversation and took matters into her own hands. She broke up with Luca and now she's brokenhearted. I didn't know how else to help her, so I came to you, hoping that maybe you could have a word with your husband, tell him that it really isn't his place to interfere in other people's lives."

Her face changes, for a moment she looks angry but not necessarily surprised.

"My husband is a good man Morgan. I know that's hard to believe, especially when he does things like this, but he is also misguided at times. He thinks that he can control those around him and that he's doing the right thing by them. I don't know where that comes from."

"I understand."

"It's what went wrong with Tyler," she says catching me off guard. "He was a good boy, don't get me wrong, but when he wanted something he would move heaven and earth to get it. It was that drive that ended up getting him killed."

"Mrs. West." I'm sure she can hear the astonishment in my voice. I don't even know why I've said her name at all.

"They all think I don't know the truth, the real reason my son is dead, the issues he had, the trouble he got in, and my husband's part in all of that. Not helping him soon enough and then covering the truth up. I may be a quiet woman Morgan, but I am not a stupid woman. In fact I'm very observant, and I can see how much Everly loves Luca, so much that she'd be willing to sacrifice her own happiness for his."

235

"Yes."

"Well it's stupid isn't it? Why should she have to sacrifice anymore because she got herself involved with this family?" she questions, turning to look out the window. It's like she can't look at me, like she's afraid I may judge her for the actions of her son and husband.

"She would never regret that, she loved Tyler too."

"Tell her I'll take care of this Morgan. Tell her not to let go of Luca, no harm will come to either of them, I give you my word." Her attention is still focused on what lies outside the window, but her words are sincere. I believe that she'll take care of Mr. West.

"Yes ma'am."

She turns back to me and gives me a smile before she shows me to the door. There's something that I've been wondering and before I leave, I turn and ask her.

"Why didn't you ever tell your husband that you know the truth?"

"He lives in a special kind of hell all his own Morgan, a hell of his own creation. Why make that any worse for him? He thinks he's protecting me so I let him have that. There's nothing I can do or say that could make him feel any worse about Tyler's death than he already does. Me blaming him doesn't bring him back, it doesn't erase any of the things Tyler did to get himself where he ended up. As a mother it kills me, I'll never be the same again. I'll never be okay, but neither will Michael, so I chose not to make that any worse and at the end of the day he was all I had left."

"I get that. I really do. Thank you for hearing me out."

"Thank you for dropping by Morgan, it was lovely to see you again."

I contemplate my next move, even though I'm a hundred percent sure that Stella will take care of our little problem with Michael, I'm not sure going to Everly with this is the best idea. I don't have complete confidence in the fact that she'll actually use this information to go back to Luca, she'd be too afraid that he'd turn his back on her even though that's ridiculous. No. Everly is the wrong person to go to with this, there's only one logical person in this whole scenario, and it's time that he hears the whole truth.

~ *Luca* ~

I spent the majority of my morning in court, God only knows I didn't want to be there today, but truth be told I don't have the desire to be most places lately. I get in my car just as I turn on

my phone and begin to check messages. I almost drop the phone when I see a text from Morgan. I haven't heard from her in a long time and when I do it's usually related to Everly.

I have to talk to you, are you free for lunch?

Gotta love the cryptic fucking messages. Do I really want to hear about anything going on with Everly right now? No. I don't, but I will anyway because that's just the kind of sucker I am.

Just got out of court, free now.

I type out a quick response and hit the send button. Not surprisingly she responds immediately.

Meet me at Laura's café. I'll b there in 10 mins.

I start my car and point it in the direction of Laura's café; I'm only about a fifteen minute drive away myself. The whole ride there I'm wondering what exactly Morgan is going to say to me. What could she possibly tell me that she thinks I need to know? I haven't heard from Everly since the night she left me. I know that she sold the house, that was easy enough to track, but I drew the line there. I don't need to get myself in stalker territory. I'd like to believe that even I'm not that desperate. Fuck I miss her though, I've cared about her for so long, it's hard not to at least try to get through to her but this was her choice and I need to respect it.

I pull into the restaurant parking lot, do a quick scan for Morgan's car, and spot it a few rows over. I shut off the ignition and angle out of the car, spotting Morgan as soon as I walk in the door. I give her a quick nod, and she waves me over to her booth.

"Hey," she greets as I take the seat across from her. The waitress is there almost immediately taking our orders which works for me because I really need to get back to the office soon.

"What's up?" I question once the waitress is out of earshot.

She takes a deep breath, looks me square in the eye, and spits it out. "You need to go get Everly."

"Where is she?" I ask, unable to hide the confusion in my voice.

"No," she says, drawing out the o longer than necessary. "I mean get her back."

This gets an eye roll from me, and to think I actually drove out of my way for this shit. "Oh God Morgan I don't want to deal with this right now. Everly made her choice. If she wants to speak to me, she knows where to find me."

"Luca." She says my name with an unmistakable tone of sadness and pleading in her voice. "I think she's scared that you're going to reject her."

This gets my attention, but I play it cool. "Why would she think that?"

"Because deep down she knows she screwed up."

"Damn right, she screwed up, but if she thinks I'm going to come back and fix it for her, she has another thing coming to her. She needs to fix it not me."

"I understand why you feel that way but you don't know the whole story, I think that once you've heard it you might feel a little differently."

The food arrives just as I'm about to reply to her. What does she expect me to do? What does she really think is going to happen in all this, even if I did go after her, Everly is stubborn as fuck. She may hold on to whatever reason she had for breaking things off with me and not let go, that's just how she operates. Would I fight for her? Yeah, I'd fight for her, I'd die for this girl, but there comes a point for everyone where you just have no more fight left in you. I don't want to drag myself through those murky waters again only to come up empty handed. Everly has never been a sure thing, she lets her fear get the better of her sometimes and when she does, she has no problem blowing her life up into smithereens.

"Alright fine. I'll bite, tell me what happened," I ask knowing that it won't make any difference but hoping that it will all the same.

"Michael West threatened to ruin your career if you didn't leave Ev."

"How do you know that?" I ask with more than a hint of tension in my voice.

"How do you think I know that?"

I fight the urge to walk out of this place, find Michael West, and rip his head off. "He went to her?"

"No, she was there; she was coming to see you and overheard the conversation."

"Fuck." I wish I'd have known this before she left me. "Okay she overheard but then she knows that I told him to do his worst, I told him I didn't care Morgan."

She nods; she knows it's true, Morgan knows I would do anything for Everly. "In her mind she was protecting you, she thinks that you've already sacrificed so much because of her that if you gave up something that you worked so hard for, you would just end up resenting her later. She thought that maybe one day down the line you'd wake up one morning and think that you threw your life away for her."

"She's crazy to think that. I love her Morgan, how could I ever regret anything that gives me a life with her."

"That's what I told her."

"I mean I get it, I can see why she thinks that what she did was the right thing, the noble thing but even still, that was my choice to make." I'm pissed at her, I want to say screw it and let it all go but I can't.

"She said she felt like a hypocrite for doing it, but there's more."

"What else can there be?"

"I think she has an underlying fear of losing you because you mean so much to her. She's afraid that something will happen to you, and she'll have to deal with the loss of someone else that she loves. I think she thought that by letting you go on her own terms it would lessen the pain."

"How's that working out for her?" I ask sarcastically.

"Don't be an ass. She's miserable all right, she puts on a brave face and does what she needs to do but she's sad and she misses you. I hear her crying all the time, and it's painful to witness."

I sigh, suddenly feeling like a jerk. "I don't mean to be a dick Morgan. I really don't, and if what you're telling me is true then yes, I'd love to go to her, to tell her to stop being a martyr and just come back to me, but if she feels like Michael's still a threat, she won't budge."

"Which is why I've neutralized him." She swirls her straw around her glass of soda and smirks at me.

I chuckle knowing that I'm about to hear an earful. "You what?"

"I took care of the problem."

"How did you do that?"

"I went to the one person who can actually bend someone like him to her will."

"You went to his wife? You do know she has no idea what really happened to Tyler right?"

"Oh Luca, she knows way more than you think. The woman is smarter than anyone gives her credit for. She knows more about what really went down than you know. She just figured her husband was trying to protect her and going through a hard enough time—she didn't want to add to that so she let him believe she's clueless."

I lean back in my seat. I can't believe what I'm hearing. "No shit?"

"No shit, and she all but promised me that she would take care of her husband; that you and Everly can be together without his future interference."

I shake my head, "I don't know what to think. I'm sorry, I know you're expecting me to run out of here in a mad dash to find her and get her back, but I just don't know."

"You're gun shy," she says with a shrug.

"You blame me?"

"No but I really think if you make it okay for her to come back, she's truly ready for you now. She's come a long way, and you started her on that path; it's only right that you be there at the end to cheer her on."

"You're a good friend Morgan, to both of us. When I was gone you were my only real connection to this place beside my parents and you never give up on Everly. She needs that, she's lucky to have you in her corner."

"She's lucky to have you too Luca, she knows she fucked up. I really believe that from the beginning, from the moment you two met in that bookstore, you were destined to be together. You just had to get through all the bullshit first, this is your chance, don't waste it."

I walk out of the restaurant feeling more unsure than ever. I want Everly—I know that as clearly as I know my own name—but the roller coaster of emotions is something that I can really do without. The interference from outside parties trying to split us up or dictate our relationship is something that I don't want to deal with anymore. A part of me wants to kill her for doing this to us, for going behind my back and making decisions for us without consulting me. But the other part of me... the other part of me wants to kiss her senseless and fuck the shit out of her for loving me enough to let me go even though it was the dumbest idea ever. Where do I go from here? I'm standing at a crossroads, and I don't know which way to go. No... That's a lie, I know which way I want to go, I just can't propel myself forward to move there.

~ Everly ~

"Hey honey, I'm hanging the last picture up in the living room and then I'm out of here."

My dad dropped by earlier this morning to help me with some of my unpacking, heavy lifting, hanging of frames and such. We've always been close but the last four years have really taken a toll on our relationship. I shut him out and he struggled to break through as any father would but I was unresponsive. Now it feels like we finally have a shot to get back some of what's been lost between us. It's why I invited him over. Well… that and I need all the help I can get right now. I hate everything involved in moving.

"Thanks Dad," I say going in for a quick hug and a kiss. "I'm going to keep putting things away, just lock the door behind you when you go."

"Sure thing," he replies, going back to his level, trying to make sure the painting he's hanging above the couch is just right.

I've been holed up in my room unpacking my mile high pile of clothes and putting them away in the closet and drawers, for the past hour. I'm about ready to give up and take a nap when I hear the front door open and close. I thought my dad left at least forty-five minutes ago.

"Dad, are you still here?" I call out to no reply. "You should probably get going, Mom was expecting you home half hour ago."

I feel his presence before I can hear or see him. I stand frozen in my spot, my heart racing as I wonder if it's just my mind playing tricks on me. A rush of warm air hits the back of my neck, his hands come to rest on my waist and my breath hitches. I know those hands, I'd know them anywhere, and I love the way they used to feel all over my body.

"Luca," I whisper, because I'm afraid if I speak any louder he'll disappear like a mirage leaving me cold and alone again.

"Shut up," he growls in my ear, gripping my hips tighter and pulling me back into his chest hard. "Do not speak, you are done talking, do you understand me."

I know I should be pissed at him for speaking to me like this, but instead my nipples perk up and a pool of heat rushes between my legs—I'm pretty sure I'm soaked. Shit, I want him now more than ever, want him to take me, make me his, do whatever he wants to me I don't care. All the fight has left me and all that's left is the overwhelming need to surrender to him.

"Answer me Everly," he demands, wrapping one of his hands around my neck.

"Yes," I reply on a breath, loving every second of this, loving how he controls my body and bends me to his will. I've missed this.

He begins to walk forward, pushing me with his body until my knees hit the mattress. I say nothing because really there are no words, I'm a little bit stunned that he's here and a lot turned on. I can't stop the gasp that escapes my mouth when he practically rips the blue sundress I was wearing right up over my head. He roughly pulls the cups of my bra down, causing my breasts to spill over the top. He's been rough with me before—wild, crazy—but this is new. The mixture of heat and anger radiating off of him is both scary and exciting.

His hands slide over my body, stopping to cup my breasts. My head falls back, coming to rest on his shoulder as he begins to knead, pull, and toy with them. My knees turn to Jell-O, forcing me to rest my hands on his hips while he continues his exploration. His lips find the curve of my neckline, sucking and tugging the skin there, placing warm kisses on me until his lips graze my ear.

"Do you like when people play games with you Everly, do you like when they make decisions for you and lie to you?"

Shit, he knows. I jerk my head up, trying to break the connection. I have no idea how, but he does and he's pissed. I have no chance to reply because he grabs my hair, pulling my head back again hard enough to make me stop but not enough to cause any real pain.

"You don't get to run away, in fact you don't get to do anything else. We're going to play this shit my way, now you do what I say. Do you get that? Nod for me if you get that," he commands, sending another rush of wetness between my legs.

I do my best to nod with his hand still gripping my hair.

"Good, I'm going to fuck the shit out of you. I'm not going to be gentle, I'm not going to slow, and if you're lucky I'll let you come. Then and only then will we talk about what happens next. Say okay Luca."

"Okay Luca," I say because I want that, all of it. I want him to fuck the life out of me, make me forget how stupid I've been, make me feel alive in the way I've only ever felt with him. And to think that I let that go. I only hope this isn't just an anger fuck for him, I hope he'll still wants me when it's over. He releases my hair, hooks his thumbs into my panties, and slides them down my legs. I step out of them obediently and wait.

"Get on the bed and kneel, hands behind your back." His voice sends a shiver through me, the sound alone nearly sends me over the edge. I put one leg on the mattress, then the other until I'm kneeling on the bed just as he ordered. He grabs my wrists and ties them up using the panties he's just taken off of me as makeshift restraints. Oh my God this is intense, the anticipation is too much, and I'm actually worried I might self-combust.

"Spread your legs nice and wide for me baby, and bend down, head on the bed, show me your pretty pussy." What kind of sick person am I that I get off on him talking to me like this in bed? What's worse is that I never even hesitate to do what he says because I know that he's about to make me feel so good. I spread open for him as far as I can without toppling over then slowly bend my torso until my head rests on the soft mattress. I close my eyes, let my mind go, and wait for whatever comes next. I haven't even seen his face yet and he still manages to get me this worked up, the anticipation is torture. I hear the distinct sound of a zipper sliding down, then the swoosh of clothes dropping to the hardwood floor.

I cry out as a flash of pain hits me when his hand comes down on my ass hard. I breathe through it keeping my eyes closed, that part of me that feeds off of this with him wanting more.

"You're never going to lie to me like that again are you Everly?"

"No."

I fist my hands, still tied behind my back as he lands another smack on the opposite side, equally as painful.

"Will you ever make a decision that affects us without consulting me again?"

"No."

"Should I keep on? The list is long of the shit I can punish you for."

"No."

"No?" he questions, sliding his hands between my legs, opening up my folds with his fingers, testing how ready I am for him. "I think you're enjoying this, you're so wet," he comments, applying just the right amount of pressure on my clit. I rotate my hips trying to maximize the sensation but he's not in the mood to make this easy on me. I let out a frustrated sigh when he stops.

"What's the matter baby, you don't like not having a choice? Getting only what I choose to give you?"

"Luca please," I beg, I get what he's doing, I know what this is about, and I'm not above begging.

"Shhh," he whispers, slipping two fingers inside of me. "I know. I'm driving you a little bit crazy huh?" He is, I'm moaning now, his fingers are working me in just the right way, exactly where I need him and when I'm so so close he pulls out of me, leaving me panting and reaching for more. As the sensations subside my breathing starts to regulate again, and he runs the tip of his index finger along my folds again getting it wet. Abruptly he slips his finger into my ass making me scream out at the invasion. Gently he begins sliding his finger in and out. I start to get used to it and begin to enjoy it. I close my eyes again reveling in the sensations, and his other arm slides under me around my waist and he kisses my shoulder as he begins to massage my clit. I'm right there again, right on the verge of an intense orgasm, and I know, I just know that he's going to stop any second now.

"Please Luca, please let me come," I beg not caring that I sound like a desperate needy woman, not even a little

247

bit. All I know is that I'm close to bliss, and I need him to take me there. He stops again making me cry out in frustration.

"Unh uh," he says giving me a slap on the ass. "Not yet. I want to feel you first."

He tugs at the panties binding my hands pulling me back slightly, angling me to his liking and then slamming into me.

"Oh fuck," I scream. He caught me off guard, I didn't expect for him to go that fast and hard. The slither of pain subsides and is replaced by nothing but pleasure. I rear back as he thrusts, meeting his every stroke, intensifying the sensations for both of us.

"That's it baby," he praises, placing one hand on my stomach and wrapping the other one around my hair using it as a rein. He pulls me up wrapping his hand at my stomach around my torso. He pulls out almost completely before slamming into me again. God it feels good, it's always amazing with Luca. He is the only person I've ever been able to be one hundred percent myself with. He's the one who makes me feel free, uninhibited, especially in moments like this when it's intense and raw, the times when I should feel shy or self conscious but instead I feel strong and beautiful, unafraid. That's what Luca gives to me.

He releases his grasp on my hair, and I throw my head back using him as an anchor.

I mumble incoherently, "Luca I'm close."

He gets it, understands what I need, and he's feeling generous now. He kisses my exposed neck and uses his free hand to apply pressure on my clit, stroking it with just the right rhythm.

"Oh God," I whimper. I feel it climbing, starting to build up inside of me.

He slows his hands, holding me back ever so slightly. "You're mine," he says roughly in my ear.

"Yes," I respond trying to hold onto the rush of pleasure just about to peak.

"Say it Everly."

"I'm yours," I cry out, and I mean it. I'm his if he'll still have me. I don't really care who tries to come between us or what anyone else thinks. Being away from him is a torture that I never want to experience again, not as long as I can help it.

"That's my good girl," he says, circles my clit one last time, and with a final thrust I'm there, gone, lost to the powerful orgasm that rocks through me. I feel him thrust one, two, three more times before he joins me coming just as hard as me. We fall forward onto the bed, a tangle of body parts and heavy breathing.

I'm vaguely aware of the minutes ticking by; I barely register my wrists being set free and my body being turned toward his. My eyes flutter open, and I get my first real look at him. His eyes lock with mine and I'm winded—I'm hit with a physical pain in my chest, sadness for what I've put us through. I look at him and see nothing but good, nothing but love and life and happiness. It's everything I've ever wanted, and I actually gave it up, threw it away. My eyes fill with tears, there's no use in trying to stop them from falling; they're justified.

"I'm so sorry," I say through the tears.

He wipes away at my tears, but they keep coming. "Don't cry."

"I was so stupid. I knew I was just being stubborn, I thought I was doing the right thing by not letting you sacrifice your career for me, but really I was just protecting myself. It was easier to get through the pain when I caused it myself."

"I know."

"I miss you."

"I'm right here," he says calming me only slightly.

"You're not angry with me?"

"Baby, I just fucked all the anger out of me."

I look at him for just a second measuring his reaction. His eyes are light with humor, the air in the room getting lighter as we both break out into laughter. He pulls me closer to him, and I take the opportunity to burrow closer as the laughter subsides.

"I need you to trust me enough to let me make my own decisions. When you heard me tell Michael to do what he wanted, I meant that. I don't give a shit about a job; I know what it's like to live without the person you want. I'd rather have you than a job any day. What would ever make you think I'd choose differently?"

"Stupidity?"

"Ev."

"So that's it? You're just going to ruin your career to be with me."

"I would have, yes, but I don't think that's really necessary anymore."

"Why not?"

"Morgan can be relentless, let's just leave it at that for now."

My eyes must show my surprise, he strokes my tear stained cheek. "That girl loves you very much. She'll do anything for you."

"I guess I owe her."

He strokes my cheek again. It's a simple touch, but with him the simplest things have the most profound effect on me. "You need to make a decision now Everly. I'm done with the bullshit. You need to choose whether you want to be with me or not."

I open my mouth to reply, but he covers it with his fingers.

"And if you choose to be with me, that's it, you're moving in with me, we're getting married, and putting all this behind us."

My heart starts to race and I sit up quickly, not caring that I'm still totally naked. "Are you asking me to marry you?" I ask in disbelief.

He wraps an arm around my waist and rolls onto his back, taking me with him. I'm straddling him, and I feel his arousal growing again. "Are you saying yes?"

"Yes." I don't even think about it, I just answer him because I know it's right — he's my future. He's the one I'm meant to be with — I know it with everything I am.

He leans up, places a kiss on my lips, and in his stealthy Luca way slides into me all in one motion. I let out a gasp when he starts to move his hips. "Then I guess we're getting married."

"Alright then," I agree with a whimper. He thrusts into me again leaving me no time to think about what just transpired. This is the way he's choosing to celebrate our engagement and who the hell am I to tell him otherwise?

"Alright," he says with a smug grin, lifting my hands up and placing them on the headboard. He jackknifes up to a sitting position, never breaking the connection, never letting me go — taking control, the way that only he can. I just hold on tight and enjoy the ride because that's all you can do with a man like Luca.

We're laying in bed together a little while later, still naked, sated, and a little sweatier than before. My mind is working on overdrive thinking about all the shit that needs to happen now that we're actually getting married.

"Luca."

His hand stroking my back comes to a stop. "Hmm?"

"I signed a lease here, paid the whole year in advance."

I let out an involuntary sigh as the stroking of my back resumes. "Your fiancé is a lawyer, don't sweat it."

"Maybe we should just live here for a year," I suggest, thinking that it wouldn't be such a bad idea. It's small but really it's around the same size as his apartment and his lease will be up before mine so it would be easier for him to get out of his.

"Can't we're closing on the house next week."

I lift my head off of his chest bringing us face to face. "Really? You bought it anyway."

"I did. I figured I needed a house anyway, and I guess part of me hoped you'd come back."

I was so stupid. I almost let this slip through my hands and I would have had no one to blame but myself. "Isn't it too late to add me on the mortgage?"

"Your fiancé is a lawyer, don't sweat it," he says with a chuckle.

"Is that going to be your answer for everything now?" I tease, shoving his chest. He chuckles but says nothing, just shakes his head. "So I should stop unpacking."

"Yes," he replies, pushing my head down so that it's resting on his chest again. I feel my eyelids start to get heavy after a little while but I call his name before I drift off.

"Luca."

"Hmm?"

"I love you," I tell him, snuggling up closer to him.

"I love you too baby," I hear him say just as my eyelids close.

Epilogue

2 Months Later

~ *Luca* ~

It's been hectic the last few months. I'm getting slammed at work, and between getting Everly out of her lease, getting her moved out, closing on this house, and then moving in, I'm glad to finally be settled in. Things between us have been amazing, every day she blossoms a little bit more, coming into her own and feeling confident about what we have. We never did hear from Mr. West again, but Mrs. West reached out to Everly to let her know she had taken care of the situation. I don't know what she said to him, but I'm grateful to her for getting him to back off.

I'm out on the patio working on my laptop and drinking a cup of coffee when I hear the glass slider open. I look up to see Everly walking outside wearing tight black yoga pants and little navy blue sweater, taking a bite out of a banana, the diamond engagement ring I gave her a few weeks ago sparkling in the morning sunlight. I should really tell her not to wear shit like that around me,

253

it only makes me want to fuck the shit out of her and the banana doesn't help the situation. I glance at her face taking in her slightly bloodshot eyes.

"Are you okay?" I question, putting down my coffee cup.

She shrugs her shoulder and pulls up the chair next to mine. I smile when she brings up her feet to rest on my lap. "I feel like shit today. I just threw up again; I think I need to go see the doctor."

It's a struggle to hold back my laughter; *this* is my Everly, completely brilliant and other times totally clueless. I've been trying to let her figure this shit out on her own because really it's amusing but clearly I need to fill her in. "Babe, I have to tell you something."

"What?" She questions tilting her head.

I cock my head to the side locking eyes with her and smile. "You're pregnant."

"No I'm not!" she declares, pulling her feet off of my lap. I can see the exact moment when the panic starts to set in. I should probably tread carefully here, but I really love when I shock the shit out of her. It doesn't happen often so I have to savor it when it does.

"You threw up what, five minutes ago? And now you're out here eating that banana like it's no big deal. We had unprotected sex that day we got back together. You remember that right?"

"It was one time," she yells, like a hostile witness on the stand and all I can do is tilt my head up to the sky and pray for patience. Denial and Everly are close friends, but this is a bit much.

"Didn't you sit through sex education in high school? That's all it takes baby. Plus it was actually two times."

"That's because *you* didn't use a condom."

"That's because I thought *you* were still on the pill." We can do this all day; it wouldn't be the first time.

"I can't be pregnant Luca; I'm supposed to start school in a few weeks."

This is where it gets tricky. "You told me you weren't even sure if you wanted to go to school now."

"Yeah but still, I'm undecided," she says, taking a final bite of her banana.

She's not going to school, I know it and she knows it. She's not really too torn up about it either. She wouldn't be lounging in a deck chair polishing off fruit if she was that upset about this whole situation. I think law school was something that she felt like she had to do for Tyler but as she comes more and more into her own I think she's realizing that it's not as important to her as she once thought it was. If I thought it was what she really wanted I'd push her into it, I'd figure out a way to make it possible, even with a baby but it's not.

I give her a minute to let it sink in before I state the obvious again. "You're pregnant."

She smiles and nods her head. "Yeah, I am."

"We'll go get you a test so we can be sure."

"We're not even married yet!" She points out with a giggle.

"So we'll get married." It's not the end of the world, whether the baby comes first or the wedding does, it'll all be fine.

"I don't want a wedding though, been there done that. Maybe just us and our parents at the courthouse."

"Okay," I agree quickly. I could care less about having a huge wedding; in fact I prefer that we not have one. I'm all for a simple laidback event.

"Oh and Morgan too," she says, breaking into my thoughts.

"Of course." I push my chair back, reach out for her hand and pull her into my lap. She comes willingly;

snuggling up to me, she places her head in the crook of my neck.

"What am I going to do for work?" she wonders out loud.

"You can always come back to the law firm. They want you back. I told Harvey we were together, and he didn't care, it's not like we work that closely together anyway." They would love to get her back at work, the place isn't the same without her there—too much shit falls through the cracks.

"This is true."

I place a kiss on top of her head and give her a little squeeze. "Or you can not work," I suggest. Yes I said it, I know...I'm a Neanderthal but she knows that shit and she loves me anyway.

She pulls her head back and glares up at me. "You would just love that wouldn't you?"

See, she knows me. "Yes, I would love that; I would love for you to stay home with our baby for a while. That doesn't make me a bad person," I say in my defense. She rolls her eyes but settles back into me.

"I could be down with that, maybe come back to the firm for now and then stay home for a while once the baby is born. It gives me plenty of time to think about what I want to do, and I know myself. I wouldn't want to leave our baby if I didn't have to."

"I like that. You know I'd never stand in the way of you and anything that you wanted."

She tilts her head back. Her eyes meet mine, and I swear I can see through her in that moment, I can see the hope in them, the love, the happiness. I love knowing that I played a part in that, that she looks at me and sees that I'm the right man for her. It's more than I could have hoped for where Everly is concerned because in another lifetime I was nothing more than the wrong man, a

256

secondary character in another man's story. I see now that it had to be that way, that we had to see how fucking horrific life can be at times so that we would be able to appreciate what we finally found in each other. I'll spend my life giving her everything that she should have had in that other life and praying to God every day that she thinks I've given her a better one. In the beginning I thought that she needed someone to save her, that she needed me to save her, but the truth is she didn't need that. What she really needed was love, to know that there was someone in the world who wanted her above all else.

~ *Everly* ~

As promised, Luca took me to the drug store earlier to get a home pregnancy test... I bought three. Luca stopped, looked at me in disbelief, then looked up to the sky and walked away. I just rolled my eyes and followed him to the cash register. Now it's been confirmed, he only let me take two of the three tests, but I can now say for certain that I'm pregnant. When I saw the
positive tests, I couldn't control it, I instantly burst into tears. Luca just pulled me into our bed and held me tight, letting me have my breakdown. I was afraid that he would think I wasn't happy about our baby but he knew, just like he always knows exactly what I'm thinking.

"You never thought you'd get the chance to be a mom did you?" he asked.
"No. I thought that dream died a long time ago. I thought it died with Tyler. I just can't believe it's actually happening."
"It's happening. We'll have two or three babies in a couple of years, how's that sound?"
"And a dog."

"And a dog."

"Thank you, for driving me crazy and bringing me back to myself. You're the love of my life Luca," I said, thinking that the last time I spoke those words they weren't exactly true. They weren't a lie either; they were just uttered on borrowed time.

"And you're mine."

Luca's in the kitchen cooking dinner, so I stroll into the home office where he occasionally works and walk over to the bookshelf. I pull one of Tyler's old books from the shelf, one of the few I decided to keep and settle into the leather couch that sits in the corner of the room. I turn to the first page and a piece of paper falls out onto my lap. I'm assuming it's a ticket stub for some kind of event he must have bet on but when I pick it up I realize it's a folded piece of notebook paper. I open it up slowly and I gasp when I take in the familiar handwriting. It's a letter addressed to me from Tyler. My hands tremble a little as I look it over. My eyes well up with tears when I notice that it was written just two days before our wedding, just days before his death.

Dear Everly,

If you ever find this letter I hope that it's years after I'm gone. I hope that you're in a time and place where whatever wounds I've left behind are healed. I'm scared babe, I have a real problem and I just don't see a way out. I don't know if I can fix what I screwed up and if that's the case you need to know that I never intended to hurt you. I never thought I'd let things get this bad, this far, or get so caught up that I would lose sight of what was really important. I've done so many things, things that I never told you, things that I'm not proud of but you... You Everly are the only thing that's right in all of the things I've done.

There are times when I can barely stand to look at you, to see the love and hope on your face because all I feel is guilt. Guilt that I've made you promises that I'm afraid I may not be able to keep, fear that I may not even make it to our own wedding. To think I might not see your face one day is the hardest thing to take. If the unthinkable happens, if I don't make it out of this, I want you to go on. I want you to get married, have babies, and see the world. Don't give up; don't hold back because he honest to God truth is I never really deserved you anyway. I was like a thief in he night taking what I wanted even though I knew it shouldn't have been mine. I don't regret it though; I'd do it all over again for you. The only thing I would change about our life together is me and what my ambition did to us. I hope you never read this letter, I hope everything turns out alright and I can destroy it, that we get the life we always wanted, but if I don't I want you to know that even if you can no longer hear my voice, I'll be right beside you, and I'll smile from wherever I am when you get the life I always wanted for you to have. I hope one day you can forgive me, I hope you know how much having you meant to me.

I love you,

Tyler

I'm hysterical now after reading it. I feel so sad for what he must have been going through, knowing that he was about to get married but worried that he might not even make it that far, and for once, since it all happened, I'm glad that we got to make it to the wedding. I'm glad that he got that one last happy moment. My heart aches for him, for all that he gave up and how terrifying those last few days must have been for him. I hiccup through a sob and then the letter is gone, pushed to the side and

Luca is there, crouched down on the ground before me his hands cupping my face.

"Hey, what's wrong? I was calling you for dinner and when you didn't answer, I came in here and you were hysterical."

"I found a letter," I tell him, trying to steady my breathing, focusing on his beautiful eyes. I slowly start to calm down. "It's from Tyler."

"Oh baby," he says, sympathizing with me. God I love this man, even now he never makes me feel bad about still caring about Tyler even though situations like this can't be easy on him. "What did it say?"

I reach over disengaging myself from him, grab the letter off of the couch, and hand it to him. "You should read it."

He sits down next to me on the couch, pulls me into his side and begins to read. I watch him as he reads, trying to decipher the emotions playing out on his face. When he's done he just holds me tighter and sighs. "Wow."

I say nothing, just nod, planting my head in his chest.

"I think he's trying to tell you he's happy for you babe, that he approves. He said it in the letter he'd be there when you got what you wanted and he was."

I let out another soft sob. "He was — I felt like I needed just a small piece of him today. It was strange; I came in here and grabbed one of his books. He's happy for us isn't he?"

"Yeah," he replies, his voice heavy with emotion. I sometimes forget now what Tyler meant to Luca, how much his friendship meant to him, that he suffered a loss as profound as mine. But in that loss, through the grief we felt, something stronger grew, something even more beautiful than what had once existed there, a union that was meant to be created even when there was doubt. I understand now that the story hadn't been completely written, Tyler was a beautiful and tragic chapter in my book, but Luca...Luca was the Happily Ever After.

About the Author

Alice Tribue lives with her husband and daughter in New Jersey. She has a bachelor's degree in communications and is currently working on her master's degree. She spends most of her free time reading, writing, and when the weather permits sitting on the beach sipping a margarita.

For more news about upcoming books, teasers, and happenings, follow her on

Facebook

http://www.facebook.com/pages/Alice-Montalvo-Tribue/216980565108887

Twitter

@AMTribue

Website

http://alicemontalvotribue.wordpress.com/

Email

Amtribue@gmail.com

Acknowledgements

To my readers, thank you for your support, your enthusiasm and your excitement for my work. It never ceases to amaze me how wonderful you all are. You inspire me daily to follow this dream.

To the bloggers who for the past year and a half have helped me to get my name out there and my books seen. There's no way I could have come this far without your help. THANK YOU!!!

To my beta readers, Stephanie Locke, Anji Albis, Kristy Garbutt, and Mindy Guerreiros. You make the writing process manageable for me with all of your honesty, comments and suggestions. Thank you so much for taking the time to help me make my books even better.

Stephanie Locke, I can't believe we did it again! Thank you for a friendship that started over a shared love for books but goes way beyond that now. Even though you like to take credit for all the awesome reads I find and you finished UT late... I hope you know how much you mean to me, you are the most supportive person I know and you get me in a way that not many people do.

Whitney Williams, OMG what a roller coaster ride we've been on over the last year. I'm so glad to have you in my corner through the highs and the lows. Your advice is invaluable and your friendship means the world to me. It's come to the point where I don't know what I'd do without our daily conversations. You make me laugh like no other, frustrate me like no other but NO ONE appreciates my dark side quite like you do. You're getting everything that I wanted for you from the first day I messaged you about Mid Life Love. I'm so proud of all your accomplishments and I'm glad I get to witness it. STAN forever!

Wendy Ferraro, my very first author friend... You are always there to lend an ear and a helping hand. Your friendship means the world to me and I always look forward to our fun times together!

Mary Wasowski, your positive energy, light, and laughter are infectious. Thank you for the chats and encouragement and congrats on all you've accomplished.

C.P. Smith, thanks for your help on this project and for helping me brainstorm when the writers block kicked in, you have no idea how much that helped me!

Tamisha Draper, Your help on this project has been a life saver. I can never thank you enough for all that you did to help me get this book out there. You literally took the reigns and ran with it. Thank you for your honesty and your amazing ideas.

Turn the page for a sneak peek of

Sins & Mistrust

By

Isabel Lucero

Alice Tribue

Excerpt from Sins & Mistrust by Isabel Lucero

Chapter One

Marc

"So, what are we getting into tonight?" I ask Nathalia.

Nathalia is a beautiful new client that got in touch with me a week ago to discuss hiring me regularly. She's a busy woman who is in the process of becoming the Vice President of marketing for one of her father's hotels. Apparently he has a franchise, and she's been learning the ropes of running a hotel her whole life. With sitting in on board meetings, and doing what her father needs her to, she says she doesn't have time to date.

"Promise you won't run scared?" she says with a wicked smile as she looks at me over her shoulder.

"I don't scare easily," I reply with a grin.

"We'll see," she states.

She turns back around and fixes her hair while looking into a large mirror on her wall. Her shiny black hair falls to the middle of her back. Nathalia is wearing a very form-fitting, black dress that dips low enough in the front to showcase her perfect breasts without showing too much.

"I wonder," she ponders, looking at me curiously.

"Are you going to fill me in on what you wonder about?" I ask with a smile.

She walks over to the couch and begins putting on her heels. My eyes move from her dainty feet, all the way up her tanned and toned legs until her dress keeps from seeing anything else.

"I hope to find out the answer myself tonight. I'll let you know when you bring me home," she finishes with a mischievous smile.

After she fastens the black strap around her ankle, she walks to me and slides her hand through the crook of my arm, and we leave the hotel room she's staying in.

"So, is this home to you?" I ask.

"Yes. I could get my own place, but I spend so much time here, that I might as well live here. Papa can never say I'm late to work," she says with a smile.

"Are you and your dad close?" I ask.

"Very. He hops around to some of the other hotels quite a bit, but I stay here. The only other one I frequent is the one in California."

I nod and decide that's enough personal questions for tonight. When we get to the lobby of the hotel, she waves to a man that's standing behind a desk near the entrance.

"Ms. LaBelle," the man greets with a smile.

"Hello, James," she responds.

"Sir," he adds, nodding to me.

"Good evening."

We walk out and straight into the car that's waiting for us. Nathalia requested that neither of us drive so that we both could enjoy our evening with drinks.

"So, Marc, tell me something about you. Like we've discussed, I plan on hiring you quite often, and I'm not naïve enough to think I'm your only client, but do you have a regular girlfriend?"

"No, no girlfriend," I answer with a smile.

"Really? But you're so handsome," she says, putting her hand on my leg.

"Well, thank you. But no, there aren't many people out there who are okay with what I do."

"Ah, yes. I understand," she says with a nod of her head. "But it is your life, no? You do what makes you happy. Does this job make you happy?"

I hesitate for just a second, but I guess I wasn't quick enough for Nathalia.

"You are not happy," she states without a hint of question.

"Sure I am. This job has made me happy for a long time."

"But not any longer. It's okay, I understand."

I ponder how she thinks she understands, when I'm not even sure I do, but I leave it alone.

"So, do I get any clues about this mystery place you are taking me to?"

"What fun would that be?" she says with a soft laugh.

"Such a tease."

"Mmm. Just you wait," she replies with a wink.

When we arrive at this mystery club, the car drops us off directly in front of the building. As I step outside and hold out my hand for Nathalia, I take a moment to gaze around the area. It's a fairly busy area with lots of foot traffic, but they don't seem to be going to the club we've stopped in front of. Everybody is making their way down the street to the other clubs or restaurants.

As I inspect the place we're soon going to be entering, I understand why nobody is interested. There's no sign, nothing to let you know what it is or that it's even open for business. It's quite dull looking, actually.

"Is this the place?" I ask, pointing at the building.

She straightens out her dress after closing the door behind her and glances at the darkened club. "Yes, this is it," she says with a laugh. "I promise there's more to it than you think."

Nathalia walks toward the building and I fall in step next to her. She raps on the door with three hard, quick knocks, and almost instantly it's opened by a large man in a black shirt and black jeans. The scowl on his face quickly morphs into a look of recognition when he sees Nathalia.

She smiles at him and he nods his head in response before we walk in. The hall is fairly dark, and another large man stands in the way with a clipboard in his hands.

"Ms. LaBelle," he says.

"Hello, Smith," she chirps.

Smith eyes me speculatively momentarily.

"He's fine," Nathalia says and Smith moves to the side and allows us in.

"Secretive place," I state.

She shrugs one shoulder in response as we walk down the narrow hall. Once we get to the end of the hall and step into the large room, I think my jaw drops slightly.

Nathalia turns to look at me with a sneaky smile on her face. "Scared yet?"

I take my time to absorb everything that's going on in the room in front of us. Directly to my right, leaned up against the wall is a couple. While this is pretty normal, what's not, is that the woman's dress is pushed up around her waist and the man has his fingers in her pussy.

Moving my gaze to the left, I see a wall of mirrors, and what grabs my attention right away are the three people standing in front of them. Well, the man is standing behind a woman who has her hands resting on the mirror. She's bent over, her dress pushed up as well, with the man fucking her from behind while she watches in the reflection. Another woman is leaned up against the mirror and has her hand down her pants as she watches.

Not everybody is half naked or having sex, but they definitely don't seem surprised or bothered by the happenings around them.

Finally returning my gaze back to Nathalia, I smile and respond. "I'm an escort. I've done or seen these kinds of things plenty of times," I say with a smirk.

She playfully rolls her eyes. "Oh, Mr. Experienced over here."

"You have no idea," I reply with a wink.

"Well, come on, Mr. Experience. Let's get a drink."

After we walk clear across the room, maneuvering through plenty of people who seem to be checking both of us out, we approach the bar and place our order.

"So, you come here pretty often, don't you?" I ask.

"Not too often," she answers as she reaches for her drink.

I place a twenty on the bar and grab my glass. "Do you always bring a date with you?"

She places the straw between her lips and peers up at me with large green eyes. "I've brought someone here once before. The other times I've been here, I've come alone."

"Do you, uh, participate?"

Nathalia lets out a small laugh. "Participate? You mean, have sex out here for people to see? No, I haven't done that. However, if you're interested, there are more private areas," she says mischievously.

"I'll keep that in mind," I answer with a grin.

As we stand near the bar, talking and enjoying our drinks, I notice a man walk out and head over to the people who are having sex by the mirrors. He leans in and says something to the man, and soon after, the man straightens up and pulls his pants back up. He gets the women who are there with him and starts walking towards the back of the room. The man who spoke to him pats him on the back and walks away.

"What's that about?" I ask, noticing Nathalia was watching the same thing I was.

"Oh, he likes to keep the sex to the other rooms. While people always do the touchy, feely stuff, he doesn't really like the all-out sex to be out in the open."

"And who is he?" I ask as I watch the man in the black suit scope out the rest of the room.

"Oh. The owner. Lincoln Cash."

I take a gulp of my drink and watch as his eyes fall on us. He does a double take and suddenly starts making his way towards the bar. I take a glance at Nathalia who is smiling in his direction.

"Thalia, how are you?" he asks in a deep, charming voice. His smile stretches across his face as he takes her in his arms.

I take another gulp.

"I'm great, Lincoln. How are you?"

"You know me," he says with a smirk. "You look beautiful tonight."

She throws him a radiant smile. "Thank you."

He turns and looks me over before asking, "Who's your friend?"

"This is Marc," she answers, gesturing towards me with her palm up. "Marc, this is Lincoln."

Lincoln extends his hand and I take it in my own. "Nice to meet you," I say.

"Mm. Likewise," he responds, and I'm not sure if he has a slight attitude or not.

We drop hands and I straighten up, finish my drink, and place it on the bar. There's a bit of an awkward silence between us three, and I can't help but wonder if they've had a relationship before.

"Well, I suppose I'll leave you two alone. I hope you both enjoy your evening. Will you be staying a while?" he asks, paying more attention to Nathalia.

"We just arrived, so I'm sure we'll hang out for a little longer."

"Good, good," he says, nodding his head. He takes another glance at me, and I hate that I can't read his demeanor. "Well, I hope to chat with you again soon, Thalia," he says, pulling her in and kissing both her cheeks.

He leans into her and seems to whisper something in her ear. When they part, Nathalia gives him a tiny nod with a hint of a smile. They communicate something in that moment, but I have no idea what.

"I'm sure you will," she replies with a smirk.

"It was very nice meeting you, Marc," he says, and this time he seems genuine.

I smile and return his handshake. "You too."

When he walks away, I turn and face Nathalia. Her eyes look at me but she doesn't move her head in my direction. She takes a sip from her straw, and then turns away from me to put it on the bar.

"Ex-boyfriend? Lover?" I ask.

It's then that she looks at me, expressionless. A moment later a smile appears on her lips.

"He wishes."

"Ah," I say with a nod.

"Is that why I felt the frigid air coming off his shoulder in my direction?"

She laughs. "Oh, I don't know. That was him being quite nice, actually."

"Do you want to dance?" I ask, changing the subject.

Nathalia smiles happily at me. "Yes, please."

I escort her onto the dance floor, and we find a nice spot near the wall of mirrors. A slow, sexy song comes on, and Nathalia puts her arms around my neck as I rest my hands at her waist.

She looks up at me with gorgeous green eyes and runs her fingers through my hair. The front of her body is pushed up against the front of mine, and as I look down at her, I have a perfect view of her ample cleavage. I lick my lips and she catches me enjoying the view.

Slowly, she turns her body until her ass is pressed up against my cock, and rests her back against my stomach and chest. She rests her head on my shoulder, and glides her hands alongside her body as she moves sexily to the music.

Her hands make their way up to her breasts and she gently and briefly gropes herself, squeezing them in a way that makes the cleavage that much more obvious. I lean down and put my mouth on her neck while I pull her ass into me, letting her know what her show is doing to me.

I hear her groan when my tongues dances across her soft skin.

Suddenly, she turns and grabs my hand, and leads me to a section of the club I didn't notice before.

She slides a panel open and I close it behind us. We're in a semi narrow area, but it's fairly long, and along the back is a wide bench and curtains to close off sections.

Nathalia goes to the back corner, and I notice there's only one other couple in here, and they're on the other end.

Once we're inside our own little cubicle, she closes the curtain and we're enclosed in a small room that has mirrors above us. Very dim lights glow from above, and the bench is cushioned. Thank God.

For a few seconds, we look at each other, the sexual energy fills the small room, and at the same time, we both lunge for the other. My tongue glides across her lips, forcing them apart. When she opens her mouth, I explore her tongue with my own.

My hands go to her face, and I bring her even closer to me. She moans into my mouth, and digs her fingertips into my ass, pulling me into her.

I nip at her lips, and she sucks my bottom lip into her mouth. I let my hands go the base of her head, and tug on her hair. She gasps out in surprise and in pleasure and then begins running her hands down my chest, fumbling with my buttons.

"Oh, sorry. I uhh…"

I turn around and notice a woman at the curtain. I raise my brows at her waiting for her to either say what she needs to say or close the curtain and leave.

"Can I help you?" I ask in a nicer tone than I want to, because what I really want to do is slide my dick inside Nathalia.

"I didn't know- uhh. I'm sorry."

She continues to stand there, but looks back behind her, and then back at me.

What the hell is going on?

Nathalia stands up and adjusts her dress, and I run a hand through my hair in frustration. It's then that the woman finally turns and leaves. I drop my head back and sigh, but then I find that I'm looking at myself in the mirror above me.

What really catches my attention is that I can see outside the room we're in and I see Lincoln standing outside, speaking with the same woman who just left.

What the fuck?

I move to the curtain and snatch it open but he and the woman are already leaving.

"What's wrong?" Nathalia asks.

"Your friend Lincoln was out here, and he was speaking with the woman who interrupted us. Do you think he had her do that on purpose?"

"Why would he?" she asks.

"I don't know."

"He might have just been checking things out. He tends to wander around and make sure everything is okay."

I sigh. "Yeah, I guess. Well, now that the moment has been ruined, what would you like to do?" I ask, pulling her body into mine.

"Hmm. Maybe we should get out of here and go back to my place," she replies as she bites down on her lip.

"I think that sounds like a great plan," I say as I lean down and cover her lips with mine.

When we part, we step out of the small room and back to the panel doors that lead to the dance floor. As we're passing another room, we hear the unmistakable sound of a woman crying out as she orgasms, followed by a man grunting.

Nathalia giggles. "I'm glad nobody heard us."

"I didn't get the chance to make you scream out my name," I reply with a grin. "If I did, everybody on this dance floor would have heard you."

She laughs. "Oh yeah? Mr. Confident too, I see." She playfully smacks my arm as we move across the dance floor and towards the exit.

Before we get to the door, Lincoln comes into view. Great.

"Thalia," he says in a husky voice. "May I speak with you before you leave?"

Nathalia glances at me, probably noticing my tense jaw. Why the fuck is this guy so dead set on interrupting our date. Is he that jealous? Maybe he had more feelings for her than she had for him. Maybe if I tell him that she and I aren't serious, and that I'm her hired date, he won't feel so insecure.

Fuck it. I'll let him suffer.

"Mr. Cash, Nathalia and I have plans for the rest of the evening. Is this matter really that important?" I ask with a fake smile as I wrap my arm around her waist.

His eyes follow my movement before looking back at me. "I suppose not."

"Great," I answer with forced enthusiasm.

I pat his shoulder as I move to pass him. His eyes look at my hand, but he doesn't say anything.

"Lincoln, I'll talk with you soon," Nathalia calls as we head to the door.

"I look forward to it," he responds.

When we get to the door, I push it open and Nathalia steps out. I chance a quick glance back down the hall and notice Lincoln still standing there watching me. We lock eyes briefly before I step outside.

Excerpt from Shelter You

Available Now!

By

Alice Tribue

Prologue

❦

"I can only give you thirty minutes to get out of here before I have to report it to my supervisors that you're gone. The clothes I brought for you are in the closet over there," she says, pointing to a long closet built into the wall.

It reminds me of a high school locker, long and narrow. At the age of 17, I've become very familiar with those lockers, having used them all throughout my years in school and they were great years, happy years, right up until the end. It's hard to believe that just a few months ago I was graduating high school, Miss Popular, top of my class, my pick of universities. To everyone on the outside looking in, it appeared that I had my whole future ahead of me. The perfect life, great grades, an amazing family, the world was my oyster. Little did they know that my future had already been decided, mapped out and planned for me. None of which I had any say in, none of which I was comfortable with.

I turn my attention back to the tall gangly woman in front of me. She's unnaturally thin, but I can almost see the attractiveness there, that she might have been beautiful once upon a time. Her blond hair is coarse, straw like and brittle, and her glasses are too big for her face, but I don't care about any of that. To me, right now she's an angel. A real live angel sent down to help me get out of an impossible situation.

"Besides clothes I was able to get you all of the basic supplies you'll need. It's not much, but it'll get you by until you can afford to buy more," she says, as I nod.

"When I leave this room, pick up the phone and call the operator. Ask for a volunteer to bring a wheelchair up to your room because you are being discharged. Once she comes up, tell her that your car is already waiting and that you need her to wheel you to the east entrance. Show her your hospital bracelet. It matches Lily's so you'll be fine; she won't know any better. She'll ask if you have a car seat, so just tell her that it's already in the car."

My heart starts to beat faster as I listen to her directions. Am I really doing this? Am I strong enough, brave enough to defy my parents, go against their wishes?

"The taxi driver will be waiting for you. His name is Seth, he's a friend of my husband's. He'll take you to the bank first. Take out every single penny that is in your savings account and then have him take you to the bus station. Take the first bus out of here, Mia. Leave your cell phone behind and get a pre paid one the first chance you get. You'll be eighteen in one month, and at that time you can call and request a copy of Lily's birth certificate. This way, even if they can track you, they can't legally force you to come back."

It takes me a minute, but I finally find my voice. "I don't know how I can ever repay you for this."

"No one should be forced to give up their child; it's wrong. Just promise me you'll be a good mom and that you'll call me if you need anything at all."

I look up at her with tears in my eyes. If not for this kind woman I'd be handing Lily over to her adoptive parents in a matter of hours. It may seem cruel of me to have promised to give my baby away to a couple who desperately wants one and then to just pick up and run away but none of this was my choice. Four months before my high school graduation I found out that I was pregnant. As you can probably imagine for a seventeen year old to hear that she's going to become a mother is shocking and scary. So I did what I thought would be the right thing, I went to my parents and asked for their help. Their solution? Hide my pregnancy until after graduation and then keep me a virtual prisoner in my own home until I gave birth. When I expressed to them my desire to keep my child they gave me an ultimatum: Give the baby up for adoption, or keep the baby but leave their house with absolutely no financial help from them. What else could I have done? I had no choice but to agree to their demands and I thought I could do it. I thought I could go through with it until I held her, my Lily, and I knew that giving her away would literally kill me—would make it difficult to go on with the knowledge that she was out there in the world somewhere, living a life apart from mine. And because of this I made her a promise and I'll die before I break that promise. I'll die before I ever let her go

Chapter 1

Nurse Kelly's plan went down exactly the way she said it would. The volunteer that came up to take Lily and I out to the car barely checked that our bracelets matched before she helped me into the wheelchair and took me down to the exit where the cab was waiting for me. Seth, the driver helped get Lily in the car seat and then got us the hell out of there as fast as he could. He took me to my house and after verifying that my parents weren't there, I ran inside. After packing some more clothes, all of my important documents and some cash that I had stored in my desk, I took one last look at my childhood bedroom and left.

Seth quickly took me to the bank where I was able to liquidate my entire savings account, a little over ten thousand dollars that I had been saving ever since I could remember. Every single dollar I'd ever been given from birthday and Christmas presents and from working at the local ice cream shop every summer was now in my backpack. Seth thought it would be a good idea to take me to a bus station a couple towns over. I wasn't about to let anyone find me now that I had come this far, so I hopped on the first available bus out of state heading to Savannah Georgia, and told myself that once I got there I could stop for the night and make a decision on where to go next.

I've been traveling for about five hours now. We stopped earlier in Jacksonville, Florida, for about an hour—giving me just enough time to hide in a large bathroom stall to feed Lily in private and grab a bite to eat for myself. I'm terrified that she might start crying and disturb the other passengers on the bus, but the continuous motion seems to help her sleep. I close my eyes and wonder how I'm going to make this work, how I'm going to be able to take care of Lily without any help. The truth behind my situation is daunting. How will I know what she needs, why she's crying, how to get her on a sleeping and feeding schedule? Will I know what to do and how to take care of her when she gets sick? What will I do for childcare when I find a job? The thoughts overwhelm me but I try not to panic. I have to keep it together for Lily, because I have to believe that a life with me is better for her than any life she could have had without me.

It's a little after ten at night when we finally arrive in Savannah. I gather Lily and my belongings and grab a taxi cab. I tell the driver to take us to the most affordable hotel in the area and a little while later he drops us off at an inn right on Bay Street. It's much too dark to explore outdoors but from what I can tell, it's gorgeous here, someplace I'd love to come back and visit one day. When I reach the front desk the clerk eyes me suspiciously as she checks me in but mercifully doesn't ask me any questions. I pay for my room in cash, grab my room key, and hop on the elevator. I get to my room as quickly as I can.

I can't help but to feel exposed when I'm out in the open, as if by some off chance someone might recognize me.

I change Lily's diaper and put her in a pink one piece pajama, turn down the bed and crawl in with her. I lie on my side with her snuggled close and offer her my breast. Kelly showed me what to do that first night after my parents had left for the evening. I remember being grossed out initially but I wanted to be able to feed her even if it was only one time. To be able to give her even just a small piece of me was important, it felt right. I'm thankful that I did it now because given my limited resources nursing her seems to be the most cost effective way to keep her fed. It doesn't take long for me to give into the exhaustion, my eyes start to get heavy and before I know it I'm asleep.

※

I was looking forward to at least taking in a few of the sites in Savannah but fear of being found or recognized kept me a virtual prisoner in my hotel room. We stayed for two days and then hopped the midnight bus to Richmond, Virginia. We stopped a few hours into the trip in North Carolina and then drove straight through the remainder of the night; thankfully Lily slept most of the way but I sat in the back of the bus and when she woke up for her feeding I was able to cover her up with a blanket and nurse her privately. It helped that almost everyone on the bus was asleep.

The hotel in Virginia is not quite as nice as the one in Georgia but it's safe, clean and affordable. I allow myself to wander around Richmond a bit more than I did in Savannah, but I keep to myself and keep my head down most of the time. I find a small pharmacy near the hotel where I pick up diapers, baby wipes, infant Tylenol just in case of an unexpected emergency, a pair of scissors and two boxes of brown hair dye. If anyone is looking for Lily and me we'll be a lot harder to recognize if I alter my appearance and making my hair darker seems like the easiest way.

"Well isn't this a beautiful baby." I look up and see an elderly woman standing behind me in the line to pay.

I instantly tense up, and go on alert. Maybe I'm paranoid. I mean, it's only a little old lady but I can't be too careful. I'm not sure if there's anyone out there looking for me. I don't know if the police were called, if the media was alerted, or if a reward was offered, but I certainly wouldn't put anything past my parents.

"Thank you," I respond quietly, never actually looking at her and hoping that she'll just leave me alone.

"Is she yours dear?" She questions, just as the person ahead of me is done paying for his items. I ignore her and quickly move up, putting my things on the counter and paying for my purchases as fast as possible. I get the hell out of there and back to the hotel in record time.

Lily begins to cry and I know that she must be hungry because she's just woken up so she can't be sleepy and her diaper is dry. I lie down in the king size bed with her and feed her until she falls asleep again. Strange as it may seem these moments with her calm me down, they give me the reassurance I need that running away was worth it. I'm beginning to feel more and more confident with her, like maybe I can do this, make this work with her and be a good mom. I think about the things I'll have to give up, the things that I have already given up—my friends, enjoying my youth. I know I should be out doing the things that normal kids my age do, partying, dating, living the college life but all of those things were taken away from me and replaced with this life instead and the thing of it is, I'm okay with that. Yes, I'm young, inexperienced and I know that making the decision to keep Lily will never be the easy choice. But when it came down to it, when I was given the option, it was the only choice.

⁂

I look different as a brunette, I barely recognize myself when I look in the mirror. I feel better to a certain degree now that I've changed my hair, coloring and cutting it shoulder length, my long blond locks were always my signature look so it will take some getting used to for me but it's what I need to do to keep my anonymity. After weighing out my options, I decided that I prefer traveling at night when there aren't many people out and about. Lily and I left the hotel in Virginia and hopped on our next bus at three o' clock in the morning driving through the night and stopping at eight the next morning in Baltimore Maryland. I decide to stop here for the night and let myself get some rest before catching my final bus into Pennsylvania. I'm not sure why I'm drawn there of all places, it was just a random choice plus it's a big enough state that I can hopefully just blend into.

By the time Lily and I finally reach our final destination, a small Pennsylvania town about forty five minutes outside of New York City, I'm exhausted but grateful that we made it here without getting caught. It's early fall and the colors of the trees here are stunning. I've never seen anything quite like it; the brilliant orange and red leaves fill the streets and it makes me glad that I chose this as the place for Lily and I to start our new lives together. I get us settled into a hotel and snuggle up close to her after feeding and changing her surprised at how connected I feel to her. Yes, she's my daughter and instinctively there should be a bond there, but I was so prepared to let her go, give her up to make my life less complicated. Looking at her now, I know that she's the kind of complication I wouldn't trade for the world. No matter how unexpectedly she was created. I close my eyes and rest. I know that I'll be up at least two times tonight to feed her and I need to be up early, I'm planning on beginning my search for an apartment first thing in the morning. Before long both Lily and I are fast asleep.

I don't know why I thought that finding an apartment would be easy. We don't need much room for now, a studio or a one bedroom apartment will work. I've been searching for days but the places I've seen within my budget dangle on the disgusting and unsafe side.

I'm running out of hope by the time I go to see the last apartment on my list. It's on a busier street but the building is clean and well maintained. A tall and slender middle aged woman meets me out front. She looks at me as if though she's surprised someone as young as me is here alone with a baby and looking for an apartment. I can tell she's not judging me, I think she's probably more concerned than anything else. She stares at me for a second with her kind eyes.

"Are you Kelly?" She questions.

I didn't want to give anyone my real name in case my family really is looking for me. When I called to set up appointments I used the first name that popped into my head, Kelly, the name of the nurse who helped me get myself and Lily out of the hospital. "Yes, I'm Kelly. You must be Janet."

She extends her hand and I reach out and take it. "Yes, I'm Janet."

She shakes my hand and quickly releases it. "Thank you for meeting me today."

"Of course. Come on in and I'll show you the apartment." She opens the front door and allows me to walk in ahead of her. "It's just down the hall and to your left."

When we reach the door she puts the key in the door, turning the knob but stopping just before she opens. "I'm sorry Kelly, I don't mean to pry but what is a young girl like you doing looking for an apartment? Shouldn't you be at home with your family?"

I know she means well but I'm not prepared to answer this question. I answer the best way I can on the spot and what I come up with is not a complete lie, just an altered version of the truth. "My family kicked me out when I got pregnant. I was staying with a friends family but it's time for me to find a place of my own."

"Oh honey, I'm so sorry to hear that. Forgive me for asking." She pushes the door open and allows me to walk through.

"It's alright. I understand what it must look like, an eighteen year old and a baby." I give her a small smile and quickly walk away from her, moving to stand in the middle of a small living room. I look around at the bare white walls and though it's small, it's by far the nicest place I've seen. It's sparsely furnished with a worn old blue couch and chair.

"The bedroom is through that door over there," she says pointing to my left. "It's pretty spacious...big enough to fit a full size bed and a crib for the little one."

I try not to read into it but her words give me hope. "Does that mean you'll rent it to me?"

"We normally require a credit check but I'm assuming since you're so young you haven't built up much of a credit rating?"

"Yes ma'am."

"And you have no furniture?"

"Not yet, no ma'am."

"And can you afford the security deposit and first months rent?"

"Yes I can."

"Alright then, I have the lease with me, if you want the apartment it's yours. You can use the furniture that's here too if you'd like and I'm pretty sure I have some old baby things that you can use. I don't live too far away. I can have my husband drop it off and set it up this weekend."

I look up at her wide eyed, stunned and seriously trying not to cry. "I don't know how to thank you. I promise you I won't be any trouble."

She simply smiles and nods at me.

By the time I leave the building, I have a lease, a set of keys, and permission to move in right away. I grab my belongings, and check out of the hotel. By nightfall Lily and I are all moved into our new apartment.

50849127R00173

Made in the USA
Lexington, KY
02 April 2016